Before becoming a bartender and crime writer, Karen Kijewski taught English at Brookline High School in Massachusetts. Her first Kat Colorado mystery, *Katwalk*, won her the Shamus and Anthony Awards and the American Best First Private Eye Novel of the Year Award. Karen Kijewski lives and works in Sacramento, California.

Katwalk, *Kat's Cradle* and *Copy Kat* are available from Headline and have received tremendous critical acclaim:

'The book is lively and entertaining throughout' *Times Literary Supplement*

'An intriguing mystery ... an engaging heroine' *The Times*

'Outstanding among today's female detectives, private eye Kat Colorado exhibits conscience and compassion, muscle and wisecracking savvy in an appealing and believable combination' *Publishers Weekly*

'A seamless syncopation of sleuth and setting that will have mystery buffs recalling Grafton and Paretsky' *Booklist*

'Kijewski's breakout book, lifting her to the front ranks, right up there with the other smartmouthed private-ey̶e̶s̶ ̶l̶i̶k̶e̶ ̶S̶u̶e̶ ̶G̶r̶a̶f̶t̶o̶n̶ ̶.̶ ̶.̶ ̶.̶ strong contender for̶ ̶.̶ ̶.̶ ̶.̶ *Kirkus Re̶v̶i̶e̶w̶s̶*

Katapult

Karen Kijewski

HEADLINE

First published in Great Britain in 1994
by HEADLINE BOOK PUBLISHING

'I Don't See Me In Your Eyes', 'I'm Killing My Troubles, One
Shot At A Time', and 'It's All Over But The Crying', are used
by permission of the author, Dan Evans. Grateful acknowledgement is made for permission to quote from this material.

10 9 8 7 6 5 4 3 2 1

ISBN 0 7472 4308 5

Phototypeset by Intype, London
Printed and bound in Great Britain by
Mackays of Chatham PLC, Chatham, Kent

HEADLINE BOOK PUBLISHING
A division of Hodder Headline PLC
338 Euston Road
London NW1 3BH

For my daughters, Maia and Sonia.
Again and with love and thanks.

ACKNOWLEDGEMENTS

For their expertise, time, and invaluable help the author wishes to thank Chief John Anderson, California Highway Patrol, and Detective Russ Martin, Sacramento County Sheriff's Department. Any errors are, of course, the author's. Thanks to Dan Evans for his musical knowledge; to Don Trethewey for background information and local color. Thanks and appreciation especially to Dianne Epperson and Linda Grant for always being there.

One

My day started off at five in the morning with a body. A body and a phone call, but not in that order.

The phone call came first. I let the answering machine pick it up.

Kat Colorado Investigations.

Damn, I'd forgotten to turn the sound down.

Leave a message after the tone.

I pulled the pillow over my head.

I'll return your call.

They don't make down pillows like they used to. I heard the tone too.

'Oh, for goodness sakes, Katy, knock it off,' Alma said crossly into the phone, 'I know you're there, you're not fooling me.' She paused. I tried to wake up. 'Katy, you *are* there?'

I sighed and picked up the phone. 'Yes.'

Alma's voice broke a little. 'Katy, the police are here.' She pronounced it po-lice. I'm not a morning person but I woke up fast.

'They say Johnny's dead but that can't be, can it? It can't. He was fine just yesterday. Fine. I made him a corned beef on rye, dark rye, with mustard and a pickle

1

just the way he likes it. So he can't be dead. Can he? No, of course he can't.'

She sounded somewhat relieved. Alma is a firm believer in the power of good home-cooked food – which is okay as far as it goes; I just don't believe it goes that far. What I do believe is police logic. For identifying a body I'd pick the police over corned beef any day.

'He *says* he's a copper. I don't know. He's just wearing regular clothes. Polyester,' she added scornfully. Alma is also a staunch believe in natural fibers.

'Did you see his ID?'

'No.'

'Alma, you let a strange man in in the middle of the night just because he said he was a cop?'

There was a long defensive silence. 'It's not the middle of the night; it's morning. Hey, sonny,' her voice faded out a little, 'let me see your ID.' Her voice came back in. 'Okay, I saw it.'

'Does he look like his picture?' A pause.

'Sonny, can I see that ID again?' A pause.

'Yes, he does. So what is he doing here?'

She asked me, not him. I don't try to figure Alma out anymore; I don't always answer her either. Anyway, he'd said why he was there, because of Johnny. My heart sank. Never mind the corned beef on rye, the dill pickles and mustard. Forget the polyester. A cop was a cop. And I was afraid. Afraid for Johnny and then for Alma. What the hell, afraid for me, too.

'Let me speak to the police officer, Alma.' I pronounced police correctly.

'Hey, copper.'

There was a little crash as she put the phone down. Alma is eighty-one and figures she can get away with stuff like this. So far, unfortunately, she's been right. Where she gets words like po-lice and copper is beyond me. I think of her as living a sheltered life. Clearly that is a misconception on my part.

'Detective Barkowski here.'

'Will you tell me what's going on, please?' I made it sound formal and dignified, as though I could control what was happening with words.

'Your name, ma'am?'

I bit back my impatience. 'Kat Colorado.'

'Your relationship to Mrs. Flaherty here?'

The impatience turned to nausea in the back of my throat. 'She's my granddaughter, copper,' I heard Alma say in the background.

'Johnny. Tell-me-about-Johnny.' I carefully spaced out my sentence, still trying to control reality with words, still not getting it.

'We haven't determined anything yet, ma'am. There was a young man found dead in Mrs. Flaherty's car this morning around three. That's why we're here. She said she had loaned her car to her grandson.'

'There was no ID on the body?'

'No, ma'am.'

Hope, like a bedraggled, soiled phoenix, struggled up through the nausea in my throat and hit me between the eyes. No ID. It needn't be Johnny. It could have been his roommate. My heart constricted again. Or the car might have been stolen. My heart eased. Stolen, that was best. I did not ask myself why anyone would bother to steal a 1973 turquoise Dodge Dart. I didn't ask because I knew the answer. They wouldn't.

'Detective, I'm coming over. You'll get a lot more out of Alma with me there.'

'I hope so, ma'am.' He sounded tired. It was a job to

3

him, a job and a body. The phoenix stumbled.

'Ask Alma to make coffee and toast. She's at her best around food.'

'Yes, ma'am. Could you get here as fast as possible?'

'Half an hour. I'm in Orangevale.' It would take me that long to get from my country part of Orangevale to Alma's Victorian in midtown Sacramento.

'Give me the phone, sonny,' Alma said imperiously.

'Katy, are you coming? You're going to clear up this nonsense, aren't you?'

'I'm coming, Alma, and yes, we'll figure it out. Give the detective coffee and a cinnamon roll or something. He's probably been up all night.' I could almost hear her gears shift from outraged citizen to caretaker. We hung up on the comforting note of food.

I climbed out of bed and into my jeans and felt my body temperature plummet a good ten degrees. The house was freezing. I lost another batch of BTUs pulling off the T-shirt I wore to bed and pulling on top layers. By the time I got to socks and shoes I was shaking. My hands were next. They froze up scraping ice off the windows of the Bronco II.

At 5:10 there was no traffic and I drove fast. It wasn't until the heater kicked in and I thawed out that my mind started working. Damn. I should have called Johnny. I banged my head against the steering wheel. Hard. That could have settled it. Why hadn't Alma called him? Or Barkowski? I drove faster hoping that all the patrol cops were at the Winchell's substation dunking doughnuts in their coffee. One cop was enough for any morning.

I took the steps up to Alma's porch two at a time. I have a key but I didn't need it, the door was unlocked.

I looked around quickly and headed for the kitchen. It was warm and cozy with an old-fashioned stove that Yuppies would kill for and Alma would never part with. It hadn't had a day's vacation in its life. Barkowski was sitting at the table with a napkin tucked under his chin and not much left of a plate of eggs, sausage, and cinnamon rolls.

He patted his mouth quickly and struggled to his feet looking a little sheepish – as if anyone would withstand Alma's cooking. I waved him down as I reached over to shake his hand. Alma hugged me from behind.

'How do you want your eggs, Katy?'

'Detective Barkowski? Oh, no eggs. Just tea please, Alma.'

'Yes, ma'am.'

'Kat Colorado. Could I see your ID please.'

He juggled his coffee about for a bit, then pulled out an ID folder and flipped it open. The badge was real. The picture was a younger Barkowski but it matched. So did the name.

'Sheriff's Department. I thought Alma said Police?'

'A cop's a cop.' Alma's contribution. We ignored her. Barkowski was getting the hang of it.

'Sheriff's Department. It was county, not city.' He flipped the ID folder shut and stowed it away.

'There you are, sunnyside up.' Alma slapped a plate in front of me and pushed me into a chair. I ate. It was easier than arguing. Barkowski grinned at me.

'More, sonny?'

'Uh . . .'

'Okey-dokey.' He grinned again.

'Did anyone call John's house?'

'Yes, ma'am.' My hand froze on its way up to my

5

mouth. Sunnyside eggs dripped and gooed.

'And?' I breathed out finally.

'No answer, ma'am.'

I shoveled the egg in, mopped up the goo with a bit of toast.

'Detective, you may call me Kat, Ms. Colorado, or even Hey You, but please not ma'am.'

'Yesm ... uh ... Ms ... uh ... Kat. It's Joe, Joe Barkoswki.'

'A good polish name,' Alma commented. We ignored that too.

'Do you have a picture of your grandson, ma'am?' He addressed Alma.

'Of course. Katy will get it.'

I got up and headed for the back parlor, the real living room/sitting room. The front was for show: for guests, funerals, and talking to police who wouldn't eat breakfast. The photo albums were all there; I pulled out the most recent. It was February now and there would be loads of pictures from last Christmas.

I spread the album out on the kitchen table, flipping pages and pointing out John. Barkowski picked out one, a good one, a close-up of John carrying Alma's Christmas tree into the house.

'May I take this?'

'Yes,' I said.

'No.' That was Alma.

'Alma.' I said it gently. 'We have to know. He'll bring it back. Won't you?' I turned to him. The words came out fierce, but I didn't mean it that way. He was unperturbed, looking at the picture.

'Of course.'

He looked at me. His face was closed and attentive,

giving away nothing. So I knew. I looked at my eggs, the yolks cold now and congealed like yellow thickened blood. The hope phoenix in my heart flapped its wings feebly and died, sinking again into the ashes. Johnny. I felt tears in my eyes, then picked up plates and walked to the sink.

'Uh, Kat.' There was sympathy in Barkowski's voice. He knew I knew. 'You're Mrs. Flaherty's granddaughter, but not John's sister?'

'No. I'm not Alma's granddaughter either.'

'Yes, you are!' Alma's voice was fierce. I scraped and rinsed the plates. God, how I loved this crazy old woman. And Johnny. Johnny, too. Tears in the dishwater.

'But not technically. Alma adopted me as her granddaughter when I was very young. We've all kind of forgotten that we're not really related, but we're not.'

'Not blood kin, but kin,' Alma said, still fiercely. 'She and Johnny are the best of them all.' Her voice broke. I left the plates in the sink and put my arms around her.

'Tell us, Joe. Tell us what happened.' I led Alma to the table and sat her down, poured fresh tea for us and coffee for Barkowski.

He looked at me, was solemn and matter of fact. 'A young man was killed around three this morning. He was sitting in the Dodge Dart registered to your . . . uh . . .'

'Grandmother,' Alma said. Her voice was tremulous. She was beginning to know now, too. She gripped my fingers tightly, her rings biting into my flesh. I didn't move.

'Grandmother,' he said.

'An automobile accident?' I asked, knowing it wasn't.

'No. He was stabbed, looks like in the car while sitting in the parking lot of the Homestead Cafe. He'd had breakfast there; a waitress later identified him as a customer. It looked like he tried to get out of the car to get help. He didn't make it, probably couldn't have with those wounds. He was losing blood fast, was dead by the time someone found him.

'The Homestead is pretty busy that time of night. A lot of people eat there after the bars close. So far we haven't found anyone who saw anything. Still, it's early yet. We'll keep looking. We'll find someone.'

Alma moaned and gripped my hand tighter. I thought about how quickly things change, how hard it is to live, how easy it is to die.

'Tell me about your grandson, Mrs. Flaherty.'

'He was a good boy.'

'Was he a student? Did he have a job?'

Was. We were already in the past tense. My heart tightened for Johnny. I got up for more tea.

'A student. He was going to be an animal doctor.'

'He was in the veterinary program at Davis,' I amended.

'What did he do in his spare time?'

'He worked there, at the lab. He was a good boy, always working.'

'A girlfriend?'

'Lots of girls, but friends. No one special, he said.'

'His friends?'

She shrugged. He looked at me. I shrugged.

'Drugs?'

'No!' she shouted. 'My Johnny was a good boy.' She started to cry. 'A good boy. Always. Katy, help me to bed. I want to rest. No more now, no more.'

Barkowski stood up. 'Can I get your address and

phone number, Miss, uh Ms. I'll need to talk to you again. Soon,' he added firmly. 'Today, in fact.'

I found my purse and fished around in it for a card. His eyebrows went up slightly as he read. At the Private Investigator, I guess.

'We need a formal ID. Maybe there's a fingerprint record. Or a dental chart?' He looked at me. I nodded.

'I don't know his dentist.' I heard my voice crack. 'I'll find out.' He nodded again.

'Katy, put me to bed. Oh Johnny, such a good boy.' She glared at Barkowski, venom in her eye, then passion in her voice. 'Get out of my house!' She tottered unsteadily, but with dignity, out of the kitchen.

'I'm sorry,' I said. 'She doesn't mean it. She's upset. They used to put the bearers of bad tidings to death, you know.'

'Huh?' He looked at me, puzzled.

'Nothing. Do you mind letting yourself out and locking the door behind you?'

He nodded, handed me a business card.

'I'll come by your office as soon as I get someone to stay with my grandmother.' He nodded again. We shook hands.

Alma was part way up the stairs by the time I caught up with her. She transferred her grip from the banister to me and I half carried her the rest of the way. Alma, my indomitable grandmother. I had never seen her like this. I put her to bed, tucked her in.

'Alma, Johnny's . . .'

'Hush, don't say it, Katy. I know, dear. Yes, I know, I really do, but don't say it yet.' There were tears in her eyes. Mine, too. 'I love you, Katy. I hope I told Johnny that, too. Recently. Often.'

'You did, always. He knew, we always knew.'

'Say a prayer with me, dear.' I sat down on her bed and waited.

'Now I lay me down to sleep...' I joined in, my words and voice filling with tears. I hadn't heard it for years but it was the prayer she had always said with us kids when we were young, when life was full of possibilities and tomorrow and death a concept we disbelieved. I kissed her wet and wrinkled cheek.

'Don't go, dear.'

'No, I'll be here. Try to sleep for a bit. Call me if you need me.'

I turned the light off and went downstairs. The sky was starting to lighten. Big deal. Bitter words, bitter thoughts. In the kitchen I warmed up the tea and sat down with a cup, the photograph album, and the realization that Johnny would never see another dawn. I flipped through pages and memories. It didn't take long to find the picture I wanted: one of Johnny and me smiling into the camera, a little rat red-eyed from the flash. He was wearing the plaid flannel shirt I had given him for Christmas. We had our arms around each other.

And, finally, I cried.

Two

At eight-thirty Alma was up again dressed in a frightful combination of red, orange, and hot pink. No black. That's the kind of thing that makes me love her.

'I spoke to Mrs. Rusher. She's coming over in a bit to stay with you.'

'That old bag? Hah. Whatever for?'

I snorted. 'That old bag' was fifty-eight to Alma's eighty-one. Nevertheless she had a point. Alma had been running rings around Rusher for years and we all knew it.

'Just for company. A warm body in tough times.' I put my arms around Alma and squeezed. She shrugged me off, back to being a tough old lady again.

'I just hope to God she doesn't bring one of those frightful disgusting salads.'

'Salads?' After all these years Alma can still throw me. Too easily, actually.

'A green gelatin job with baby marshmallows, mandarin oranges, and Miracle Whip. Though it beats me how she can call that slop a salad.'

I stared at her. 'Alma, this is California, not the Midwest.'

'*I* know,' she said with dignity. 'Tell *her*.'

11

The doorbell rang. I often feel, when I'm with Alma, that life takes on a soap opera quality. I opened the door to Mrs. Rusher and something in an aluminium mold. It was lime green with baby marshmallows and mandarin oranges. I averted my eyes.

'Hello, dear,' Mrs. Rusher effused. 'And how are we? Ah, never mind. Here. I brought a little something.'

'Letty, you shouldn't have,' Alma said, and meant it. Her words had an ominous ring. I jumped into the conversation, peacekeeper at heart.

'Thank you so much, Mrs. Rusher. How very thoughtful.' I received the lime-green-marshmallow-orange-aluminum offering and bore it off to the kitchen. As the door swung behind me I heard Mrs. Rusher challenging Alma to cribbage at a penny a point. Empathy and compassion are not Rusher's strong suits; neither is common sense. As I came out I heard Alma take her up on it. Playing a competitive game with Alma is like throwing a Christian to the lions. Money or Christians, color it gone.

'Two cents a point or nothing,' Alma announced in a spirited fashion. Rusher placidly, and foolishly, agreed to it. Shortly after that I left.

It was a short hop over to 7th and G and the Sheriff's Department. Barkowski was out. Detective Henley, his partner, saw me instead. Unlike Barkowski, who was clean-cut, trim, and athletic, Henley was burly, hefty, and going to seed. His belly hung over his belt and there was dandruff on his shoulders. None of it matched the rich baritone voice that greeted me.

'Ms. Colorado? My pleasure. Come in, be seated. We're hoping you can help us fill in background and detail.'

'I hope so too. I loved John very much.' I gulped. 'Did you make an ID from the photograph?'

He nodded. 'I don't think there's any doubt, although we still need a legally definitive identification. His fingerprints are not on record. Perhaps you know who his dentist was?'

'No. You need to talk to his father, Walter Benson. The last I knew he was living in Marysville. Here's the number I have. I tried earlier but couldn't reach him.' I handed him a slip of paper.

'Now, you are not exactly family?' His eyebrows arched with the question. There was a sprinkling of dandruff in them.

'No, Alma Flaherty took me under her wing when I was about nine. She considers me her adopted grand-daughter, as I consider her my grandmother, but the tie is one of affection, not of blood, or legal arrangement. John's mother, Sophie, was Alma's niece. She died at least ten years ago.'

'But,' he looked at his notes. 'Mrs. Flaherty referred to John as her grandson?'

'Yes. She called both of us her grandchildren. John was really her grandnephew. They were very close.'

'What can you tell me about John's father?'

I sat for a long minute. 'He is a successful business-man, active in his church and community, well liked and respected. He has never fit in with the family very well, perhaps because he is an aloof and reserved man.' There was more; I thought it but I didn't say it. 'He and John were not close; John has been on his own for years now. Holidays were always at Alma's and Walter was never part of them, although he was invited.'

'Other siblings?'

'A sister, Michaela, who ran away from home some years back. There was something odd about that but I don't know what. John rarely spoke of her, but when he did it was with affection. I knew her, of course, but not well. John and I were close as adults, not as children.' My voice thickened a little.

Henley wagged his head sympathetically. A few more flakes of dandruff drifted down, a stray gray hair landed on his shoulder.

'What can you tell me about John's friends, associates, girlfriends?'

'Nothing. We didn't move in the same circles or talk much about that. John was almost twenty-three. I'm thirty-three. Our ties were family and affection. I was kind of a big sister to him, occasionally helped him out.'

'Of trouble?'

'No, small stuff. Money to get him by, or helping him with his car – it was always breaking down – or taking care of his dog.' I put my head in my hands; Ranger, one more thing to see to.

'How did John spend his time?'

'He went to school, worked at the lab there and part-time for a local vet.'

'Enemies?'

'No, it was impossible to dislike Johnny, unless, well, no . . .' I shook my head.

'What?' His voice was mellow; his eyes had sharpened.

'John had a couple of run-ins with some of the animal rights activists who vandalized the lab research facilities. They set animals free and ruined projects. John had a very scientific mind and supported humane animal research. He thought of the protestors as unreasoning fanatics but not, I'm sure, as enemies.'

'Do you know their names or anything about them?'

'No.'

Henley asked me a bunch more questions about John's daily habits, work routine, and so on that I couldn't answer. Then it was my turn.

'Did he eat alone at the Homestead? Was there any indication that he met or had plans to meet someone?'

An eyebrow went up. 'Apparently he ate alone and, no, we have no evidence of a meeting but we are, of course, considering that possibility.'

'Or that he was set up or staked out?' The eyebrow came down. No comment. 'Homicide in the commission of a robbery? His wallet was missing, I understand.'

'Yes, it was missing. No, we haven't come to a conclusion; the investigation has just begun. We are considering all the possibilities you mentioned.'

'And others?'

He nodded. I sighed and gave up. If cops don't want to talk to you they don't and that's that. I'd had plenty of experience with it.

'May I, or someone in the family, remove his personal effects from the apartment?'

'Of course. We have his address book and a few other items. They will be returned to you when we are through with them.'

I nodded.

'Did anyone stand to gain financially from his death?'

I shook my head. 'I can't imagine it. I'd be surprised if John had more than what was in his pocket and a couple of hundred in a checking account.'

'Okay. I guess that's it, then. For now at least.'

I stood up. So did Henley. Dandruff drifted down

onto his cuffs. He shook my hand warmly. The dandruff floated, airborne. Pigpen with a shoulder holster. I liked him.

'Thanks for your help.'

'Yes, I hope . . . we want . . .' I gulped and swallowed.

'Yes, yes, we'll be in touch.' He patted me kindly and ushered me out. A stray gray hair settled on my shoulder.

I stood on G Street in front of the Sheriff's Department in a cold February wind and wondered what to do next. Finally, cold all the way through, though still not as cold as Johnny, I started back to the car.

Work, I guess. The report. I had told Alma not to expect me until dinnertime. I headed back across town to my midtown office. I have a cubbyhole in a not very fixed up or fashionable Victorian on the perimeter of the fixed up and fashionable Victorian renaissance area. Rent is cheap, parking easy, the business address okay.

I parked the Bronco out front and walked up the steps into the building, past the secretarial service and old Mr. Addison's adding-machine repair shop. The door to my office was open. Someone sat at my desk reading my mail.

Three

'Charity.' I was too burned out to react further.

'Kat. Well, it's about time! Where have you been?'

'How did you get in?'

'Mr. Addison. I explained it was important.'

On cue Mr. A. walked in. He was always walking in, never busy. How could he be, fixing adding machines? The earth spun on a different axis now; we all had calculators. Me, too.

'Hi, doll face.'

'Hi,' I said numbly.

'Kat, what's the matter? Where have you been?' Charity got up and headed for me. She's my best friend and, while not awfully observant, does, when she notices, care. 'You look like hell,' she said kindly.

'You do, doll face, you do,' Mr. A. chimed in.

'I was at the Sheriff's Department, before that at Alma's. John, my cousin (that's what we called each other in our peculiar family nomenclature), was killed last night. Early this morning actually.'

Charity and Mr. A. swooped down on me like well-meaning but predatory birds and smothered me with pats and comforting noises. I collapsed into the nearest chair.

'Don't ask,' I said. 'Not now, not yet.' I heard the snap-snap of jaws clicking together. I closed my eyes. In the background the Coke machine thunked, a pop-top popped, and a cold can was thrust into my hand.

'Drink this.'

'Whatever happened to St. Bernards and brandy?' I murmured, but they were mumbling in the background.

'Kat,' Charity said, in her healthy-person-talking-to-the-crippled voice, 'I'm taking you out to lunch.'

'Thanks, but no, Charity. I've got work to do.'

'No, you don't. I listened to your messages and read your mail and there's nothing that won't wait. Oh, except Hank called; we had a nice chat. You're supposed to call him back.'

I opened my eyes and looked at her in astonishment. Opening my mail, listening to my answering machine? That was pushing it, even for my best friend. She had the grace to blush.

'She's right, doll face. Go on, it'll do you good. I'll keep the home fires burning.'

'Mace's, we'll go to Mace's.'

I closed my eyes again. 'Charity, I'm not dressed for Mace's. Burger King, yes, Mace's, no.' Mace's is elegant, refined, and high priced, all the things I'm not.

'Nonsense, you're with me. C'mon Kat, it'll do you good – you need food.'

She was right. Two bites of egg hours ago hadn't filled up the hole in my stomach. Not that food would either – Johnny was part of that hole. I swallowed hard.

'Food,' I agreed, 'and alcohol.'

'You got it, doll face.'

Between them they steered me out the door and toward Charity's BMW. Charity had a schizophrenic personality. Half the time she's a country girl, working with her cutting horses and smelling of sweat and manure; the other half she's a Yuppie in silk suits and a Bimmer. Maybe being a hotshot advice columnist does that to you. I sank into the (real) leather upholstery and closed my eyes. Charity ground the gears getting into first and we lugged off.

'Why don't you get an automatic?' I asked, my eyes still closed.

'It's not done.' She sounded shocked.

'Who cares? You can't drive a standard for shit.'

'Kat!'

I made a rude noise. Then I fell asleep. I didn't realize it, of course, until Charity woke me up in the Pavillion's parking lot. I knew where we were right away because of all the Mercedeses, Volvos, BMWs, and Acura Legends.

'Hungry?' Charity asked shyly.

I smiled. She loved me and this was her way of showing it. What the hell. 'Starved.' And it was true.

She smiled back and we climbed out of the car and strolled past the inanimate sculptured ladies sitting by the fountain, across the parking lot, and into Mace's.

Four

It was early. There were tables but we went into the bar first. Old habits die hard and I had been a bartender for years. A cocktail waitress glided over to our table and floated napkins down.

'Bombay martini up, very dry,' Charity said.

'White wine.'

'Ummm, good stuff,' Charity added, at a loss for further description. She was a connoisseur of gin, not wine.

'We have a chardonnay, a sauvignon blanc, an elegant fumé blanc, a Johannesburg Reisling and . . .' her voice floated on and Charity and I looked at each other. I raised my eyebrows and sent a telepathic cosmic shrug message. Charity grinned.

'The chardonnay will be fine.'

She rattled off some chardonnays and I picked one at random. Then she glided off, thank goodness.

'Kat—'

'No, let's not talk about it anymore. Later I'll be ready again, but not now.'

'Okay.'

'What's up with you?'

'StarBroke's ready. God, he's beautiful! We're going

to a show next weekend. He'll take every ribbon there.'

I smiled. 'And?'

'And I'm bored, Kat. There's more to life than cutting horses. But, shoot, I don't know what. After Sam—' She broke off and we stared at each other.

The drinks glided over and settled in front of us right in the center of their napkins. Sam was her husband, estranged husband. He'd died while I was investigating what he'd done with two hundred thousand dollars of their money. Charity had hated him more than she loved him, but still . . . she missed him. The human animal is an unfathomable creature. And cutting horses, even those like StarBroke, doesn't fill the void inside that a person leaves. I felt the hole inside me again that Johnny had left.

I picked up my wine glass. '*Salud.*' Charity tossed off her martini. I recklessly followed suit with a good half of my chardonnay.

'What else, then?' I asked.

'I don't know.' She looked puzzled. 'But I need something.'

The waiter appeared and dazzled us with specials. I felt my eyes glaze over.

'Order for both of us, Charity. Another white wine for me, please. Chardonnay,' I added quickly before he could get started on the list.

Lunch was good. I didn't pay much attention to what it was, but I enjoyed it.

'Kat, you're not supposed to eat the garnishes.'

'Mmmm. I'll eat your kiwi if you're not going to. Fork it over.' She sighed. I grinned. 'I suggested Burger King.' Her elegant shoulders shuddered.

'Dessert?' the waiter asked.

'No.'

'Yes.' We said it at the same time just as we always do.

Charity ordered for both of us. Naturally. She eats both desserts – which undoubtedly explains why I'm slim and she's round.

'A little shopping?' she asked on the way back to the car.

I laughed. On a scale of one to ten shopping is a minus two for me and Charity knows it. 'Back to work.' I waved good-bye to the sculptured ladies.

'Okay. I guess I should go to the office, too, pick up the mail and whatever.' We drove across town in contented, stuffed silence.

'Thanks for lunch, Charity.'

A quick hug and I was out of her car and up the stairs. Mr. A. was nowhere around. Thank goodness. I slipped into the office, closed the door, flipped the lights and computer on, and picked up my mail. I badly needed a dull, boring, business routine. The mail was nothing so I sorted through my notes and continued drafting my report on the background investigation I was doing for a possible corporate merger. Engrossing stuff.

That was why I didn't hear the door when it opened.

Five

'On the outside it says Kat Colorado, Investigator.'

I looked up from the computer at the slim, long-haired, blonde teenager who stood slumped against the door frame. She had ugly eyes and a strident voice. I nodded.

'Are you Kat Colorado?'

'Yes.'

The ugly eyes appraised me. 'You don't look like a private eye.'

I shrugged. 'What do you want: a pipe, notebook, and magnifying glass? Maybe a Hawaiian shirt and a .357 Magnum?'

She sneered. 'Are you any good?'

'You're planning to hire me and you want references?' I inquired politely.

'Anything to drink around here?'

'Coke machine down the hall.' She stuffed her hands in her pockets and disappeared, reappeared with a Coke.

'You can get your own if you want it.' She made her voice challenging. 'I'm not getting it.'

'I assume you want something from me. Most people are a little more polite.'

'Not me. I'm a bitch.'

'Yes.' I tended to agree with her. 'You are.'

She nodded with satisfaction. 'Grown-ups hardly ever admit that, you know.'

'That a kid's a bitch?'

She nodded. 'They say, "Oh no, you're not. You're an okay kid. You've probably had a tough time but we can straighten it out." '

'That's not it?'

'No. Yeah. Well, maybe. I've had a tough time, but mostly I'm a bitch.'

'Why?'

'What do you mean why? Because I am.'

'Or because you've decided to be.' She stared at me. 'Does it get you what you want?'

'Yes. No. No, my body gets me what I want.' She flipped her long hair back and stuck out her pointy little tits.

'What do you want?'

'What do you mean?'

'Just that. It's not a tough question.'

She looked confused. Her hair fell forward again and across her face. It made her look as young and vulnerable as she no doubt was somewhere under that tough facade. It almost tugged at my heart. I kept it out of my voice.

'Okay, how about: Why are you here?' Enough of the social chitchat.

'Why do you think?'

'I don't know. I don't even particularly care.'

I'd had a tough day and this kid was not making it any easier, though she was making it easy to be rude. Very easy. I turned away from her and went back to work at the computer.

There was a pause, not a long one, and then a Coke can slammed into the wall. It whipped past my ear and trailed soda over my shoulder. I took it full in the face on the rebound; I made myself count to ten.

'That showed you.' Her voice was full of malevolence and satisfaction.

'It showed me nothing except that you're rude and don't know how to act. Get out.'

I sounded calm but I was ready to kill. And I sure as hell couldn't understand why any of the grown-ups she knew thought she was an okay kid. She didn't move. I told her to get out again, and I didn't sound nearly as reasonable.

'I hate it when people say things like that. I hate it. Why do you do it?' Her voice came out in a whisper. 'Turn around, can't you. Look at me.' I counted to ten again; it was an effort. Then I turned. 'Why do you say it?'

'You're acting like a bitch, and you think that's good. It's not. You don't know what you want and you're not asking the right questions, so you won't find out. That's not good either. You're here because you want something, yet you throw a Coke at me. That's stupid. You don't want me to like you and I don't. What do you care what I think?'

Her eyes were big, dark, and full of hate. Her hands twisted and begged and pleaded. Her hands won out.

'I need your help.'

'Ask me.'

'Will you help me?'

'Please.'

'Please,' she whispered.

'Get a towel from the bathroom down the hall. Clean up the mess.' Hate flashed in her eyes again, on and off like emergency blinkers, but she went. She came back with two towels, one for me, and did a barely adequate clean-up. Then she sat down across from me.

'They found Lisa.'

'Who's Lisa?'

'My friend.' The hate drained out of her eyes. 'They found her dead. I read about it in the paper.' There was a long silence. 'She wasn't a bitch. I wasn't a bitch either, not with her. They don't know her name, but I know it was her. By the clothes and the watch. They said it in the paper and asked people to come forward and tell. They say that, come forward. It's stupid. How else would you come – backward, sideways? That's how I feel – backward, sideways.' She put her head in her hands.

'Did you?'

'What?'

'Come forward?'

'No. I'm afraid.' She was whispering again. 'Somebody killed her. Other people got killed too. They could—' She broke off. 'She had a watch on.'

'A watch?' I shook my head, puzzled. She'd lost me.

'In the description they said she had a watch. Well, I gave it to her, it was a birthday present. She'd always wanted a Mickey Mouse watch. She told me once and I remembered and I got her the best one I could find. The arms were Mickey's arms and the hands were really hands, white ones.' She moved her hands in doll-like fashion back and forth to the beat of an unheard tick tock.

'She was my best friend. I loved her and now she's dead. I know she is even though I don't want to believe it. It was a battery watch; I bought a battery that would last for two years. Now she's dead and Mickey's still running. His hands go around and around on her wrist and they tell her when it's time to get up and have lunch and meet me, but she never sees and never hears. They just go round and round on her dead arm.'

She stared at me, her eyes big and wide and dry. 'She's dead. Somebody killed her. I could be dead too. Other girls have died.'

'Tell me about it.'

'Do you know what I am?'

'I've got a pretty good idea.'

'I'm a hooker.'

I nodded.

'I'm scared. Help me. I don't want to get dead.'

'I'm not a social worker; I'm an investigator.' An investigator running out of patience, I thought. 'Talk to a social worker. Or a cop. I'll help you find someone.'

'They'll just send me home.'

'Good. That's where you belong.'

'I can't.

'Hah.'

There was a long silence. When it stretched past my patience I went back to the computer.

'I can't. Don't you see? I can't. Oh, fuck you, I can't.' She started crying.

I stopped working and watched for a while. 'Why not?'

'I don't have a home. My stepfather, he started coming into my bed. My mother slapped me and called me a whore when I told her. Then she threw me out and told me not to come back. At least on the street I get paid for it. And nobody slaps me.'

'No?'

Her eyes dropped. 'Now *you're* being a bitch,' she whispered.

'Okay,' I sighed. 'I'm sorry. But I'm still not a social worker and I don't have a magic wand to change your pumpkin into a coach. What do you want from me?'

'Help. And I want you to find out who wasted Lisa. I'm scared I could end up like that.'

I thought about it. 'If I decide to help you, you have to cooperate. That means you're off the street and you don't throw Coke cans at people's heads.'

'I threw to miss,' she whispered.

I stared at her, a cold hard stare, a cynical investigator stare.

'I was a pitcher.' She was still whispering. 'Softball. If I wanted to hit you, I'd have hit you.'

I kept right on staring.

'Okay. Yes. I promise.'

'All right. I need to make a phone call. Why don't you go wash off about a quarter pound of makeup and wait for me in the hall.

She opened her mouth to snap back and I watched, waited. Finally, defiantly, silently, she got up and left. The door shut just a little too loudly behind her.

I picked up the phone, crossed my fingers, and punched buttons. Bingo, Charity was still at her office.

Six

Only hindsight is 20/20. In hindsight I would not only have locked the office door, I would have slapped up the Out-to-Lunch sign and maybe the Going-Out-of-Business one as well. Instead it was two o'clock on a Tuesday: Johnny was dead; there was a teenage hooker gunking up my bathroom with makeup; Charity was on her way over to my office again.

I turned the computer off, pushed the keyboard aside and rested my head on my arms.

'Are you all right?'

I sighed. 'No' was the only answer to that. I straightened up again.

'What's your name?'

'Lindy.'

'Last name?'

'I don't have one anymore.'

I shrugged and didn't press it.

'Look, are you going to find out about Lisa?'

'Lindy, I'm already behind in my work, and I've got a lot on my mind right now. I'll go with you to the police if you want. That's their job and they do it for free.'

She sneered. 'I hate cops.'

'Okay. But they're the ones to see about dead friends.'

'You know what I heard a cop say once? He said we're throwaways. Our parents throw us away, somebody throws us away. Then we're just like Kleenex. Guys blow their nose and shoot their wad in us and then they throw us away too.'

'Nobody's going to give you the respect you don't give yourself.'

'Fucking cops.'

I raised my eyebrows. 'You're not on the street now, Lindy.'

'Stupid cops. I'm not going to them. So will you find out for me about Lisa? I'll pay you, I've got two hundred dollars.'

Great. I sighed. Kat Colorado, licensed private investigator, working for a teenage hooker on a two-hundred-dollar-trick-money expense account. That would knock 'em dead in Peoria.

'Okay? Two hundred dollars?'

'That's only one day. Less.'

'But it's for Lisa . . . you'd be helping . . . it's not just a cold business deal . . . there'd be satisfaction and stuff . . .'

She ran down and stared at me helplessly, suddenly very young and vulnerable in scrubbed face and hard, sharp, hooker clothes.

'I am not the Salvation Army. Satisfaction doesn't pay my bills any more than it pays yours.'

'Bitch.' She spat it out.

'You're the bitch.'

'Slut.'

'No, you're the slut, too.' She stared at me and her eyes filled up with hate again.

'I'll make a deal with you, like I said.' The hate

stayed. 'I'll see what I can find out. In return you stay off the streets and go back to being a kid again. You try,' I amended. 'Maybe you can't pull it off.'

She stared at me, then scuffed her shoes. 'I can do whatever I want to.' She paused. 'But how am I going to live?'

I tried not to smile at the contradiction in the last two sentences. 'I'll help you figure that out.'

'Oh.'

'How old are you? Fourteen?'

'Fifteen.'

'Lisa too?'

'About. Yeah. Maybe fifteen and a half. I dunno. We didn't talk about stuff like that, stuff that happened before we met.'

That stopped me. Of course it was unimportant stuff: age, last name, where you lived, stuff like that. I shook my head trying to clear it.

'Okay. Do we have a deal?'

'I guess.' She looked at me defiantly. 'Yeah.'

'Shake on it.'

I held out my hand and we did. In walked Charity. The timing was perfect. I couldn't have choreographed it better myself.

'Charity, Lindy, I'd like you two to meet.'

They eyed each other warily. Naturally. They were different life forms from different planets.

'Charity is a very successful advice columnist. She owns a ranch and breeds horses and is looking for a new project. Lindy is a hooker with no home, a dead friend, and problems.'

I paused and took a deep breath.

'Charity is always looking for someone to fork hay,

31

brush horses, and shovel shit.' Charity made a low sound in her throat that sounded like a moan; no, maybe a growl. 'Lindy is looking for a temporary home. I'm trying to wrap up this deal and get back to work. What do you think, folks? Do we have a plan?'

They both looked at me as though I'd lost my mind and was now, clearly, beyond hope. Okay, I hadn't really banked on them buying it the first time around. I sat and waited for inspiration that didn't come. They stood and stared sullenly at me.

'Nothing ventured, nothing gained,' I said at last. It was feeble, I knew, but it was the best I could come up with on the spot. No response.

'Charity begins at home.'

A flicker of guilt in Charity's eyes.

'A friend is someone you'd do anything for.'

A flicker of something in Lindy's eyes.

The silence lengthened. Like taffy at a taffy pull it stretched out, longer and longer. You keep thinking it's going to break but it doesn't.

'All right,' I said finally, at the breaking point even if the taffy wasn't. 'I guess the deal's off.'

Lindy and Charity scuffed their feet. I took a page out of their book and stared sullenly.

'Okay,' Charity heaved a heavy sigh of resignation that I thought was a bit melodramatic.

'Lindy?'

'Yeah, okay.' She heaved a sigh too. Great. They were going to have things in common.

I stood up and walked around my desk. 'That's settled then,' I said. They stared at me. Then I waited happily, expectantly, for them to leave. Not much happened.

'Is this right, Kat?' Charity said at last, sounding

worried. 'Shouldn't we talk to youth services or whatever they're called?'

'We should.' I agreed.

'They'll send me home.' Lindy's voice had a high, sharp edge to it.

'Or to a foster home.'

'I'll run away.'

'Will she?' Charity asked me.

'Probably.'

'Damn right I will.'

'We'll try it this way for a bit. We can work it out later, formalize it. I know a social worker who will help.'

'Hmmm.' Charity sounded dubious.

'For a week?'

'Oh, I guess.'

Silence again.

'An advice columnist?' Lindy ventured out this time. 'Could I help you write answers to your letters?'

'I don't know. Could you?'

'Maybe. I know a lot about problems.'

They sort of smiled at each other.

'Do I really have to shovel shit?'

Charity nodded. 'I have lots of horses and their stalls need to be cleaned out.'

'They go in their stalls?' Lindy sounded outraged.

'Horses don't use litter boxes, Lindy,' I explained in what I thought was a kind tone. She glared at me.

Charity jumped in. 'What do you think about going shopping for some clothes?' I had to hand it to her. She did a great job of keeping her look and voice non-committal.

'Terrific! Oh.' Lindy's face fell. 'I can't, I promised Kat the money.' She looked at me.

'No. We made a deal instead.'

'I'll buy the clothes: clothes, room, and board in exchange for work,' Charity offered.

'Why don't we put your money toward Lisa's burial in case we can't find her family?' I asked.

Lindy's eyes lit up. 'I'd like that. Would you keep the money for me? I want to do it, but I don't always trust myself.'

I nodded and she reached into a cheap vinyl handbag and brought out a wad of dirty, crumpled bills. I wondered how many tricks it represented.

'Would you like a receipt?'

'No, I trust you.' It felt like some kind of a milestone but I was too tired to figure it out so I let it go.

'Do you have a picture of Lisa?'

'Yeah. Not a good one though; it doesn't look a lot like her. We were just goofing around in one of those picture booths. Here.' She fished around some more in her purse and held out four dog-eared photos.

'It was right after I got her the Mickey Mouse watch.' Her voice tightened. 'That's in the picture, too.'

She was wrong about the likeness. The girls were clowning around for the camera but they were alive, happy, and recognizable. And they looked like girls, not hookers.

'How tall is Lisa?'

'About the same as me, maybe a little shorter.'

'Five four?'

'Yeah.'

'Weight?'

'She was skinny. Always eating and trying to stay over a hundred pounds. Me, I gain weight if I look at a Twinkie sideways.'

34

'How did she usually wear her hair?' In the picture her shoulder-length, dark brown hair was partly down, partly caught up on the top of her head with a clip.

'Like that, or down, or pulled in back.'

'Brown eyes?'

'Yeah. She called them her spaniel eyes. Said she could make ten bucks more by saying nothing, making her eyes sad and just looking at a john. They fell for it. I saw it happen lots of times.'

I nodded. I believed her. Lisa's eyes were the kind you see on a Save-This-Child picture. They seemed to take up half her face and sucked you into their unspeaking depths, made you want to feed her oatmeal and cream and give her money. And fuck her, I thought grimly. Maybe kill her, too.

'Do you know what she was wearing?'

'I'm not sure. There was a sweatsuit missing. Gray with pink stripes. Probably sneakers, white high-tops.'

'Jewelry?'

'She had a gold chain with a locket and a pinky ring with a heart on it that she almost always wore.'

'Any distinguishing marks?'

'No. Well, yeah. She had a mark on the back of her leg where she backed into a heater. It was a rectangle a little darker than the rest of her skin.' She reached down and touched the back of her right calf.

'Right leg?'

'Yea. No. Well, I think so. I'm not sure.'

'Where did you live? And Lisa? Did the two of you live together?'

'You don't need to know that.' The hostility was back.

'Sure I do. You think that I'm a magician, that I can pull answers out of a hat like rabbits?'

She threw me a hard-edged stare and I threw it back.

'I need to know where you guys lived, if you had a pimp, as much as you can tell me about her regulars, her everyday habits, all that kind of stuff.'

She twitched her head nervously back and forth. Her hair flowed and flopped. Charity stared at us open-mouthed.

'Really, Kat,' she began. I flipped a stare, hard-edged like a Frisbee, over to her too. She caught it full in the face and shut up.

'Yeah, really.' Lindy's voice was an ugly echo of Charity's.

I shrugged. 'Up to you. I can check, see if we have a possible match based on this description and the pictures. If you want to find out about her death I'm going to need more to go on.'

'I can't,' she whimpered. 'I could get hurt too. Or killed.'

'Okay.' I shrugged again. 'Whatever you say. She was your friend.' Lindy made an animal sound low in her throat.

'Kat—' Charity began. I glared at her again. She shut up.

'Think about it, Lindy.' She wouldn't look at me. I was acting like a tough, but I didn't blame her for being scared. Burning your bridges is always scary. So are a lot of things on the street.

'I changed my mind.' Her voice was frosty, like a cold Coke on a hot day. 'I'd like a receipt after all.'

'Okay.' I moved behind my desk and opened a drawer.

'No, wait. Never mind.' She kicked my desk. 'I, uh, okay, I'll think about it.'

I nodded. 'We can talk about it more if you want to. It might help.'

She snorted and looked away. We all stood around saying nothing. It was a fifteen-second pause that felt like five minutes. Charity broke first – she's probably a nicer person than either Lisa or me. Certainly more compassionate. And more polite.

'Errr, how about an ice cream?'

No response.

'Maybe a double scoop?'

I grinned. Charity's answer to stress is food. Stress, sorrow, frustration: Charity's answer to a lot of things is food, especially desserts. She's two inches shorter than my five seven and probably has twenty pounds on my one hundred thirty. She won't tell me, not that I care. Anyway, it looks fine on her.

She stretched a smile across her usually serene Madonna face, ran her fingers through blond hair, opened her blue eyes wide, cleared her throat nervously and tried again.

'Err, what the heck, maybe a triple scoop? Anybody?' Her question trailed off into the dusty corners of my office.

'Sounds good.' I lied, I was still stuffed from lunch. 'I'd like to but I've got to finish this report and then go over to Alma's.' I looked at Lindy.

'I wouldn't mind,' Lindy said at last and grudgingly. 'How about one of those places where they have lots of neat flavors? Like bubblegum.'

I shuddered. Teenagers.

'Or coconut sherbet?' I offered.

They shuddered. 'Bleah. Yeech.' It was hard to tell who said what.

'Chocolate, chocolate dip chip,' said Charity.

'Caramel pecan fudge twirl,' said Lindy.

I beamed at them. If Lindy could shovel horse shit they were going to get along fine.

'Don't drip ice cream on the new BMW, kid; you're dead meat.'

Lindy looked at me nervously. I winked. She tried out a smile but it slipped off her face before she could convince anyone but a store dummy.

'Oh, Kat,' Charity chided. Lindy tried the smile again, with more success this time.

'Have a good time, you two. Eat a scoop for me. Amaretto chocolate carrot cheesecake maybe.'

'Bleah,' they said in unison. I grinned and waited, still hopeful and expectant, for them to leave. Nothing happened. I walked over and hugged Charity good-bye.

'I don't suppose I could hug you?' I asked Lindy. She stared at me for a long time.

'We could shake hands,' she said at last. And smiled. It lit up her face like fireworks on a dark night. We shook.

'Baskin and Robbins?' Charity asked.

'Leatherby's is better.'

'No!'

'Yes!'

'Is not.'

'Is too.'

They headed out. I said good-bye, but no one noticed. Ice cream, the great suspender of social amenities. I walked over to my desk and sat down, flipped on the computer, waited for it to boot up. A stack of grubby greenbacks stared at me, George on top, dour-faced and serious as usual.

I counted the money, two hundred and fourteen dollars, stuck it in an envelope, and put it in the floor safe. The computer prompt blinked invitingly at me. I ignored it. A teenage hooker with an attitude problem, a dead girl with a live Mickey Mouse watch, a murder investigation, and Johnny. Swell. I flipped the computer off again.

I should turn the girl and the information over to the authorities, but I couldn't, wouldn't. I was the child of an alcoholic single mother and I'd been abandoned too many times. Now I can't turn away the Lindys and Lisas who fall into my life. They might not have anyone else. If Alma had turned me away . . . but I didn't finish that thought. It was too painful.

I got up carefully, carefully didn't kick my chair back against the wall even though I felt like it. Then I went next door to see if Mr. A. wanted to amble down the block for a beer at the local dive. It beat ice cream. It beat crying over lost lives: Johnny's, Lisa's, maybe Lindy's. I wondered where Michaela was.

And I wondered if helping Lindy could ease the pain of losing Johnny. I hoped so.

Seven

The beer didn't help, of course. It never does. So I came back and stared at my computer and the report some more. Then I gave that up too.

I called Henley just before five. Not to bug him, just to give myself the sense that I was doing something.

'I got a hold of Walter Benson,' he said. 'He didn't seem real broken up.'

'Hard to tell with Walter, but I'm sure he was inside. Outside he's got all the emotion and empathy of an ice cube.' Henley grunted. 'He wouldn't show what he felt to a stranger anyway. Anything else come up?'

He grunted again. 'I don't have the coroner's report yet but I'll tell you what I think. It doesn't look like there was any kind of struggle. My bet is John knew his attacker and felt at ease with him. Or her. He saw no reason to feel threatened or to be on guard.

'Let's say some guy John knows comes over to the car. John starts to get out of the car and the guy lets him have it. Quick and easy. And quiet. John falls back in the car, the guy shoves him in, shuts the door, and walks away. It's all over in a minute or less. Nice,' he added, then rumbled and cleared his throat as he remembered who he was talking to.

'His wallet was gone,' I pointed out.

'Could of been to throw us off. You see what it means?'

'We're back to motive.'

'Yeah.'

'Only if it was someone he knew. John was very open and friendly. Trusting.'

'Would he get out of his car to talk to a stranger?'

'He might,' I said sadly.

'Well, just for fun, let's play with . . .' He stopped and cleared his throat embarrassedly.

'It's okay, I understand.'

He grunted. 'Sorry. Let's hypothesize that John did know his attacker.'

'Back to motive?'

'Yeah. Got any?'

'No. I thought about it but I can't come up with anything more than I told you earlier. I'll talk to Alma tonight, maybe she'll have an idea.'

He grunted. 'Okay. Stay in touch.'

'Henley.'

'Yeah.'

'Thanks.'

'Yeah. You're welcome. Be talking to you.'

Alma did have an idea and she dropped it on me like a bomb. But not right away. For an hour I felt like a civilian in an air raid, waiting and listening, all tense, fevered, and expectant – all the time praying it will come, that the bombs will drop and the planes leave. Then, if you're not dead, you can go back to bed and to sleep.

'Alma!'

'We'll eat first, Katy. It's always best to talk about these things on a full stomach.'

'What things? What are we talking about?'

'Set the table, dear.'

'Arghh!'

Alma looked at me reprovingly.

'I won three dollars and forty-five cents from Mrs. Rusher today. I beat her at cribbage, casino, and canasta,' she announced with satisfaction.

'It's okay to talk about your gambling winnings at dinner but you can't talk about Johnny?'

'Could you dish up the stew, Katy? I'll get the garlic bread and salad.'

I gave up. We talked about the inconsequential things that Alma brought up, one after another.

'How long should I wait before I return Letty's Jell-O mold?'

'Until you finish the Jell-O, I guess.' It wasn't like Alma to ask such an obvious and dumb question.

'It's history.'

'You ate it?' I was amazed.

'I had a little for lunch,' she said in her most heroic voice. 'It was only polite.' I agreed. 'But I tossed the rest out as soon as she left. It was only sensible.' I agreed with that too.

'Alma?'

'We have ice cream and cookies for dessert, Katy.'

'No thanks, maybe later. Could we—'

'After the dishes.'

I sighed. We did the dishes.

'Tea, dear?'

'Yes, please.'

'Now?' I asked when we were finally settled in the

sitting room with a pot of tea and a plate of macaroons.

'Now,' she agreed.

'Do you know of any reason why someone would kill Johnny?'

'Just the money.'

'What money?' I gaped at her, unfortunately doing my half-witted goldfish impersonation.

'Sophie's money.'

'Sophie had money?'

'Quite a lot of it, actually.'

'How come I never knew about this?' I sputtered, choking briefly on a bit of macaroon.

'Really, Katy,' Alma admonished me. 'Decent people don't talk about things like that.'

That's right. I forgot. In Alma's book decent people don't talk about money, sex, or going to the bathroom. They do it, they don't talk about it. I sighed again.

'Let's talk about it now. For Johnny's sake.'

'Yes.' She paused to collect her thoughts and sip tea. 'Johnny's grandfather, Sophie's father, James, who was your grandfather's brother, had a number of walnut orchards in Marysville. He did well, very well indeed. When he died he left all three children provided for.'

'How much?'

'I imagine it was at least a hundred thousand for each of them. And property, I think,' she added, vaguely.

I whistled. 'And that was what, twenty-five years ago?'

'Thirty. Even conservatively invested it would amount to quite a lot now.'

I did some mental arithmetic and agreed. It would be a nice chunk of change.

'Sophie couldn't touch the principal. James set it up that way.' I raised my eyebrows in a question. 'Partly

because she was a girl and he was old-fashioned; he
didn't do it for the boys. But mostly it was because
he didn't trust Walter and was vehemently opposed to
their marriage. He thought Walter was a scoundrel and
an opportunist. I must say James seems to have been
wrong about that.'

'What happened to the money when Sophie died?'

'It's in trust for the children, Johnny and Michaela.'

'Principal or interest?'

'All of it, the whole works.'

'And if either one of them died?'

'It went to the other.'

'Nothing to Walter?'

'No.'

'Not even if both children died?'

'I don't think so. Anyway, that seems a bit far-fetched,
doesn't it?'

'Yes. It does.' But I thought about it some more
anyway.

'When does the money come to them?'

'Twenty-three, I think. Sophie thought twenty-one
was too young.' We stared at each other. 'Michaela's
twenty-one,' Alma said, 'and Johnny would have been
twenty-three in April.' We stared at each other some
more. A tingle started inside me. It was excitement,
horror, and revulsion all mixed up and ugly. I shivered.

'Johnny knew about this, of course?'

'I'm not sure. He knew he would get something, naturally, but I don't think he knew how much. Sophie and
I agreed it would be better for the children if they
didn't know. She wanted them to make something of
themselves on their own, not depend on family money.

'They knew Sophie had money of her own but I think

44

they thought it was just enough for occasional extras: sports equipment for Johnny, and music lessons and instruments for Michaela. Sophie never threw money around and Walter took care of all the family expenses.'

'So Michaela doesn't know either?'

'I can't see how. She was seventeen or so when she left home.'

'Johnny could have asked Walter?'

'Yes.'

I thought about it a bit. 'First thing tomorrow morning I look into this.'

'No, not first thing.' I stared at her. 'First is Michaela. Find her, Katy.'

'Alma, you don't just find someone. She's been gone for at least four years and no one's heard from her.'

'Find her, Katy. Try. Johnny is her brother and she should be here for the memorial service. It's only right. I know she'd want it.' Her eyes filled with tears. 'She's living; Johnny's dead. He can wait now.' The tears started spilling over.

'I have been wrong, Katy. She is Sophie's daughter and I should have been more of a mother to her. I owed Sophie, and the child, that much. Indeed, I loved her when she was young, such a dear child, but teenagers are so difficult.' She sighed. 'Still, that was mistaken. I should have been more of a mother to her . . . Oh me, find her, Katy.'

'All right. But now? There are a lot of things that I should—'

'Now. It is *For-the-Family*.'

There it was finally, the sacred pronouncement. I couldn't, wouldn't argue. Alma had given me the only family I'd ever known after my little sister died.

'Katy?'

'Yes.'

'You'll do it?'

'Yes.'

'First thing?'

'First thing tomorrow. Now I'm going back to the office to finish a report that's due.'

'Oh, dear.' She smiled wanly.

I smiled back. 'Call this number.' I scribbled a number down. 'Ask Tim to take care of the animals.' Tim is my twelve-year-old neighbor and helper. 'I'll sleep here tonight. Be back as soon as possible.' I leaned over and kissed Alma.

I finished up the report, stuck it in a manila envelope, and slapped a page of stamps on it. The PO makes a small but steady profit off me because I'd rather over-estimate the postage than make a trip down there.

Then I called Hank. Hank's a detective with the Las Vegas Metropolitan Police. We met last summer while I was working in Vegas for Charity and have been together ever since. If you can call me living in Sacramento and him living in Vegas 'together.' We both have ridiculous phone, gas, and travel bills.

No answer on his end. Bummer.

I called Charity. No one was there but the machine. They were out having fun in the barn, I supposed. The machine and I had a little chat. I said I'd be busy for the next few days but I'd be in touch by the end of the week. The machine said nothing.

The almost antique clock sitting on the mantel of the almost fireplace in my office told me it was 10:25 and the clock was at least fifteen minutes fast. What the hell, cops work twenty-four hours a day. Henley and Barkowski were not answering. I finally got through to someone and left a message for one of them to call me at Alma's the next morning.

Then I called Johnny's number, hoping his roommate would be there; hoping he'd be willing to briefly take care of Ranger, a lovable research-project-reject dog that John had adopted; hoping he could tell me something new and helpful. I got to base on the first two and struck out on number three.

'Kat, I wish I could help. John was my best friend. He—'

'I know,' I said into the silence. 'Thanks. Did he say anything about what he was doing that day?'

'I never even saw him. I spent the night before at my girlfriend's. By the time I got back in the morning he was gone. I have no idea. Kat, the police asked me about drugs.'

'Yes. They asked me too.'

'John despised the drug scene.'

'Yes.'

'I can't believe it's anything like that.'

'No. Me, either. What else? Did he owe someone money or vice-versa? Bad feelings over a girl? Trouble at the lab?'

'They asked me that, too, and no, nothing I know about.'

'Did John ever talk about the money he was coming into?'

'Was he? When?'

'On his twenty-third birthday.'

He was silent, thoughtful for a while. 'Yes and no. One night a couple of weeks ago he had a long talk with his dad. Parts of it were pretty angry – John shouted quite a bit. He said that by the terms of the will the money was his, absolutely, on his twenty-third birthday and that he would do what he wanted with it. He said something about making his own decisions regarding investments, that he appreciated his father's advice but that he was capable of handling it fine. Something like that.

'Then he asked who the other executor was. I heard him repeat the name of a bank official and a bank but I didn't pay any attention to it. We talked about it a bit but I didn't learn much more.'

'Hmmmm.'

'Does that help?'

'Right now anything does. Did the subject ever come up again?'

'No. Course we didn't see each other much. I'm over at my girlfriend's a lot. I wish I knew more, Kat, I'd like to help.'

On an impulse I took him up on the implied offer. 'Ned, I know it's late but could I come by? I'd like to look through John's things.'

'Now?'

'Now.'

'Oh. Well, yeah, sure, I guess. I'm studying for a big test, I'll be up for a while.'

'Half an hour then. See you.'

'Yeah, see you. Hey, Kat, how is your grandmother?'

'Okay, but not good.'

'I'm sorry. I wish – Aw, hell!'

And that about summed it up all right.

Eight

It was an impulse I almost regretted as I hung up. It was late, I was tired, and Davis was a good twenty miles down the freeway. Almost regretted, not quite. It was for Johnny.

They lived in an older house near I and 4th that had been carved up to cash in on every possible student dollar. A while ago it had slid into looking dilapidated and sad, the paint peeling, the steps sagging. The yard was worse, run-down and dispirited as though lack of interest had made the half-living things there give up hope. There was a rotting pumpkin from Halloween still sitting on the porch, its toothy smile a distorted sad grimace.

Ned answered the door on my first knock. He had a pencil behind his ear and the TV on. The 'M*A*S*H' helicopter was landing for the four millionth time.

'Come on in, Kat.' He shrugged his shoulders and waved his hands around a bit. 'Make yourself at home, look at whatever you want. You know where John's room is?' I nodded.

'Do you have a few minutes, Ned?'

'Well, yeah, I guess. I have this test though.'

'I know. What's been on Johnny's mind this last month or so?'

'Nothing much. Just the usual stuff.' He paused, looking at me helpfully. Obviously he was going to need prompting, prodding. I prompted.

'Was he mad or upset about anything?'

'The animal rights guy, I guess. What was his name?' He looked at me. I shook my head. 'Gil. That's it. He was passing leaflets out in front of the lab one time. John took one, read it, and then told him it was full of distortions and misinformation. The guy called him a liar and a murderer. That kind of pissed John off.'

Ned looked at me and I nodded. 'Understandably.'

'Yeah. Well, John kept trying to talk to him in a rational way and Gil kept hollering "murderer, killer, slaughterer," that kind of stuff. He compared John to Hitler, Genghis Khan, and Lady Macbeth. Kind of stretching it, don't you think?'

I thought so. Definitely. Lady Macbeth was out of her league there, never mind John. In the background Hawkeye raised the ante at poker and tossed down an extra dry martini. Maybe that was stretching it, too, but we'd gotten used to it.

'Anyway, they got into kind of a shoving match. The guy's leaflets got dumped and he landed on his butt. John wouldn't fight him – he's just a little guy, a lot of hot air in a skinny little frame.

'I guess Gil picked himself up and moved back a little, still hollering, threatening John, too.' Hawkeye won the hand and left to check on a patient. Then some guy with a calm soothing voice started talking about stomach acid and Rolaids. I wished I had some. Ned ran down and waited for the next prompt.

'With what?'

'Huh?'

'Threatening him with what?'

'Oh, nothing in particular. He said he wished John would get all cut up like those poor animals and then he'd be sorry and that some day he'd get his and he, Gil, just hoped it was pretty damn soon.'

That sounded fairly particular to me, that or I was missing something.

'Just general stupid stuff like that. He probably didn't even mean any of it, probably was just trying to salvage his pride. John had made him look pretty dumb and ineffectual.'

'Did you tell the police about this conversation?'

'No. What is there to tell?'

I looked at him and blinked. One of us was in a different reality. The same train did not stop at both of our stations. Briefly I wondered what the name of his station was: Lotus Land, Ivory Tower, Ostrich Island?

'Ned, he threatened John, said he wished John would get cut up, would get his. John was stabbed to death not long after that.'

It was Ned's turn to blink. Hawkeye talked to some poor blown-up kid and told him he was going to be all right. Then the kid died. Hawkeye looked like he needed some Rolaids. So did Ned. I probably did, too.

'I don't think he really meant it, do you?'

'I don't know. That's the kind of stuff the police figure out.'

'You think I should tell the cops?'

'Yes,' I said firmly. 'I do. Here's the guy you want to talk to.' I fished Henley's card out of my wallet and copied down the name and number. Ned looked at it like it was a hand grenade with the pin about to fall out. The 'M*A*S*H' music played.

'Okay. But they'll probably think it's stupid.'

'No,' I assured him. 'They won't.'

'Okay.' Still dubious.

I tried to come up with the next prompt. Ned knew things he didn't know he knew. There was more to come, I was betting on it. 'There was a girl, a new girl.'

'You think so?'

I nodded firmly. I'd just made it up, so firmness was called for.

'Yeah, maybe you're right. I don't think they were real involved though. He talked about her like she was off limits, married maybe, or at least had a boyfriend.'

'Where did he meet her?'

'I don't know.'

'Name?'

'Don't know that either.'

'Did they see each other often?'

'Not as often as he wanted – he was pretty hot for her. Once, twice a week maybe, and always during the day. Lunches, beers after work, that kind of thing.'

'What does she look like?'

'I never met her.'

'Did he describe her?'

'Said she was beautiful.'

Great. Big help. That narrowed it right down. 'Does she live around here?'

'I guess. I think she might be at Davis.'

'In veterinary medicine?'

'I don't know. Look Kat, I've really got to hit the books. Tomorrow—

'One more.' He frowned. 'Why did John get into an argument with his dad?' Ned laughed and that surprised me. Why?

52

'Same old stuff every guy his age gets into with his old man. His dad is a stockbroker or something, knows how to manage money. He's pretty conservative, too. He wanted John to leave his money in these safe long-term investment accounts so it would be there for the future. He even said he'd match a percentage of it to help John start his own veterinary practice when he finished school.'

'Sounds pretty generous.'

'Yeah, it was. And John was happy about it, he appreciated it. I guess they hadn't always seen eye to eye.'

'Why did they quarrel?'

'Because John said he wasn't going to take his father's advice. He was going to spend some of it, quite a bit, I gathered. He said he really needed the money for something but it was a good investment and he'd get it back.'

'What?'

'I don't know. Me, I would have bought a Maserati.' He grinned. 'But not John.'

'No.'

'Look, Kat, maybe some other time but now I've got to study.'

'Thanks, Ned. You've been swell. Tell the cops all this: Gil, the girl, the discussion with Walter.'

'Walter?'

'His dad.'

'Yeah, okay.' He didn't sound convinced, he didn't sound eager. I hoped he was willing. Ned drifted off to his room and I headed for John's.

Except for a sense of sadness and violation I didn't find anything. The sadness I probably brought with me; the violation came from other people going through his things. I found nothing personal: no notes, no journals, no letters, no nothing. I flipped on the computer and pulled up the directory. Everything looked school related. I jumped into a few files that seemed like possibles and then some at random. Nothing.

Nothing in his pockets, desk, bureaus, or under his pillow. Either there was nothing or the police already had it. Then I sat and thought about how well I knew Johnny and how I didn't know him at all. The Johnny I knew wouldn't shove a guy, even a jerk like Gil, and toss his leaflets around. Or run with a married woman. Or spend large sums of money on something a conservative stockbroker would disapprove of. The Johnny I knew was easygoing and kind, careful with his money, and on the moral straight and narrow.

And the Johnny I didn't know? But that was it. I didn't know.

On my way out I tapped on Ned's door. I thanked him again but that wasn't the reason. The reason was I wanted his girlfriend's number. Ned didn't look pleased but he gave it to me.

'Sally doesn't know anything. They hardly knew each other.'

'Okay. I'd just like to talk to her.' If she didn't know anything like Ned didn't know anything, I could learn something.

I let myself out the back door. I didn't have to call Ranger, Johnny's dog, he came running. I hugged him and told him about Johnny. I cried. I didn't mean to but I did. His ears drooped, his tail stopped wagging, his eyes got empty and lonely. Maybe it was just the sadness in my voice. Maybe not. I said good-bye to Ranger, told him I'd come for him as soon as possible, then headed for A. J. Bump's Saloon on G Street.

I called Sally, Ned's girl, from there. She sounded glad to hear from me or maybe it was just from anyone.

'Sure, you can buy me a drink, two or three in fact. I'm supposed to go over to Ned's but screw him, drinking with you sounds like more fun. I'll meet you at the bar in ten minutes.'

It wasn't ten, eight maybe. She was bouncy and pretty and I had a hard time matching her up to Ned. She ordered an Alabama Slammer and I gave up trying.

'It's about John, right?'

'Right.'

She nodded. 'It had to be. I don't *know* anything but I've got ideas.'

'Good. I'd like to hear them.'

'Johnny was deep, you know what I mean?' She slugged down a third of her Slammer. I didn't but I nodded. 'Some people you can tell what's going on inside by how they are outside. They match, the inside and the outside, you know? But John wasn't like that. On the outside he'd seem all calm and cool; on the inside, he'd be boiling away. Like a pot of boiling water. When the lid's on you can't tell it's boiling; you take the lid off and, oh brother.' Sally shoved her cherry to the bottom of the tall glass with her straw, then stabbed it, fished it out and ate it.

'What was he boiling about?'

'Well, that's the hard part.' She finished her drink. 'Can I have another one of these?'

'Sure. As many as you like.'

'Thanks.' She sighed. 'I love them but they're too much for my budget and Ned's kinda cheap.' At four bucks a pop and the rate she was drinking them that was understandable. The bartender put another Slammer in front of her and she started in on it.

'I think he was angry a lot. I think he'd had a tough time in some ways and had had to work real hard to make things come out the way he wanted them to. Most of the time he kinda understood that that's the way life is but sometimes I think he'd get mad, mad that things were such a struggle.

'Then maybe he'd think about how things didn't seem fair and sometimes he'd take it out on other people or situations. Like that animal rights guy. He's a jerk, yeah, but even so it seemed John was kind of hard on him. You know what I mean?' She looked at me, intelligent brown eyes over an Alabama Slammer.

And once again, no, I didn't. Easygoing, light-hearted Johnny mad inside? Boiling away unseen like a volcano you think is extinct but is really just biding time?

'Ned said you two didn't know each other very well.'

'Well, we all hung out together a lot. And a couple of times when Ned went to bed early John and I stayed up real late and talked. We knew each other. Ned doesn't like to admit it because he was a little jealous that we got along so well. Maybe he was afraid that I could have gone with John instead of him. And maybe I could have if John had shown any interest, but he didn't.' She ended on a note of regret and finished her drink, then raised her eyebrows at me. I nodded and she ordered another.

'Was there a new girl in John's life?'

'Yeah. He told me about her but he didn't say much. He was kind of strung out about it. Either she was holding him off or the situation was.'

'Situation?'

'Like she was married or with a guy.'

'Do you know her name?'

'He mentioned it.' She frowned. 'I remember thinking it was a really dumb name. It didn't match the kind of person I'd have put him with in my mind.' She frowned again. 'Belinda, that was it. And sometimes he called her Bella, too.'

'Did you meet her?'

'No.'

'Know what she looked like?'

She shook her head. 'Oh, wait. He said that she had real short dark hair sculptured around her head and that only a *very* beautiful woman could wear her hair like that. La-di-da.' She ended on a spiteful note and swung her hair back.

'Did he say anything else about her?'

'No. I asked too. He wouldn't not say, but he kinda slid off and changed the subject. I got the message.'

I finished my beer as Sally finished her drink. 'Did you drive?'

'Bicycle.'

There's a reason why drinks have names like Slammer, Kamikaze, B–52. 'I'll drive you home. We can put your bike in the back of my car.'

She smiled. Her teeth were a little crooked. Her eyes too. She'd consumed a lot of alcohol in a short time. 'Okay, good.'

I dropped her off and got back on the freeway. Traffic was still heavy. I–80 lightens up sometimes for about ten minutes between three and four in the morning. Sometimes. The eighteen-wheelers were roaring by in the fast lane so I poked along in the slow.

I had a lot more information but it all fell in the

column labeled speculation, not fact. It figured but I didn't know how.

Maybe that figured too.

Nine

The phone rang at seven-thirty the next morning. It was Henley sounding chipper and putting me on the spot.

'Ms. Colorado, I got your message. What's up?'

What was up? God knows. Not me, it was seven-thirty. I put my brain in gear and revved it, tried to shift up. Henley waited patiently.

'I found out something yesterday from Alma.' I cleared my throat, trying to get rid of the early morning sleepy sound.

'Yeah.'

'Money. Motive. John stood to inherit a bundle on April eleventh, his twenty-third birthday.'

Henley whistled. 'How much?'

'I don't know. The principal was at least a hundred thousand thirty years ago. Sophie, John's mother, inherited it from her father, James Budroe. She couldn't touch the principal and probably didn't spend much of the accrued interest. John would have gotten half of it on his birthday. Michaela inherits on her twenty-third birthday in two years. She'll get it all now.'

'Where is she?'

'Don't start on Michaela. That's another long story and you need to talk to Alma first. She doesn't think

59

either of them knew anything close to the amount of money involved. They knew their mother had extra "fun money." That's all.'

'Is Mrs. Flaherty busy now?'

'God knows, Henley, I'm barely awake. I don't know what *I'm* doing, much less anyone else.'

He laughed.

'Alma's eighty-one and doesn't get out much. Can you come by at eleven-thirty? I'll tell her to expect you for lunch.'

'Uh.'

'She's at her best around food. Trust me.'

'Good cook?'

'The best.'

He sighed happily. 'All right. I'll be there.' He started to sign off.

'Wait, there's more.' My mind was working finally, though not in high gear. I told him about my conversation with Ned and asked about Gil. I gave up more information than I got but he finally came across with a last name for Gil and an address in Davis. Then I sicced him onto Walter.

'I think it might be interesting to see the will, find out who's managed the money all these years, see how it's accounted for now.'

'Yeah,' said Henley, 'it would be at that.'

'It sounds like Walter and a bank acted as executors.'

'I'll check it out. Anything else?'

I thought and couldn't come up with anything. It was 7:35. Hot tea sounded good. Damn. I knew I was forgetting something, I just didn't know what.

'Ms. Colorado?'

'No, I guess not.'

'About Michaela?'

'Later, detective,' I hedged. 'Talk to Alma first.'

'Right. See you later then.'

'Yes, but not today. I've got family business to take care of.'

'No problem.'

No problem? I thought that was overly optimistic on his part, but then he didn't know the whole story. Neither did I, but I wasn't feeling optimistic. We hung up and I took a bath in Alma's block-long, claw-footed tub and woke up some more.

'What now, dear?' Alma asked me as she plied me with choices for breakfast.

'I go home and change and then head for Marysville. I figure I'll start with Walter even though he probably won't be much help.'

'I mean what do you want for breakfast. You can't have a full day on an empty tummy.'

I sighed and wondered how many hundreds, thousands, hundreds of thousands of times I'd heard that. I'm rarely hungry in the morning but I didn't bother to argue it. I know when I'm outnumbered.

'Oatmeal, please.'

She cooked it with raisins and firmly placed a banana in front of me. I ate it all. I even drank my milk and I hate milk, especially for breakfast.

'Alma, tell me about Michaela.'

She thought for a while. 'She was a quiet child. They both were but Johnny got to be more outgoing as he grew up and Micha never did.'

'Micha, I'd forgotten that.'

'It was her mother's name for her. Nobody really called her that after Sophie died. She was eleven and she took her mother's death hard. I tried to help but I wasn't driving much then and Walter rarely brought the children over, though I asked him to.' She sighed.

I stood up and put some water on to boil for fresh tea.

'I was wrong, Katy, I should have tried harder.'

I leaned on the stove and watched the pot which, naturally, didn't boil.

'She was a beautiful child, so like her mother. They both had wonderful big eyes and thick curly brown hair, though Sophie's turned gray at the end with her illness.' She started to get teary.

I took my eyes off the pot, so it boiled. Then I made tea.

'Oh, Katy, I should have tried harder!' I sat her down and pushed a cup of tea in front of her. 'She was so talented. She took violin lessons and later guitar, too. And her voice, oh what a voice. The angels in heaven would bend down to hear her sing and cry at the beauty of it.'

She gulped down her tea and held out her cup for more. I swear the woman has an asbestos lining to her throat. 'She was good at tennis, too. She could really flap that stick around.'

'Swing that racket,' I said automatically. She ignored me.

'I was wrong, Katy, I should have—

I was tired of hearing her recriminations. 'Alma—

'Now you listen to me, young lady.'

Whoa. Listen? I almost saluted.

Her face softened. 'I'm sorry, Katy. I forgot who you were and what year it was for a moment there. Crying over split meatloaf.' She sighed. I blinked. 'And it never does any good.'

'Spilt milk, Alma.'

'No, thanks, dear, black as usual.' She held out her teacup. 'Please.' I got up and refilled it, left the pot on the table.

'She was such a dear, sweet child and then something went wrong when she was a teenager. I know all teenagers are difficult but it was more. Something was wrong and I didn't—' She sighed, the kind of sigh that pulls your heart apart at the seams a bit and afterward leaves a dull ache where it doesn't quite come together again.

'In this world of ours, Katy, there is good and bad both. Every good thing you do changes the balance in the universe. I know that you know this, dear. I know that you do what you do partly because of it.'

I looked at her, startled. I hadn't thought about it that way.

'Even though you probably don't use words like good and bad.' She sighed. 'But that's what it is, and it doesn't matter what you call it.' She sighed again.

'I see myself as one for the good, but oh my, my sins of omission haunt me. We are responsible for what we see as well as what we do. To see a bad thing and ignore it is wrong and it changes the balance. The balance changed in that child and I ignored it.'

I gazed at Alma, dumbfounded at this combination of Old Country and New Consciousness. I said nothing. Fortunately.

'Find her for me, Katy. I don't want it to be too late.'

'It could be.'

'Yes, I know.' There were tears in her eyes. 'I've got to try.'

'All right. Tell Henley all this and anything else he asks. Don't play cops and robbers with him, Alma, the police are on our side.' She looked hurt and innocent but I wasn't taken in by it. Or rather I'd been taken in too many times before.

'And don't let him in without seeing his ID either.'

'No,' she said sweetly, 'or take candy from strangers.'

I shrugged. Henley was on his own.

'I have a problem teenager on my hands.'

She raised her eyebrows.

I shook my head. 'It's a long story. No time now.'

'Bring her over here.'

I shook my head again. 'She's better off in the country; I've parked her with Charity and the horses. She's one of the reasons I don't want to leave town just yet.' Alma raised her eyebrows even higher. 'And Johnny's the other reason,' I added.

She shook her head. 'The dead must wait on the living, Katy.'

In my mind Lisa and Johnny gazed wistfully at me. I promised them that I wouldn't forget, that I'd be back. That was it. Damn. I'd forgotten to drop Lisa on Henley. The wistful changed to reproachful and I made more mental promises.

'Katy? Katy, are you there?'

'Yes.'

'What now?'

'Home to change and then Marysville. Will you be all right today? And tonight if I don't get back?'

'Yes.'

'I'll call later.'

'Do you think the detective would like it if I made biscuits to go with the stew?'

'Sure.'

'And a custard pie for dessert?'

'He'll love you forever. Save a piece for me. And don't put too much nutmeg on top like you usually do. Cinnamon is better anyway.'

She made a face at me as I kissed her good-bye.

Ten

Marysville is only about thirty-five miles away but it's close to an hour's drive, a bunch of it two-lane, half of it country. You can get stuck behind a good old boy doing forty mph in a pickup real easy. Some days I mind, some I don't. This was a day that I wouldn't have minded. No pickups and I made it in under fifty minutes.

Walter has been a stockbroker for years. My theory is that he looked like one when he was born and naturally gravitated toward the profession. In his twenties his temples were going gray. In his thirties his hair went from gray to white. He could have my vote for Mr. Distinguished, but distinguished is where it ended. In his case beauty, as Alma was fond of pointing out, was only ankle deep.

Neither one of us is very charitable about Walter. Neither one of us is being very fair. So it goes.

I hadn't called ahead for an appointment. Walter hadn't cared much for anyone on Sophie's side of the family after her death and it was unlikely he had changed. I figured I had a better shot just breezing in.

I found his office easily, as stolid, respectable, and stuffy as ever. Old-fashioned even. Some of Sophie's antiques had made it down there too. The place reeked

66

of money and stability. I zipped up my purse as I went in.

Walter greeted me formally in a friendly, respectful way that was guaranteed to charm your socks off and snap your wallet and checkbook to attention. It had been a long time and he didn't recognize me.

'Hello, Walter, it's Kat Colorado, Alma Flaherty's adopted granddaughter.'

The friendliness and formality took a hike. The real Walter stepped forward, cold, distant, stuffy.

'What do you want?' His tone implied that, were he not a decent church-going man, he would have shown me out. With ease. With pleasure.

'May I sit down?'

I settled into a lovely overstuffed brocade number without waiting for an answer. Good thing, since the answer would probably have been no. Finally, grudgingly, he sat down assuming an Abraham Lincoln Memorial pose. Without the kindness, wisdom, or compassion.

'I'd like to extend my sympathy to you on John's death.' I almost choked on the words, on the tears, but I got them out. I was brought up right.

He nodded. 'Thank you.' A man of few words. 'What do you want?'

'Alma has asked me to act for her. You know how she loved Sophie and the children. She is very saddened over John's death and wants me to find Michaela. Naturally I hope you can help us.' I indulged in a bit of wishful thinking there.

His face turned a dark red and his cheeks mottled up in an interesting, if unattractive, way.

'I wish I could but I know nothing about her. She is

my daughter and I have tried. I want to help, want to do whatever I can; I only wish I knew where she was and what I could do.' A classic example of paternal affection and concern. I was impressed, but not too much.

'She shamed herself and her family, me especially. As far as I am concerned that doesn't matter, she's still my daughter.' He looked concerned.

Shamed? I wonder about people who think in those terms. 'How did she shame herself?'

'That is none of your business, nor would it be fair to Michaela to bring it up.'

The mottled effect disappeared. The red flush deepened and turned slightly purple around the edges. I watched with interest. It was like viewing a sunset, watching the shift and change of color.

'Do you have any idea where she went when she left?' He shook his head. 'How about friends or family that would know?'

'No, I don't think so. She didn't even keep in touch with John, perhaps because he wouldn't have—' He stopped in mid-sentence. I wished he hadn't done that; he was just getting to the good part.

'What about her friends here? Did she leave a note or anything behind that would indicate where she went?'

'At the risk of repeating myself I will say again that I don't know. I wish I could help but I can't.' He started to rise. Good thing I don't get discouraged easily.

'I find it difficult to believe that she never tried to contact you. Seventeen is awfully young to be on your own. She never wrote or phoned for help or money?'

'I wish she had,' he said sadly.

The colors in his face changed again. He seemed sad but he didn't look sad, or maybe it was the other way around.

'Surely John heard from her at least once or twice? They were very close.'

Bull's-eye. The balance of red and purple shifted. He opened his mouth and then shut it again.

'What happened, Walter?'

I leaned forward. Abruptly he stood up, moving so fast he jammed his thigh on the desk corner in his haste to see me out. I let him croak out a few sentences before I stood up. Even with lifts in his shoes I'm an inch taller than he is.

'Unfortunately we'll never know.' He choked over the words. 'First Michaela, then John. What a blow to a father's heart! I wish—'

I waited with interest for the wish but he caught himself, thought better of it, and stopped.

'If you will excuse me, I must try to work. My regards to Alma, of course.' He had to look up slightly to see me. There was spittle in the corner of his mouth. I tried to understand and be sympathetic but it sickened me.

'Thanks for your help, Walter. You've been swell.'

With the best of intentions I sounded sarcastic, and maybe I was a little. I walked out of the office leaving the door ajar for him to close behind me. He didn't slam it.

I can never decide whether I am heartened or disheartened by my opinions on human nature. Disheartened I think. They're mostly pretty cynical. A semi growled by, grinding gears. I took a deep breath and filled my lungs with a gulp of pollution-ridden, hydrocarbon-laden air. It was a wholesome change from the atmosphere inside. Then I thought about what I'd just heard.

What can a sixteen- or seventeen-year-old do that is that bad? Marysville is a smallish town of twelve thousand. And quiet. Not a gang-filled, crime-ridden urban center. Kids around here think they're wild and rebellious when they throw returnable pop bottles out the window of a moving vehicle. Shamed herself and her family? It sounded archaic, like the nineteenth century, not the twentieth.

Drugs? Alcohol? A boyfriend? Pregnancy? I climbed into the Bronco and headed for Marysville High. It seemed as good a place as any to start. I vaguely remembered where it was. Vaguely didn't cut it so I played hit or miss for ten minutes until finally it came back. I drove past Ellis Lake, under the railroad tracks, parked and headed into the school.

A rather spare fiftyish woman who looked like she'd caught too many kids smoking in bathrooms and had to stop smiling with the weight of it all greeted me politely. Her eyes didn't meet mine. Probably afraid I'd haul a cigarette out of my purse and light up. Not a chance, I could have told her, but I skipped it in favor of business. I changed my story around a bit too.

'I'm looking for a young woman, Michaela Benson, who was a student here four years ago. Sometime during or shortly after her senior year, she ran away from home. There has been a recent death in the family and it's important that I find her. I wonder—'

The phone rang. She put her hand on it. 'How sad.' And picked it up. 'Excuse me please.'

Not having much of a choice, I nodded. I tried not to fidget. There was a ruler on her desk.

'Yes?' She hung up and turned back to me.

Did I have to start over, I wondered. 'I'm looking for Michaela. May I speak to her counselor or—'

'Sign here in the visitors' book. Counselors' offices are down the hall to your right.'

The phone rang again. She didn't bother to excuse herself this time. I thanked the side of her head, signed the book, and walked.

I asked the first counselor I came across. She was a bit harried but friendly and willingly looked it up for me. 'Bob Evans,' she announced.

'Is he still here?'

'Oh yes. Next office down.'

I thanked her and went next door. I was on a roll. He was there.

'Mr. Evans?'

A sweet, round owlish face somewhat hidden behind thick horn-rimmed glasses peered at me. He had a receding hairline and a corduroy jacket with suede elbow patches, a male version of the old-maid schoolteacher type.

'May I help you?' He half stood. I introduced myself and we shook hands.

'I'm hoping you will remember a former student.'

'Try me. If it's not too long ago . . .' He let his voice drift off.

'Michaela Benson.'

A look of concentration settled in on his face, then a smile.

'Michaela, I remember. Quite a special girl—' He broke off. 'May I know why you're asking? She's not in trouble, is she?'

'No, or not that I know of. Her brother died and her

grandmother wants her home for the memorial service. She left home four years ago and no one has heard from her. I assume you knew that?'

'That she left home, yes.' His glasses slipped and he pushed them up again onto the bridge of his nose.

'You said she was special?'

'Yes, bright and very gifted musically. She was a quiet girl but with good friends. Everyone liked her: teachers, other kids, everyone. She was a good student, hard working, friendly, motivated to do well and go to college. And then—' He broke off.

'And then things changed,' I finished for him.

'Yes.'

'How? Why?'

'I don't know but it seemed like she became distant and withdrawn overnight. Her grades went down suddenly and sharply and she quit hanging out with her friends. The only thing she did was her music. She continued her lessons, sang in chorus, and practiced as much or more than before.'

He paused. 'Her father stopped that. He refused to allow her music until her grades improved again. He meant well, meant to encourage her in her studies, but it had just the opposite effect. I was very much against it and told him so.' Another pause. 'He is not the kind of person who listens well or takes advice.' A charitable and sympathetic evaluation of Walter.

'What did Michaela say?'

'Nothing. She wouldn't talk, at least not to me or to her teachers. She became sullen and uncommunicative and then dropped out of school three months before she would have graduated.'

'What do you think?'

He pushed his glasses up and stared at his knuckles. 'Drugs?'

'I – no. No, I don't think so. She didn't hang out with any of the other – No, I don't think so.'

'A boyfriend?'

'Could have been. She was friendly with a number of boys but there didn't seem to be anyone special. At least not here at the high school.'

I nodded. 'What does that leave us?'

'Trouble at home?' He made it a question.

'Like what?'

'Well, it can't have been easy for the child with her mother dead.'

'No, but she was used to it. Sophie died when Michaela was eleven.'

'Sometimes fathers have a difficult time when their daughters turn into young women. They become overly strict, find it hard to let them date.'

'Did Michaela and her father get along?'

'Err, I don't know.' He was nervous. 'I realize I don't have enough information to generalize so I, err . . .' His voice ran down weakly. It sounded like his batteries were dying.

'Mr. Evans, you started to tell me something and stopped. Why?'

'Errr,' was his articulate response. Hook the man up, jumpstart him, I thought. I was annoyed.

'What were you implying?'

His face reddened. 'Nothing, nothing at all. You'll have to excuse me now. I have another appointment.'

I stood up.

'See if you can locate Susie Goodnough. She married a boy named Barton. Susie was Michaela's best friend.'

I thanked him for his help and gave him a card. He reddened again and was pushing at his glasses as I walked out. He had given me an idea that I didn't like much.

Not much at all.

Eleven

I found Susie Goodnough Barton in the phone book:
Steve and Susan. She was home. So were at least two
children judging from the noise. I explained the situation and asked if I could speak with her. She sounded
happy about it, happy, interested, and concerned. The
directions she gave me were good. I got there in five
minutes.

Susie opened the door with what looked like a two-
year-old in her arms. A three- or four-year-old zoomed
recklessly around in the background. She wore her hair
in pigtails and had a light blue T-shirt with vertical
numbers on it, 9–8–7–6–5–4–3–2–1–Baby! It looked like
blast-off time to me.

'Susie? Kat Colorado.'

I held out a hand but the toddler snagged it before
she could. We shook hands solemnly.

'Actually I go by Susan now. Please come in. Excuse
the mess. I haven't had a minute all day.'

I looked around. There was a picture book open on
the coffee table with a graham cracker sitting on it, a
small wooden trike tipped over on the living room floor,
and a lone white sneaker in the hall. Mess is a relative concept.

'Will you come into the kitchen? I hope you don't mind, I was just making lasagne for dinner. Joey, stop that!' She pulled the medium-size child off the small child and looked at me inquiringly. I assured her I didn't mind.

'How can I help?' she asked after I was settled into a kitchen chair with a cup of freshly brewed coffee in front of me.

'Bob Evans said you were Michaela's best friend.'

'Bob Evans?'

'A counselor at Marysville High.'

'Oh, *Mr.* Evans. Yes. Well, he's right. I was. Or at least I was until she dropped her friends.'

'What happened, Susan?'

'I don't know all of it. I honestly don't. I've asked myself that question enough times. Robby, no! No biting.' She disentangled the two children, tucked the smaller, Robby I think, under her arm and looked around distractedly.

'Here, do you mind?' She plopped the child into my lap without waiting for an answer. Just as well. It could easily have been yes.

'I do hope this one's a girl. Steve wants a little girl so bad. Me, too, but I don't think I can go through this again.'

I nodded sympathetically. Robby chomped down on my finger. I pinched his jaws. Hard. His mouth flopped open and he looked at me in astonishment. 'Do that again, kid,' I hissed into his ear, 'and you're in big trouble.' I doubt that he understood the words but he caught the meaning and scrambled to get off my lap. Susan was layering lasagne thoughtfully.

'Tell me what you do know,' I said.

On went a layer of ricotta, mozzarella, and meat sauce. 'I'm sure Mr. Evans must have told you how she changed?' She looked at me and I nodded. 'I was her best friend and I didn't know what was going on. She wouldn't tell me. It's not that I didn't ask either. I did, over and over.'

'Drugs?'

'No, I don't think so. Maybe.' She hesitated. I let it slide for then.

'A boyfriend?'

'Yes and no. There was one guy she liked but—' She shrugged. 'What she really wanted was to go to music school. Me, I wanted to get married and have babies.'

She smiled ruefully. 'Now I wonder, but then I didn't. Steve and I were already going together. Not Michaela. I couldn't believe it when she started blowing it so badly, her grades and all.'

'Did you ask her?'

'Yes, of course.'

'And?'

'And she told me to go to hell, which was as unlike her as everything else.'

She was silent for a long time. Me too. There was something more, I just didn't know what.

'There was one thing.'

And here it comes, I thought.

'She came over one day and asked if she could spend the night. We did that all the time – it was no big deal. Of course I said yes. I asked her about stuff but she still wouldn't talk. Then in the middle of the night I woke up and heard her crying. There were twin beds in my room. I got up and went over to her bed, got in and held her. She cried like she was going to break into pieces. I told her she had to talk to me, to tell me what was going on. So she did, part of it, anyway.'

Susan took a deep breath. We looked at each other. She considered. I waited. Finally she spoke.

'She made me promise not to tell and I haven't, so I hope that you . . .' She looked at me inquiringly. I nodded. 'She told me that she was pregnant, that her father was ashamed of her and was sending her to Minnesota to a church home for unwed mothers. She cried and cried.

'I asked who the boy was. She wouldn't say. She said it was just a guy and she didn't see him anymore. I wondered about it a lot. I think I know.' I raised my eyebrows.

'He wasn't a boy, he was a man, especially to us. We were so young. He was a musician who played in a bar in town. She thought he was wonderful and a great artist. He wasn't, of course. We were very naive then,' she said apologetically. I nodded and thought how refreshing that was. I didn't know any naive seventeen-year-olds.

'She about worshipped him. It wasn't good and I told her so. He was twenty-five, way too old for her. And then she started sneaking out at night to be with him. He got her into the bar where he was playing and got her drinks, maybe drugs. I don't know about that for sure, but maybe. He did them, I know. She quit telling me stuff when I said she shouldn't go with him.

'Of course Mr. Benson found out and he hit the roof. He's against sex, drinking, smoking, drugs, you name it. And,' Susan added hastily, 'in this case he was absolutely right. It's just too bad he was so strait-laced and came down on her so hard. He was a good father but he didn't know how to be a mother. Michaela really needed a mother then.' She sighed.

'I think the poor man was desperate, that's why he sent her to Minnesota. Michaela said he was ashamed, but it wasn't that simple. He cared, and I'm sure he was trying to do his best to get her away from all the things he saw as bad influences. And they were,' she added. 'Very bad. He was absolutely right about that.' She sighed again. 'Poor Mr. Benson. Poor Michaela.' The kids stopped squabbling for a moment and the silence was loud.

'I told her she was crazy to go to Minnesota. It wasn't that big of a deal after all – girls have babies without being married all the time. She cried even harder. I said that she should go to her grandmother. She cried some more. All she did was cry. She didn't tell me any more, just cried. I fell asleep there in her bed, hugging her, but in the morning when I woke up, I was alone. She was in my bed.' Susan patted the last layer of noodles carefully in place.

'After that she wouldn't talk to me, she wouldn't even look at me. She left town several days later.'

'And that was it?'

'Yes. No. She wrote me once from Minnesota.'

I let my breath out slowly. I hadn't realized I was holding it.

'It was a letter that made me cry again for her. She thanked me for being her friend, and she was sorry the way things had turned out between us, that it was her fault, and that she wished me the best. I wrote back but I never heard from her again.'

'Did you save the letter?'

She nodded. 'I don't know why, but I did. Would you like to see it?'

'Very much.'

She went to get it, leaving me with the children. They were fine until she walked out the door. Then they fell on each other with a ferocity that made Cain and Abel more understandable to me. I separated them several times. It seemed to take Susan forever.

'I couldn't find it after all.' She was slightly out of breath. Damn. 'Nothing but the envelope.' She held it out, return address in bold print. Good. I sighed in relief; I was back in business.

I copied the address down, thanked her, and left. She gave me a long message to give to Michaela but Joey and Robby drowned out most of it. I smiled and nodded and waved to the three of them and to Blast-Off Baby.

On my way out of town I grabbed a milkshake and fries. A grease and carbo boost seemed like a good idea. With luck it might last me halfway home.

It didn't, but I didn't notice. Gunshots make you forget details like that.

I passed up Highway 70 to Sacramento where it cuts off 65. I'd decided to go home, not to the office. Highway 65 is four-lane for a bit, then two-lane most of the way back. I dialed into automatic pilot and was stuffing the french fries and milkshake in.

I caught the Trans Am first in the rearview mirror, moving erratically and driving too fast. It started to pass me on a long straightway. There were three kids and at least two guns. I figured that out later. I was sure about the kids, not about the guns. All of them seemed to be moving and making noise. The first bullet caught me unaware as it thunked into the body of the Bronco. The Trans Am was next to me, the road ahead clear in my lane. An old Chevy pickup was headed straight for the Trans Am.

I hit the brakes and dropped back, zigzagging a bit. The pickup hit its horn and brakes, the Trans Am its accelerator. They cleared by four inches easy. The old boy in the Chevy was wide-eyed and white-faced and looked like he was about to have a coronary. I understood the feeling. The Trans Am left us in the dust. I got a partial on the plate, CA 1MZD2 something. Enough for an ID, although chances were good it was stolen. Real good.

The old boy in the truck didn't stop and neither did I, not until Wheatland, another six miles down the road. Being a sitting duck on a country two-lane is not my idea of fun. In Wheatland I parked in front of a gas station and walked across the street to a cafe.

I asked for the phone and the bathroom. A dumpy cashier stared at me and pointed to her right. I was wearing the milkshake and chocolate is not my best color. After a largely unsuccessful attempt at cleaning up I phoned in an anonymous tip to the cops. I gave them the kids, the guns, the make and color of the car, and what I had of the plate They wanted more, cops always do, but I didn't feel like sitting around waiting for them to show, then answering questions for the rest of the afternoon. Wearing a milkshake puts me in a bad mood.

I paid attention the rest of the way, no more automatic pilot, but nothing happened. It doesn't usually when you're on alert. It took me thirty minutes to get home.

There was a hole in the side window of the Bronco, one in the windshield, and at least two in the body. Good-sized holes, we weren't talking cap pistol here. It didn't make me feel great, but being shot at never does. I poured myself a glass of wine on the way to the bathtub and tried to figure it out. Kids? Maybe. A connection to what I was digging up? I couldn't see it. Basically I came up with nothing, which was not encouraging.

My cat, Xerxes, wound himself around my ankles, talking and begging for attention. I turned the tub on and patted him briefly, then peeled my clothes off. Xerxes settled down purring and licking my milkshake shirt; we both love chocolate. I got into the steaming water. The phone rang but I ignored it and the answering machine clicked in. I slid under the water and blew bubbles. I was fed up with thinking about other people's problems and coming up with zip for answers.

After my bath and a snack I called Hank. I didn't expect to find him at home and I didn't. I didn't find him at work either. I left a message even though I got the secretary with an attitude problem and I knew he wouldn't get it.

'Your name, please?'

I gave it to her. She knows it, of course: my name, my voice, my hair color, probably my social security number. And my place in Hank's life. That's the part she doesn't like.

'And your message?'

'Just tell Hank I called, that I'll be out of town on business for a few days, but I'll call him when I get back.'

'I'll let Detective Sergeant Parker know.'

She stressed his rank. La-ti-da. She didn't call him detective sergeant any more than I did. Attitude problem again. Her attitude was that no one was good enough for Hank but her. Her problem was that I had him. That's life; too bad she wasn't more philosophical about it.

'Please be sure he gets the message.'

'Of course.' Icy notes dripping through the phone line.

Yeah, right. He never got messages I left with her. It would turn up in his out basket sometime next July under a batch of to-be-filed case folders. I wished, again, that he'd get an answering machine at home. Oh well, I'd done my best.

I called Alma and checked on her. Then I called Charity to beg a ride to the airport tomorrow. I didn't feel like leaving a car riddled with bullet holes in the parking lot – better to leave it in my driveway at home. Charity offered to bring her truck by for me to use when I got back. I accepted gladly. It would smell of horses but it beat bullet holes any day.

Twelve

It wasn't quite five but already the day had been too long and I was ready for bed. No such luck. And thoughts of Johnny were still pulling on me. Lisa, too, and Lindy. They were turning out to be more of a distraction than I'd bargained for.

I pushed Xerxes, my fifteen-pound lovable meatball cat, off my lap and reached for the phone again. Somebody grabbed it on the first ring.

'Mr. Richards?' I trilled. 'This is Sunshine Cleaners to confirm that we *will* be there at eight in the morning. Did Mrs. Richards decide if she wanted the sofa and loveseat done as well? Since we'll *already* be there the charge is minimal and the results, I *assure* you, are gratifying.' I paused for breath. The voice on the other end was high, not very masculine, and sounded like a raggedy starter motor trying to catch.

'What? Huh? Who? Hey, you got the wrong number. There's no Richards here.'

'Why,' I said brightly, 'can I interest *you*, Mr.—' I paused.

'Jones,' he said automatically.

'Mr. Jones. We have a three-room carpet special this week and for just a *wee* bit extra we'll do your sofa and loveseat. Do you have a sofa and loveseat, sir?'

He snorted. 'Loveseat. Lady, I don't even have carpet. Tore-up lino is what I got.' He hung up.

Okay. Gil was home. Xerxes jumped into my lap again and butted his head against my hand, letting me know I could scratch his ears.

It seemed like a better idea than going to visit Gil but it would have to wait. I dumped him, stood up, looked for my purse and car keys, and headed out. Davis again. I–80 again. With luck Gil would be home for dinner and the evening and I would catch him.

His house was even more low rent than Ned and John's. More hopeless, helpless, and dilapidated. The paint was peeling off the front door, the knocker had a screw missing, the door to the mail slot was history. I knocked and waited.

The guy who answered the door also answered to Ned's description of Gil: a skinny little shit.

'Gil Jones?'

'Yeah.'

'My name is Kat Colorado.' I stuck out a hand and he took it automatically. 'I hope I'm not intruding but I'm very interested in your work with the Activists for Animal Rights and think it would make a good article. Do you have a few moments for an interview?'

'Not exactly.'

'It won't take long.' I shifted the notebook under my arm and put one foot inside the door.

'I guess. I'm just fixing dinner. You don't mind?' I shook my head and followed him in, wondering if I was walking behind Johnny's killer. It was a counter-productive line of thinking so I dropped it.

The kitchen was a mess. Dirty dishes were piled on the counter; a mop, a paint bucket, and a brush with red paint dried thickly in its stiff bristles crowded the sink; the windows were curtainless and dirty. There were three chairs, only one of them clear. He waved me to it. The stench didn't hit me until I sat down. I was on top of a pile of garbage. I hitched the chair over; it helped some but not much.

'Coffee?' He picked up a mug off the counter, upended it, shook something out, poured coffee into it, and offered it to me. The something might have been a cockroach.

'No thanks.' I was firm.

'Suit yourself.' Gil reached for a can of generic pork and beans and looked around for a saucepan. 'Damn,' he muttered. 'This place is a dump.'

He kicked a cupboard, found a spoon and began eating the stuff cold out of the can, leaning against the counter. I watched in appalled fascination, momentarily forgetting my reason for being there.

'Yeah?' he asked, his mouth full. I got my notebook and pen out.

'How large is your group and how long have you been in existence?'

'Five of us. Six months,' he said with his mouth full. A half-chewed bean sat on his chin, then slid down. It left a trail like amber snail slime.

'Are you students?'

'Concerned citizens.'

'What is your target?'

'The research and teaching facilities at Davis. What they do is criminal!' Half-chewed beans spewed from his mouth. I slid my chair back into the garbage. It seemed preferable. 'They slaughter innocent, helpless creatures, pets – yours and mine. They're as bad as

Hitler!' He was off and running. When he paused for breath I jumped back in.

'It is my understanding,' I said mildly, 'that they follow humane guidelines and are in compliance with strict standards set and enforced by federal, state, and local agencies. Surely the teaching and research is in pursuit of a higher quality of life for both animals and people and not—'

That was as far as I got. Gil started ranting and raving again: four-letter words figured strongly; references to murder and slaughter abounded. For a man advocating peaceful treatment of animals his verbal violence was considerable.

'Goddamn fascist pigs paid off by the medical industrial establishment – ' I blinked. That was a new variation on an old theme. 'All God's creatures have a right to life and a natural life span. We should goddamn experiment on the goddamn experimenters.'

They were exceptions, presumably, to the right to a natural life span theory. I assimilated that one in silence.

'Let *them* go under the knife. That might change their goddamn minds.'

It was a perfect lead-in and I took it. 'I understand that John Benson, a young man who worked at the lab and with whom you had a run-in, was murdered last week. Did your group claim any responsibility for that?'

'What the hell are you talking about?' He slammed the can of beans down and stared at me in astonishment.

'You were overheard threatening Benson. Your words were, "I hope you get cut up just like those animals." Shortly after that he was found stabbed.'

'Are you crazy?' he shouted at me. There was drool on his chin blending with the bean trail.

'Are you?' I countered, but I didn't really want him to answer. There was a wild, unconnected look in his eyes, like Manson on a good day.

'Look, lady, I didn't like Benson. That's a fact and that's no secret. Man, if he was on fire I wouldn't cross the street to piss on him. I'm even glad he's dead, yeah, I am, but I didn't kill him. We're not butchers, they are.'

He advanced on me waving his spoon, jabbing it in my direction to make a point. 'They,' jab, 'are,' jab. 'We might do a little free advertising,' he pointed to the paint brush and bucket. Now there was foam in the corner of his mouth. 'But not *murder*. Who the hell do you think you are, anyway?'

I stood up. I knew who I was and I knew I'd had enough. Too much.

'Get the fuck out of my house,' he screamed at me as I headed for the door, notebook in hand. The spoon hit me in the back. I turned the door knob and didn't let myself react. 'Butchers, slaughterers, murderers, that's what you all are. Murderers!'

He was still screaming as I closed the door. I didn't take the steps two at a time but it cost me emotionally. He may not have been certifiably insane but he was a few bricks shy of a load. Quite a few.

My hands were shaking as I unlocked the Bronco. How many times had he used the word murder or murderers, I wondered. And I wondered, too, at the irony of a violent man talking about peace, and humane treatment, and the sanctity of life.

I wasn't sure that the violent could live in peace. I was sure that they could kill.

Xerxes was glad to see me, but not as glad as I was to see him.

Thirteen

I was on the plane to Minnesota by eight-thirty the next morning. I'd tried telephoning the Weyland Home for pregnant young women first but it had rapidly, like within thirty seconds, become apparent that I wasn't going to get anywhere. Bureaucratic runaround was the name of that game.

'I'm sorry we can't discuss our clients. At Weyland Home we don't do that.'

There was more.

'No, I'm sorry but I can't even confirm that.'

Good stuff.

'No, the person with the authority to authorize it is not here now. Even if she were, she wouldn't.'

It went on like that for a while. I got tired of it first. It was my dime; I hung up. Anyway, I'd never been to Minnesota. I wondered if Lake Wobegon would be too far out of the way.

Sacramento is one of those it's-damn-tough-to-get-anywhere-from-here places. We landed in the Twin Cities about one-thirty local time. Everything was white except for the sky, which was gray. I rented a car and walked out into monochrome. Nothing about California clothes, even the best ski jacket, meets the challenge of a Minnesota winter. It's the difference between bush league and major. I shivered all the way to the rental car.

No place looks like old times anymore. Fast food and used car lots have homogenized much of America into a kind of bland and boring unanimity. It's hard to tell one town from another, one state from another. Crossroads was a small town without much charm. I stopped at a gas station to ask directions to the Weyland Home. The kid there didn't know it by name but we nailed it down on the address and the description.

'Oh yeah, that place.' He leered. 'It's for girls in trouble.' He leered again and rubbed his hands. 'Run by some church. Man, they *never* get out.' Disappointment was written large on him, and not just on his face. He rubbed the palms of his hands on his jeans. 'Never.' There was a pimple on his chin about to burst. I thanked him and left.

It was out of town, an old two-story house on a large lot with acres of snow around it, probably corn or grain in the spring. An impressive wrought-iron arch loomed over the driveway. The letters at the top of the arch spelled out WEYLAND HOME. I drove through and parked in the semicircle in front of the house marked VISITORS' PARKING. Mine was the only car. Not an auspicious beginning.

As it turned out I was just in time for tea.

'Miss Colorado, you say?'

Actually I'd said Ms. but clearly that was not in her vocabulary.

'I am Miss Weyland, Miss Margaret Weyland. My sister is Miss Penelope Weyland.'

I nodded and was willing to put money on the fact

that no one in this century had called them Maggie and Penny. Miss Margaret was seventy, maybe older, and as well tended as a fragile hothouse flower. She looked about as fragile as reinforced concrete.

'I understand you have questions. Naturally I hope we can help you but now it is tea time. You understand, I'm sure, how important it is for us to maintain a rigid routine for the dear girls.'

I nodded but it was a lie. I wasn't sure I understood at all. Or maybe she'd just lost me on 'rigid routine.'

'You will join us, of course, for tea?' She asked the question the way a general asks a question and had already turned away by the time I answered.

'Thank you, with pleasure.' It was another one of my compromises with the truth.

She nodded and led the way out of the front office and into a large sitting room, comfortably if prosaically furnished. An immense old-fashioned tea urn stood on the sideboard. It was surrounded by platters of whole-wheat-bread sandwiches and fresh fruit. About twelve girls sat, silent and subdued, with their hands folded in what was left of their laps. They looked at me with interest. I sucked in my already flat stomach and smiled.

'Good afternoon, girls.'

'Good afternoon, Miss Margaret,' they chorused.

I stared. 'Good morning to you, good morning to you. We're all in our places, with sunshiny faces . . .' a refrain from grammar school, drifted through my mind. Nobody smiled. Nobody looked happy. Nobody spoke. With the exception of Miss Margaret and me, everyone was pregnant.

'Jenny, you will pour. Mind that you don't drip. Elizabeth, the sandwiches; Laura, the fruit.' The girls hauled themselves out of their chairs and did her bidding. Naturally. Few people thumb their noses at wardens.

Miss Margaret led us in a prayer and then we ate and drank in silence and joylessness. Another prayer and the girls were dismissed. I was hungry but I didn't eat much. The girls did better. Of course they were eating for two.

'Now, how may I help you, Miss uh . . .'

'Colorado.'

'Yes.'

I told her. I played up the tragedy, the distraught and grieving family, the search for Michaela in time for the memorial service. It was a good story and brought tears to my eyes. My stories often do that to me.

'Well, I can look up the records but I think you would be better off talking to Nurse. She has the *most* remarkable memory.' Miss Margaret beamed proudly. 'If you will wait here I will send her down.' I waited and watched a dour-faced elderly woman clad in white clear the tea things.

Nurse looked like a female version of the Grim Reaper. The more I saw of her the sorrier I felt for the girls; talking with her did nothing to dispel that illusion or change my feeling. The last time she smiled had probably been sometime in the Truman administration. Early Truman administration.

'I remember the girl. She was not well-behaved.'

'Did she seem troubled about something in particular?'

Nurse stared at me, amazed at my obtuseness no doubt. 'They would hardly be here if they weren't troubled, now would they?' There was contempt in her voice.

'Did she ever mention anything specific?'

'No, but we don't encourage that kind of thing here. The girls are to pray, eat well, exercise, and maintain a healthy attitude. That is all.' Her lips snapped shut. Her heart, no doubt, had done that years ago.

'Do you have any idea where she went when she left?'

'If a girl is eighteen it is, of course, no concern of ours.'

I looked at her without moving or speaking. We faced each other down. I won, but it was close; she was a tough old bird.

'I believe she may have left with another girl, Julia Hyde I think her name was. Their babies were born about the same time. It often happens that the girls become friendly with others whose babies are due approximately the same date.'

I thanked Nurse for her help and went in search of Miss Margaret, names, and addresses. Instead I found Miss Penelope. I recognized her instantly as the guiding light behind the concepts of unbreakable rules, no talking, laughter, or information being given out. She didn't recognize me from our phone conversation. She didn't take to me either. I got the Hydes' Chicago address out of her. Then I tried for more: impressions of Michaela and Julia, of what they saw in their future, of how they felt about giving up their babies. 0 for three on that and I was out.

On my way to the bench I asked Miss Penelope if I could visit with the girls a bit and get a feeling for how the house was run. She obviously didn't think much of the idea.

'My niece,' I murmured with a mental blush, chagrined as usual at how easily lying comes to me.

Miss Penelope shifted gears. 'Of course.' A figure slipped by on the sidelines. A gnarled, wiry hand shot out and nabbed it, like a lizard snagging a fly. 'Jenny, will you show Miss Colorado about?'

'Yes, ma'am.' Jenny slid a smile across her face and looked as though she'd rather swallow razor blades. Miss Penelope moved off briskly to the office and a ringing phone.

'What would you like to see, Miss Colorado?' she inquired politely.

'Mostly I'd like to talk to you, to some of the other girls too, if possible. And please call me Kat.'

'This way,' she said, still with excessive politeness. We headed up a wide wooden stairway. She used the banister to pull herself along. 'Did you know that the house was left to Miss Margaret and Miss Penelope by their father? He was a wealthy farmer here but I guess he lost everything in the Depression.'

She looked at me with a question and I nodded, confirming the Depression.

'Miss Margaret and Miss Penelope never married.' Our eyes met in mute comprehension. She giggled. 'They chose to give the house to the church and stay here and do God's work.'

Maybe, I thought, or maybe they couldn't afford to keep the house on their own and donated it in return for a lifelong home and a small pension. And of course God's work meant different things to different people: St. Francis walked barefoot among the poor; Jim Bakker had an air-conditioned doghouse and screwed his secretary; Miss Margaret and Miss Penelope made miserable the lives of the young women in their care.

'The church?' I asked.

'Fundamental Further Church of Christ First.' She wrinkled her nose. 'Or something like that.'

I nodded. Close enough. What I'd seen and heard fit in with a fundamentalist Christian sect.

'It's still called the Weyland Home?'

'Yes.'

'For wayward girls?'

She looked at me surprised, grinned suddenly. 'It seems like that, doesn't it?'

'Very much so.'

'Most of us are only here for four or five months, but they're long months.' She pushed open a door to a common room. Six heads bobbed up and looked at us. It was absolutely silent: no TV, no radio, no stereo, no girl talk.

'Girls, this is Kat. She wants to know about life around here. She's okay.'

A chorus of groans greeted Jenny's announcement. Then they told me. The home was clean and warm, the health care adequate, but the philosophy and joylessness of it reminded me of Lowood Institution in *Jane Eyre*. I asked them.

'Jane who?'

'Eyre.' I was about to explain.

'You know,' someone said, 'the woman on the *Hello America* program, or something.'

'Oh.' Puzzled faces.

'No. Not really.'

'Huh?'

I decided to skip it. 'What's life like here?'

'It's not what it is; it's what it's not.' There was a burst of agreement with Jenny's statement.

'No boys.'

'No TV.'

'No phone calls except from your parents.'

'No music.'

'No movies.'

'No fun.'

Everyone laughed.

'A sound mind in a sound body.'

Boos.

'Food, exercise, and a healthy attitude.'

Groans.

'And prayers. Don't forget prayers.'

More groans. A few rude noises. I grinned at them and they grinned back.

'We don't usually sit around and laugh.'

I shook my head. 'Not good. What do you do?'

'We knit.'

'Or crochet.'

'Needlepoint, too.'

'And we're supposed to put our minds into the silent contemplation of the error of our ways.'

'And pray to be better young women.'

Jane Eyre again. The Misses Weyland and their church were in a time warp. The twentieth century had crept up on them and they hadn't even noticed. The inmates looked at me expectantly and I looked back.

'You seem okay to me. Everyone makes mistakes. Making a mistake doesn't make you a bad person.'

'You're the only one here who thinks that,' a voice said quietly from the back.

'How about you? What do you think?'

It was a challenge. Nobody answered.

'Get it together. Be yourselves. They can push you around on the outside but not on the inside. Nobody can make you stop thinking your own way, or laughing and living your life.'

'Yeah, how would you know?' The question, the voice was hostile.

'You want to see my scars?' The silence stretched out. 'My mother was an alcoholic. I had to take care of myself and my little sister. My mother was too drunk to go to my high school graduation. I found her when I got home; she'd broken her neck falling down the stairs. I paid my dues.' I kept my voice neutral.

The silence folded itself up and enveloped us.

'What can we do?' someone asked hesitantly.

I shrugged. 'Don't let them get to you. You're only here for a few months. Keep your sense of humor. Write your own script.'

'Huh?' It was a collective response.

'You've got no TV, movies, music, telephone, letters, or boys. So, tell your own stories. Talk to each other.' I would have said more but the door opened behind us and the expression on their faces warned me.

The room fell silent. I felt the presence of Miss Penelope behind me. I didn't have to turn around to confirm it, the temperature in the room had dropped.

'Well,' she said. She sounded like an executioner testing the edge of her blade, an executioner not entirely satisfied with what she found.

I turned and smiled. 'Miss Weyland, thank you so much. I appreciate the time you and the girls have given me. It has been most helpful. I think,' I turned back to the girls, 'that you need a motto.'

They stared silently at me. I moved forward so that Miss Penelope was well behind me.

'Fuck 'em if they can't take a joke.' I mouthed the

words, pantomimed them a bit. The girls laughed, they couldn't help it. I turned around to find Miss Penelope staring balefully at me.

'God bless this home,' I said. The girls echoed me. It was hard to argue with that so she didn't try. She knew I was lying, she just had no way to call me on it.

'*This* way, Miss Colorado,' she intoned majestically, and led the way to the door. Fishing around in my purse I followed meekly. I handed a dozen or so business cards to the girl nearest me and, I judged, nearing baby blast-off.

'Stay in touch.' I winked. They would have winked back but Miss Penelope turned around too fast.

'Remember the motto.' I waved good-bye after my parting shot and heard a suppressed giggle. Miss Penelope snapped around again.

'God bless our home,' someone said piously.

'Wherever it is,' I added.

'*Come*, Miss Colorado.' Miss Weyland was getting a bit snappish. Her bony fingers fastened around my wrist. They were cold and clammy. I turned and winked again. This time I did get a few winks in return.

I like to think I would have made a promising revolutionary.

Fourteen

It was over an hour's drive back to the airport. I was tired and hungry and had a lot on my mind, Julia Hyde for instance. I did not much want to go to Chicago but I did want to connect with her. I decided to stop at a motel, get something to eat, and make some phone calls.

First the airlines. Ordinarily you can't get to Sacramento without going someplace else: Chicago, Denver. Once I got stuck overnight in Salt Lake City, and it changed me, as a place like Salt Lake City will. This time I had to beg them to route me through Chicago. And they charged me extra for it. Next time I don't beg.

Then I called the Hydes. I reached Mrs. Hyde and started to tell her who/what/where/why and when. It wasn't necessary; I had her sympathy right off. It turned out Michaela was a favorite of hers.

'I like her a lot. She is a very sweet girl, but troubled. I tried to talk to her but she wouldn't discuss anything but music. My, but she is gifted. She used to play the piano for hours before she and Julia moved out.'

'She and Julia are roommates?'

'They were; not now, but I don't really know what happened. Let me give you Julia's number. You need to talk to her.'

I thanked her. She made me promise I would call if I needed anything or if she could help Michaela.

'And if you come to Chicago and need a place to stay, you must come here. Promise me.'

I promised. We hung up and I wished I'd had a mom like that. If wishes were fast trains, we'd all be someplace else. When I got done wishing, I called Julia.

Julia was out but, her roommate assured me, would be home in a couple of hours. And no, she'd never heard of Michaela. I said I'd call back. I called Sacramento next, hoping to catch Rafe, hoping he'd pick me up at the airport. He's a good friend, but unpredictable, unreliable. He was out. Of course. Phooey. I went in search of food and found a pleasant restaurant with oilcloth tablecloths. I didn't know they still made oilcloth.

I won't say that all food in the Midwest runs to meat, potatoes, and gravy, with iceberg lettuce salads and Jell-O, but a lot of it does. All of it did there. I had chicken fried steak. The waitress tried to bring me more mashed potatoes and gravy and scolded me for not eating my Jell-O. I could see carving it but not eating it. I bought a candy bar for dessert on the way back to the motel.

Julia was in and caught the phone on the second ring. 'Hi, I've just talked to my mom. She called. How can I help you?'

'I have a three-hour stopover in Chicago tomorrow. Could we meet at the airport? I'll pay for your time and expenses of course.'

Yes and no. Yes, we could meet; and no, I couldn't pay her. What were friends for? She sounded just like her mother and I liked her already.

'Tell me where you're coming in and I'll meet you at

the gate. It's real easy to lose someone at O'Hare. I've got Day-Glo red hair; you can't miss me.'

Julia was right; I picked her out of the crowd with no problem. Day-Glo didn't do it justice, though; it was the kind of red that stunned you, rolled you over, then hit you again as you picked yourself up.

'Did they call you Red as a kid?'

She grinned. 'Only once, 'cause I popped them but hard. I've got the temper that goes with the hair.' She held out her hand. 'I'm glad to meet you. Michaela was a good friend of mine. I hope I can help.'

'Was?'

'Well, is; it's just that I haven't heard from her in a while and I don't know what's going on.'

A businessman bumped into me with a suitcase and mumbled something that didn't sound like an apology.

'People are so rude.' Julia said it in a loud voice.

'Let's go find someplace quiet. Lunch?'

'Okay. C'mon, this way.'

She strode off and I followed. A lot of other people were tempted. With that hair she was like the Pied Piper and we, the mesmerized. But not rats, or children. Over lunch Julia talked and I listened.

'We met while we were doing time.'

Startled, I looked up from my shrimp and rock-hard avocado salad. She laughed.

'That's what we called being at the Weyland Home, "doing time." '

'Understandable.'

'I didn't mind it so much. I takes a lot to get me down and anyway I wanted to be there, or somewhere away from Chicago and my family. I chose it, so it was different for me, but Michaela hated it. She's very sensitive, much more sensitive than I am. It was music that kept her on track. They had a piano there; she'd never played but she taught herself. It was amazing.' Julia flipped a pound or two of thick red hair over her shoulder. I tried to bite into the avocado again and almost chipped a tooth.

'We had our babies at about the same time. Boys,' she said softly. There was a catch in her voice.

'Was it hard?'

'Yeah, for me, a little. Not for Michaela. She said she closed her eyes and wouldn't even look at it. "It," she called him. She didn't want to know anything about him except for the blood type or something. That was odd.' She frowned. 'She never saw her baby, or held it, or asked about it, but she wouldn't sign the release papers right away.' She frowned again.

'They made quite a fuss about it, but she stuck to it. Actually she told them to fuck off. Either she got what she wanted or she wasn't going to sign the release papers. Miss Margaret about had a fit.' She looked at me and shrugged slightly. 'Michaela and I talked about almost everything but she wouldn't talk about that.'

'And afterwards, after the papers were signed?'

'We neither one of us knew what to do, but at least I had a place to come home to.'

'Michaela didn't?'

'It sure didn't sound like it, so I talked her into coming back with me. I went back to school and she hooked up as a singer with a local band.'

'What kind of music?'

She shook her head. 'I can't remember. Anyway, she didn't stay there long. She moved on to a group that did kind of jazz, kind of blues. I don't know, I'm not very good at music. She liked that group but there was a problem – she wouldn't sleep with some guy in the band and he wouldn't let her alone.' She shrugged. 'That's life for you; it can be a bummer, huh? So she left. She has a beautiful voice, you know?'

I nodded. I didn't know, but I'd heard and I wasn't surprised.

'Anyone who heard her wanted to come back and hear her again. Or hire her away to join their group. She was a siren. The word would get out and wherever she was playing she would pack the place. Sometimes the guys – musicians, especially men, are real prima donnas – couldn't take that.

'Michaela is smart, but not street smart. She didn't know how to handle stuff, was always botching things up. I tried to help, she tried to learn, but it just didn't come easy to her, not like the music.'

'Was that a good time for her? Did she seem happy?'

'Well, yes and no. We had a lot of fun together but there was a blue side to her that never quite went away. Still, it was a pretty good time.'

'What about other friends or a boyfriend?'

She shook her head. 'I was her only close friend. She knew a lot of musicians, and there were men who wanted to get to know her better but she wouldn't let them, wouldn't give them the time of day.'

'Did she ever speak of her family?'

'No. And I never saw any letters or heard of any phone calls. It was like they didn't exist. Oh, except for her brother; she mentioned him a couple of times. I got the feeling that she loved him and that they had been close. I don't know if they were still. There was something real strong there: sorrow, anger, maybe something else, but I couldn't figure it out. She wouldn't talk about it, and after a while I learned not to ask.'

'When did she leave?'

'About six months ago. She said that Chicago was too big time for her, that she needed something smaller, slower.'

'Where did she go?'

'Back home. California.'

'Home?'

'California, anyway. I don't know. What's home?'

'Marysville? Sacramento?'

She shook her head. 'It doesn't sound familiar.'

'Do you ever hear from her?'

'She calls sometimes, never writes. When she calls she asks how I'm doing. And she asks about my mom – she and my mom like each other a lot. She asks about our other friends and about my school work, that sort of thing.'

'What about her life?'

'She doesn't say much. Just that things are okay, that she's in music again.'

'Jazz? Blues?'

'No. Country western, I think. We laughed about it. She said she never thought she'd do country.'

'Has she ever mentioned a place?'

'No. Yes. Does Hangtown mean anything to you?'

I nodded. 'It's northeast of Sacramento. Back in Gold Rush days it used to be called Hangtown. Now it's Placerville.'

'She said something once about doing a bunch of clubs in the valley. I don't know what valley. Does California have a valley?'

I was dumbfounded. Easterners do that to me. 'Yes.' It was an understatement. 'Several.' I turned around, looking for a clock. My plane wouldn't leave on time of course, but I would have to pretend it would and be there. I picked up the check and we started out.

'She had a stage name, did you know that?'

'No.'

'Micha. No last name, just Micha.' It was a jolt hearing Sophie's affectionate name for Michaela as a child.

Julia walked me back to the gate. 'Will you stay in touch? Please tell Michaela I want to hear from her. She can call collect, or whatever – '

I promised and gave her my card, said good-bye and got on the plane. We made it back in record time – early, the pilot proclaimed proudly, because of a tail wind. Incredible. I deplaned with equal speed.

'Kat!'

I heard him before I saw him. Rafe was here. Good. I let out a sigh of relief. I'd called him again from Chicago and he'd promised to pick me up, but Rafe was about as reliable as an old car on a cold day. He slouched over, draped an arm around my shoulders and hugged me. People stared. They always do.

'Hey, babe, what's new? I heard about John. I'm real sorry.' He squeezed my shoulders again.

'Thanks, Rafe. How's Alma?'

'Good. I took her out to bingo last night. She beat the crap out of a bunch of Catholic ladies with blue over-permed hair and crosses clutched in their hands. Had to hustle her out of there before the lynch mob formed.'

Rafe is given to exaggeration, and hyperbole is a concept unknown to him – he thinks it's the norm. For him it is. That's one reason people notice him. The other is that he's drop-dead gorgeous, six-two, with blond hair and blue eyes. I'm the only woman I know who is immune to his charm and beauty. Maybe that's why we're such good friends.

'Afterwards we went to the Pine Cove.'

'Huh?'

'Alma and I.'

'You're kidding. Why?'

'She was a little down. I thought she needed cheering up.'

Rafe's the only one I know who would take an eighty-one-year-old lady to a neighborhood bar to cheer her up. I was speechless for a bit. I've known Rafe for years and he can still do this to me. Over and over. It drives me crazy.

'Did it work?' I asked at last.

'Yeah. She had two Manhattans and a massive amount of popcorn. And flirted with an off-duty cop. They loved her there. She made me promise to take her back. Have you got a bag, Kat?'

We were approaching the baggage carousels and the front exits. It doesn't take long to walk Sacramento Metro Airport.

'Just what I'm carrying.'

He was parked in the loading zone right out front. No ticket. Rafe gets away with stuff like that all the time. I used to wonder but now I take it for granted.

He and Alma have a lot in common, which is probably why they are friends. I guess friends is the word for it. Terms like cohorts, even partners in crime, occasionally occur to me. They don't talk like ordinary people, like ordinary friends.

'Alma, if you were forty years younger, I'd chase you till you dropped.' That is Rafe's idea of gallantry and idle chitchat.

'If I were twenty years younger, I'd let you,' is Alma's idea of a reply.

They'd been bantering and palling around like this for a while. It had started with Rafe taking Alma out one evening to play bingo or bunko or some game where old ladies were allowed to get wild and holler. Rafe had loved it and it became a regular thing with them. First talking and bingo. Now it was Pine Cove and drinking. God knows what was next.

'Alma wants me to teach her to shoot pool.' There was my answer. I reflected glumly on my hard-drinking, popcorn-eating, pool-shooting grandmother. 'How about you, Kat? Want to grease out at Mack's and rack up a few?'

'I'm too tired, Rafe. I want to go home and relax.' And call Hank, I thought guiltily. 'Let's go to Alma's first, though.'

We climbed into Rafe's 1969 black Corvette and blasted off. He made a big show of driving cautiously for me, caution not being a component of his everyday reality. He was being cautious and quiet both and, naturally, it made me suspicious. He's quiet about as often as he's cautious.

'What aren't you telling me?' I asked.

'Hmmm?' He pretended he was absorbed by traffic, which was a joke. There wasn't any.

'Rafe?'

'Oh, she's fine. Don't worry.'

'Who?' Alma? Charity? My mind raced, reeled, with the possibilities.

'She doesn't want you to worry.'

'Rafe!'

'Somebody tried to kill her.'

I froze up. It takes a lot less than that to worry me. A whole lot less.

And I still didn't know who.

Fifteen

'Who?' I asked it again.

'Alma.'

I didn't say anything for quite a while. I couldn't. My teeth were clenched, my hands gripped, my mind and imagination out of control.

'Kat.' Rafe patted my knee gently. I couldn't answer. 'Kat.'

'Tell me,' I said at last.

'A guy got into her house yesterday morning. I figure it was through the back door. That's how he left, anyway. You know how Alma never bothers to lock it?'

'Dear God,' I breathed, and hated Alma for being trusting and hated me for not, and for hating Alma.

'He came up behind her in the kitchen where she was cooking. Had a gun.' My teeth clenched again, tight enough to make my fillings ache.

'She didn't hear him, of course. She was listening to one of those stupid talk shows blasting away on the radio. He had to holler at her. She turned around and asked him what he wanted. For an answer he waved the gun under her nose. She turned back to the stove, picked up a skillet full of grease, bacon, and sausage and threw it in his face. Hit him a good one. He went down. Alma tromped his gun hand and tried to get the gun.'

I groaned. I've often wished she wouldn't watch so many cops and robbers shows. They give her a lot of bad ideas.

'That didn't work so she went next door to Rusher's, leaving the guy in the floor in grease, sausage, and pain.'

'And called the cops?'

'Rusher did. Alma called me.'

I sighed. Yeah. Right. Why bother with the police and sensible procedure when you can call in the vigilantes? 'Did either you or the police get there before the guy left?'

'No.'

'Could the police tell you anything?'

'Could they? I don't know. They didn't.'

No, of course not. I wouldn't tell Rafe and Alma anything either. 'I don't like it, Rafe.'

That was an understatement.

I told Rafe about getting shot at in the Bronco. He didn't like it either. That was obvious, and another understatement. We neither of us had a clue, never mind an answer.

That was equally obvious.

Rafe pulled up in front of Alma's house. I took the steps two at a time, rang the bell, and fumbled through my purse for a key. The back door is never locked but the front door is. Can't beat that for logic. Alma got to the door before I found the key.

'Katy, dear, come in. How are you? Tell me about your trip.'

'Alma.' My voice choked over a little.

'There, now.' She patted my hand. 'Come into the

kitchen and we'll have tea. I'm just baking a pie.' Rafe padded along after us making appreciative noises at the prospect of food. Pavlov's dog has nothing on Rafe in stimulus/response time when it comes to anything edible.

'Tell me, Alma.'

And she did, although really it was more of a dramatic rendition, skillet and all; it was entertaining but not particularly enlightening. I found myself muttering, 'The facts, ma'am, just the facts,' but no one paid any attention. Nothing new there for either Alma or Rafe.

'Don't forget the phone call,' Rafe said.

Alma frowned. I could see that it had already been placed in the to-be-forgotten slot. Her eyes slid back and forth between us.

'Cough it up, Alma.' I was firm.

'This morning a man called me and told me not to be a meddling old busybody. He told me to keep out of things that didn't concern me or I'd be sorry. Imagine! Calling me *old*, indeed.'

'Did you recognize the voice?'

'No.'

'What did it sound like?'

'Like he was trying to sound tough and mean.'

'Did he?'

She hesitated. 'Yes.'

'Alma, I don't like this, not one bit. It's time for you to lock your doors, keep quiet and out of sight, and—'

'Certainly not.' She was indignant. 'What are they going to do, kill me?'

'Well, yes, actually.' My voice, I noticed, sounded almost apologetic. 'I think that's the idea someone's trying to get across.'

'To hell with them, Katy.' I winced. I swear, but I hate it when Alma does; it just doesn't seem right. And she does it all the time; I should be used to it by now. 'I'm not going to let anyone push me around.'

'Why don't you move in with—'

'No, I won't leave my house.' I stared helplessly at her. 'I'm a stubborn old woman, Katy, and that's that. Anyway, Rafe will stay here with me for a while, won't you?' She turned to him.

'Sure.' He grinned, visions of sugarplums dancing in his head.

I nodded numbly. It was better than nothing. A lot better, actually. Of course if she survived, the end result would be an obdurate old woman hopelessly addicted to Manhattans, stale popcorn, the Pine Cove, and shooting pool. I sighed.

'We could go out and shoot a little pool this evening if you like?' Rafe, always helpful, echoed my thoughts.

'Good idea.' Alma perked right up.

I sighed again. Why couldn't I have a grandmother who made doilies and read *Reader's Digest* large-print books?

'Rafe, run me home, will you?'

'You're not staying for dinner?' Alma looked surprised, Rafe looked astounded. I shook my head.

'I've got too much to do. Maybe tomorrow.'

We left it at that. I did. They didn't. So I had to tell every detail of my trip twice. Then Alma wanted me to speculate. She fussed and dithered and was still going strong when I kissed her good-bye and dragged Rafe out to the car.

It was a silent ride. I was lost in thought and Rafe finally gave up trying to entice me into conversation.

He pulled up in front of my house and behind Hank's '65 Mustang. My heart did flip-flops. I jumped out of the car and headed up the path, remembered my bag and came back. Just in time I remembered to thank Rafe and say good-bye. He winked at me.

'Hank,' I called as I opened the door. 'Where are you?'

Mars, Hank's black, mostly black Lab, came bounding out to greet me. I dropped my stuff and headed for the living room patting the dog. The situation was not promising. As far as I could tell, and it didn't take an investigator's smarts to figure it out, Mars was the only one excited to see me. Hank sat in the middle of a bunch of empty beer cans and glared morosely.

'Where have you been? I was worried about you, Kat.' He didn't sound worried, he sounded mad. Looked mad, too. 'I called and left messages. You didn't call back.'

'I—'

'What am I supposed to think?'

'Hank—'

'I was worried, Kat.'

'Goddamn it, Hank. You know I can take care of myself.'

'Yeah, right.' He glared morosely again.

I glared back. I can. Mostly. It was debatable sometimes, I admit, but I didn't feel like getting into that can of worms.

'Most people don't have five bullet holes in their vehicle.'

Hmmm, good point. He mashed a beer can into a neat little pancake and stared at it before carefully placing it on the coffee table. We glared at each other.

Damn. We were fighting before we'd even kissed hello.

'You just broke in?' I hadn't given him a key yet, an irrational, independent streak of mine I couldn't quite get over.

'Yeah, and it was tough, Kat. I reached through the hole in the bedroom screen, unlatched it, opened the window, and climbed in. Thirty seconds, tops. Nice, tight setup you have here.'

Mars bumped against me and started licking my hand. He hates it when we fight. Me too.

'Lighten up, Hank.'

I started for the kitchen to get a glass of wine. Mars followed me. Behind us we heard the sound of beer cans being pulverized. Mars and I stared at each other. I got out some crackers and cheese and cut up the cheese, flipping Mars the moldy parts. Hank came up behind me and put his arms around my waist.

'Kat, I'm sorry, sweetheart, but I was worried.'

He kissed the back of my neck and the top of my head and held me tightly around the middle. Mars bumped my knee begging for more cheese. I stood, silent and frozen, waiting for Hank's kisses to thaw me out a bit.

'You didn't call or answer my messages – '

'I did, Hank.' I hugged him back and stood on my tiptoes to kiss him. 'Your dip-shit secretary probably deep-sixed it like she always does.'

He ignored the interruption.

'So I came up, Kat—' He broke off. 'We had an agreement that you wouldn't pull this kind of shit.'

So much for the sweet talk.

'I didn't pull any kind of shit,' I said, and it was mostly true. 'I left a message for you with your secretary, the one who never gives you my messages. Did you get it?'

'No.'

'Hank, *do* something about her. Anyway, if you'd get an answering machine at home I wouldn't—'

'Damn it, Kat, I hate those machines. I won't have one.'

'Okay, just don't complain if I can't get a message to you.'

He yanked the refrigerator door open and pulled out a beer. It sprayed slightly as he popped the top.

'Hank, I'm sorry.'

It was hard to choke out but it was true. I was sorry. Still, I couldn't change my life, or my job, or make Hank not be afraid for me. His wife had been killed by a guy trying to get to him; he couldn't get over it, or over the fear of losing me.

'Did you figure out I was okay?'

'Yes, probably anyway.'

'How?'

'The house looked the same as usual, your bed was made, the messages on your machine recent and on-going, there was no blood in the Bronco. Lots of stuff.'

'And Tim came by to feed the animals and told you I was out of town on business?'

'That, too.'

We laughed. I leaned back in his arms and relaxed. It scares me having someone to care about me, to worry over me, but I like it too.

'Hank?'

'Mmmm,' he said into my hair.

'Let's go unmake the bed.'

We made love and Mars ate the cheese and crackers.

Sixteen

'There's no food in the refrigerator, Kat.'

I stretched out lazily in bed and then started to climb on top of him. Food? Who cared about food? Hank's stomach growled. So there was my answer: six-one hunks who've been on the road for hours did.

'Did you drink all the beer, too?'

'Yeah. Let's go shopping.'

'I think there's a jar of spaghetti sauce, maybe some canned beans and stuff in the cupboard.'

'Shopping,' he repeated firmly.

'All right.'

Hank's a real find: smart, kind, and loving; tall, dark, and handsome, too. How do I love him? Let me count the ways. One, he's a great cook. Well, no, that's not actually number one . . .

'Kat, you getting up, sweetheart?'

Hank stood over me as I lay and daydreamed. He was slightly damp still from the shower and had a towel wrapped around his waist. I tried to pull it off but he was too quick for me.

'Somewhere out there is a steak with your name on it, or halibut simmered in wine with cream and shallots, maybe chicken with . . .'

I got up. I'm only human.

'Maybe I'll make a banana cream pie while you cook dinner.' Banana cream pie is Hank's favorite dessert and he's putty in my hands when I make it. I can bake, I just can't cook.

'What's this?' His fingers caressed my shoulder and the bruise there.

'Oh that.' I thought about it and didn't know. It could have been the Coke can Lindy bounced off me, or maybe I hit the steering wheel dodging bullets.

'I've got a lot to tell you, Hank.'

'You talk. I'll drive.' He hugged me. 'Do you think you ought to get dressed first?'

'Damn, but you detectives are sharp. Don't miss a thing, do you?'

He smacked me on the bottom as I pulled on my jeans.

The trip to the store wasn't long enough for all the details. I hit the highlights: Johnny's death, Lindy and Lisa, my search for Michaela, the attacks on Alma and me. As I finished I felt the albatross on my shoulders flap his wings and lift off. It felt good to have Hank beside me. Real good.

'Halibut?' I asked.

'You got it.'

'Spinach and mushroom salad?'

'Sounds good.'

'I'm glad you're here, Hank.'

He put his hand on the back of my neck and we drove the rest of the way in companionable silence. Silence full of promise.

I spent the next day with Hank but first I made a number of phone calls, looking for Michaela. No dice.

She didn't have a listed or unlisted phone number and none of the bars I called had heard of her. I wouldn't find out anything on a Monday or Tuesday either, not until later in the week when live music was happening. Then I could talk to people. So that was that.

Hank was leaving the following morning and we took the time for each other. I needed a sane and sensible person to talk to and filled him in on everything I could think of. Everything. It was hard when he left, but it always is. We had gotten used to it.

Johnny, Lindy, Lisa, Michaela: I felt like a juggler with too many balls in the air. I called Henley first. He was in and sounded pleased to hear from me. I didn't think it was my charm.

'Glad you called, Ms. Colorado. Why don't you come on down to the office? There are a few things I'd like to talk to you about.'

There are never RSVPs in invitations from cops. They assume you'll come. Usually they're right. I still didn't think it was my charm.

'Okay. I've got some stuff for you, too.' He grunted, hiding his enthusiasm well. 'I'll be there within the hour.' He grunted again. End of conversation.

I called Charity. No answer, so I set off for Henley's office.

'You're not going to like this,' Henley said when I appeared at his office door.

I shrugged. 'I'm tougher than I look.' He waved at a chair.

'Sit down. John Benson's death looks like the result of a drug deal gone bad.'

My knees felt like they'd stopped working and I plopped into the chair. Shit. I wasn't that tough and he was right: I didn't like it. And I didn't believe it. I said so.

He shook his head. 'Listen first. I know how you feel. We found half an ounce of cocaine in the car. A lot of it was packaged in one-half and one-gram packets, typical for drug sales.' He looked at me to see if I was following. I was. 'We also found a sizable amount of Ice. You know what that is?' He asked it grimly. I nodded and my heart sank. It's a potent form of crack.

I stared at him. I knew my face was white. It had to be, all the blood had drained down to foot level. 'I find it very hard to believe,' I said at last, and I hated myself for it, and for not flat out saying, 'I don't believe it.' I wanted to but I couldn't. I'd heard a lot of new things about Johnny recently and I didn't know what to believe.

'Yeah, well,' he shrugged. 'We found drug residue in the trunk and behind the back seat too.'

'Hey, Henny, you wanna go to lunch?' A detective in shirt sleeves with suspenders and a shoulder holster stuck his head in the door. Henley shook his head and the guy disappeared.

'Henny?' I asked. It was the only thing I could think of to say.

He flushed slightly. 'Naw, don't call me that. It's Bill. Look, Kat.' He paused. I was still sitting there stupidly. 'Look, we haven't bought it yet either. We're still checking it out.'

'It could be a plant.'

'Could be, but why?'

I didn't have an answer to that so I didn't answer. He paused politely, then continued. 'We're not jumping to conclusions, we don't do that. We'll check it all out.

We didn't find anything at his apartment. If his lifestyle doesn't include drug dealing, then we'll keep looking.'

I nodded again. It had hit me hard. I realized I wasn't being an investigator, I was being a family member. Henley knew it, too; he was going easy on me.

'We checked with the Davis police. Several people, researchers particularly, have reported threats recently. The Activists for Animal Rights took credit, if you can call it that, for the threats. We're looking into that pretty carefully too.'

I nodded. 'Gil Jones?'

'He's on the list.'

Good, I thought. He should be.

'You interested in what we got on Walter Benson?'

I nodded again, me still the whupped dog and him the nice guy flipping me bones.

'Clean as a whistle. The money left in trust for the Benson kids is all present and accounted for down to the last cent. It's invested in low-risk, moderate-yield accounts. Half of it is tied up in longer term, slightly higher yield accounts, presumably since the Benson girl doesn't get it for another two years; the rest is liquid or due to be by John's birthday, so the investment options would have been his. All on the up and up and squeaky clean.'

I nodded. Alma had said that Walter never spent, never mind misspent, Sophie's money. And God knows he's good at managing the stuff.

'And Michaela inherits from John?'

'Yes.'

'Directly? She doesn't have to wait until she's twenty-three?'

'No. Directly.'

'Who inherits if something happens to Michaela?'

'Why?' His eyebrows went up. 'Is something going to happen to her?'

'How should I know? I'm just asking out of curiosity.'

'Rhonda Porter.' He waited for my reaction. There was none. 'Well?'

'Haven't a clue, unless – ' I shrugged. 'I wonder if it's little Ronny.'

'Little Ronny?'

'A niece of Sophie's. Not little anymore either. She and Michaela are about the same age and used to play together as children. I haven't seen her for a long time, years. Sophie was always very fond of her.'

'Find out.'

'May I use your phone?' He nodded. It rang nine times before Alma answered.

'Katy, dearest, you know how I hate it when you ring during the soaps.'

'Sorry. It won't take long.'

'Luke is about to have an affair with his stepsister, only she's really his half sister but he doesn't know. They're kissing. Next it'll be sex and incest,' she added with satisfaction.

'Not on the soaps?'

'And he's been exposed to AIDS.'

'Luke's a homosexual?' Henley stared at me. I mouthed the word soap at him but I don't think he got it.

'Bi. Who would have thought of it? He seemed so manly.'

'Alma, what's Ronny's last name?'

'Ronny?' She sounded puzzled. 'Which soap?'

'No soap. Sophie's niece.'

'Oh. *That* Ronny. Porter, why?'

'Did you know that she inherits if something happens to both Johnny and Michaela?'

'Did I? Hmmm. I think I did. Sophie was always very fond of her, I can't think why now. I thought she was a rather spiteful, mean little thing. Dear, I've got to go. That bitch, Jolene, is on and she's one of my favorites.' She said good-bye and hung up without waiting for mine.

'Did you get that?' I asked Henley.

'Rhonda Porter is Sophie's niece.'

'Yes.'

'Who's homosexual?'

'Bi. Luke, but that's soap opera, not real life.' Henley digested that in silence.

'You said that you had something to tell me?' he asked me finally.

Mentally I tried to shake myself alert: out of drugs and soap opera. Henley looked at his watch although he didn't look hurried. His stomach growled. Oh, lunch time. I pulled out the photos of Lisa and Lindy, sorted through them and passed over the clearest of Lisa.

'I have reason to believe that the girl with the dark hair and eyes is one of your unidentified bodies. If she is, her name was Lisa, fourteen or fifteen years old, a runaway hooking here in town.'

Henley looked at me warily. 'How do you know this?'

'Information from a client.'

'We need to talk to your client.'

I nodded. 'I agree, but I can't do that at this point. If and when I can, you will.'

'How did your client find out about it?'

'It was in the paper: description etcetera with an if-

122

you-can-help-call-the-Sheriff's-Department-at-this-number request.'

'He didn't call?'

'No, but I have the information and I'm passing it on to you.'

'All of it?'

'All I have right now.'

'Can I keep the picture?'

'Yes. And, Henley.' He looked at me stolidly. 'See if the girl had a Mickey Mouse watch on.' I paused to get the essentials straight. 'Also, I'd like to know how she died, what—'

'Yeah, right,' he interrupted me in a not very promising tone.

'And if the watch is still running,' I added. He looked at me strangely.

'I'll see what I can get on it.'

'And let me know?'

He sighed. 'And let you know.' He sat and rocked back in his chair for a bit. 'Look, Kat, in this business we go for the obvious. And chances are that's going to be it. A teenage hooker gets killed, it's because the street is a rough place for a young girl, I don't care how tough she is. And this girl,' he gestured toward the picture, 'doesn't look tough.

'Six out of ten women who are homicide victims are killed by their husbands or boyfriends. Most homicides are committed by someone the victim knows, often well.

'In this case that's probably not it. She's the third prostitute to die in the last nine months. All were young, pretty, and dark-haired. All of them were strangled. I think this one was too. We've probably got a psychopath with young dark-haired, pretty hookers on his mind.

Like I said, we start with the obvious. If there are great criminal masterminds, I've never met one.'

He pushed back his chair, folded his hands across his ample belly. 'Now stupidity, ask me about stupidity.' But I didn't have to ask, he rolled on. 'Guy and a gal pull a gas station robbery. While the guy's pulling the heist, the girl's filling out a Win-a-trip-to-Hawaii blank which she drops in the box. We were waiting for them when they got home. Another guy did a bank job and wrote the holdup note on the back of a deposit slip. Not *any* deposit slip, his. Some criminal mind.

'We close seventy-five percent of homicide cases and we know who did a lot of the rest of them but we can't get the evidence or crack a phony alibi.' His stomach growled again and he stood up. 'I'm going to lunch. Want to come?'

I stood up too, and shook my head. 'No, thanks, I'm not real hungry.'

He grinned. 'I lost my appetite once, August '68, first guy I'd ever seen was—'

'Shut up, Henley.'

'In the trunk of a car for four days in hundred-and-ten-degree heat.' He grinned.

'What a sweet, sensitive, caring guy you are.'

'Yeah, that's what the wife says.' He pulled on his coat. A few flecks of dandruff settled on the dark blue polyester. We walked out together.

'Hope your burger chars and your ice cream melts,' I said glumly.

He laughed. 'I'll let you know.'

'And find out if the Mickey Mouse watch is still running. Remember that.'

He shook his head and got suddenly serious. 'You're

getting too close, Kat. Stand back, push off a little.' He squeezed my arm. A gray hair floated past.

'Yeah.' He was right, I knew he was.

I just couldn't do it.

Seventeen

Charity and Lindy were waiting for me when I got home. No, that's wrong. Waiting implies passive behavior, and nothing could have been further from the truth.

'Hi, gang,' I said as I walked into the kitchen. Charity waved. She hates to talk with her mouth full.

'Hey, Kat,' said Lindy, stuffing a four-inch-diameter chocolate chip cookie into her mouth. 'Lunch time. Are you hungry?' Unlike Charity, she had no inhibitions about talking with her mouth full. And, obviously, neither of them had any compunctions about making themselves at home. I wondered, again, why I had given Charity a key to my house.

'Mmmm, this is great, Kat. How come you had so much good food around here?' Had was the operative verb all right. They were laying waste to my groceries. It was like watching human trash compacters at work.

'Doesn't she usually?' Lindy asked.

'No. Yogurt, hard-boiled eggs, apples, stuff like that.'

'Yeech.' Lindy pulled on an oven mitt and hauled out an extra-large pizza.

'Pizza, Kat?'

'No.'

Bloated, smelly, four-days-old-in-the-trunk-at-a–110-degree bodies danced in front of my eyes. Damn Henley.

'You don't look too hot.' I shuddered. 'You ought to eat.' Lindy smiled tentatively and sweetly at me.

First bodies, and now a teenage hooker mothering me. There was a limit. I shuddered again. 'I'll have some juice,' I said finally.

'Okay.' Lindy opened the freezer door. 'Nothing good, though. No Hawaiian Punch, or grape juice or—'

'There's orange, apple, and cranberry.'

'Yeah. No Hawaiian Punch. Nothing good.'

'Hawaiian Punch is a juice substitute. I bet nothing in it ever waved at Hawaii.'

'Calm down, Kat.'

Charity was looking at me solicitously. Right. I was losing it over nothing. Too many bodies: Johnny, Lisa, and now Henley's stiffs. 'Cranberry, please.' I said it in subdued tones.

Lindy clattered around and then put a glass of juice and a slice of pizza in front of me. I drank the juice and pushed the pizza around my plate for a while. Then I ate it. I ate the next slice she gave me and had to fight for the third. Charity and Lindy don't mess around when it comes to food; they strap on the feed bag and go for it.

'Dessert?' Lindy asked.

'Chocolate chip cookies in the cupboard and part of a banana cream pie in the fridge,' I answered.

'Uh-uh, they're gone.'

'Gone?'

'History.' Charity and Lindy had the grace to look a little guilty.

'You had a dozen cookies and banana cream pie

before lunch and you *still* fought over the last piece of pizza?'

They shrugged.

'Ice cream?' Charity asked Lindy hopefully.

'No, I looked already.' The phone rang.

Lindy is not a shy teenager. She opened the cupboard door and picked up the phone at the same time. 'Hey, there's more chocolate chips in here,' she said to no one in particular. 'Hello,' she said into the phone. 'Yeah, she's here. Hang on.'

'For you.' She thrust the receiver at me and ripped off the top of the chocolate chip bag with her teeth. 'Who is it?' she snatched the phone out of my grasp to ask, then grinned, handed it back. 'Somebody in a bad mood.' She grinned again. I didn't grin back. The phone was already squawking at me.

'Katy, for goodness sakes, who was that person?'

'Hi, Alma, I'm fine thanks, and how are you?'

'Katy.' Alma's voice was reproachful.

'It's a long story. I'll tell you later. How are you?'

'Pooh. Have you found Michaela?'

'No. Nothing's changed in the day and a half since I talked to you.'

'Katy, dear.' Her voice was even more reproachful. I sighed. Guilt, the poor man's mind control. 'And Johnny?'

'The cops are working on that.'

'What have they found?'

'Nothing definite yet.' I opted for half truths and left out the drugs.

'Katy, you're not going to leave it up them?'

'Yes, I am. Mostly. That's their job and they do it well. Much better than I can.'

'Oh, dear,' Alma said and hung up. I stared stupidly at the receiver for a moment, then Lindy kindly took it from me and replaced it.

'It must have been Hank. I wish he'd come more often,' Charity said.

'What?' I asked, still stupid.

'Hank, I wish he would come more often.'

'Yes, me too. Why?' I asked curiously.

'Food. You always have food around when he's here. That was a really good lunch. I love it when you have food.'

Had, I thought glumly, looking at the pile of dirty dishes in the sink. It was down to the usual: yogurt, a bag of apples, half a carton of milk, probably sour. And Lindy had almost polished off the chocolate chip stash.

'Did you find out about Lisa yet?' she asked, stuffing the last handful in and throwing the wadded-up wrapper at the trash can.

'You missed.'

'Yeah, so?'

'So, pick it up.' We glared at each other. She finally did.

'So, did you?'

'I spoke to a detective this morning. He'll let me know if the young woman in the description was Lisa.'

'Cops, fucking cops!'

'Lindy!' Charity shrieked.

'Don't even start,' I said in a dangerous way. They looked at me and calmed down appreciably.

'I thought you were going to find out.'

I shook my head. 'Private investigators don't solve murders, cops do. It's only on TV and in the movies that cops look dumb and PIs run around being super sleuth.' She didn't look convinced.

'In real life cops solve murders; PIs do the kind of stuff cops don't have time for. That's the way it is, kid.' She sneered. I sighed. I'd about had it with both Lindy and Charity for the day. 'I'm still working on it, Lindy. I'll ask around, talk to people. For that I need some information.' She looked nervous.

'Like where you two lived. And worked. And hung out. I need descriptions of Lisa's regular johns.'

'I don't want to talk about it. I don't want to think about it. That's behind me now.' She said it on a virtuous note, but underneath I heard something else.

I shrugged. 'Okay. I can't do much then. Think it over.' We'd been here before and we both knew it.

'Fuck you!'

'Yeah. You really have a way with words, Lindy. Keep it up, kid, you'll get to first base one of these days.'

She stared defiantly at me. 'Fuck you! Fuck you, fuck you.'

'Probably strike out a lot first though,' I amended. She started to cry.

'Shall we start over?'

'Fuck you!'

'Have a nice time at the horse show, Charity. See you both when you get back. Why don't you toddle along now? I've got things to do.' I nodded and made myself smile, then turned and started out of the room.

'Okay,' Lindy said on a gulp. I kept on going. A loud wail started behind me. I kept right on, sped up actually.

'Kat.' I was out of the kitchen and halfway through the front room. Almost home free. 'Kat – please.' Damn. I stopped but I didn't turn around. 'Kat, I'm sorry.' She said it so softly I could hardly hear. I waited.

'I said I'm sorry! Okay? Okay?' she hollered.

'Okay.' I turned around and came back.

'Now what?'

'Now we try to work together to find out who killed Lisa.'

Her eyes filled with tears. 'Yeah. Okay.'

'Did you live together?'

'No, but we wanted to. Next month – We'd planned – It's like the Mickey Mouse watch –' She was crying now. 'The plans are still real. In your mind they go on ticking just like the watch but Lisa, Lisa, she's not there, so the plans are shit,' she finished bitterly, 'just shit.' Charity fidgeted uncomfortably. 'And plans don't count. They don't count if there's no one to make them with.'

'Where did you live?'

'At the Halfpenny Motel with two other girls.'

'And Lisa?'

'At the Hideaway.'

'I don't know the names. Where are they?'

'Auburn Boulevard.'

'Around Bell Street?' She nodded. It was an area generally known as the stroll. A lot of girls lived and worked there.

'You worked the stroll?'

'Yeah.'

'Both of you?'

'Pretty much. Sometimes we went downtown in the J Street area, but mostly we worked the stroll.'

'Give me the names of a couple of girls I could talk to.'

She hesitated a long time. 'Don't tell that I –' she looked the question at me.

'No.'

'Trinka. She knows what's going down.'

'Anyone else?'

'I – no.'

I let it go. 'Lisa's regular johns? Think carefully, Lindy. This is a big one.'

She nodded and looked serious. 'Yeah, it's just that – fuck! – ' Charity moaned softly. Lindy slid her eyes across to Charity, then back. 'Oh, sorry. It's just that – that I don't know. There weren't too many regulars, most of the guys were from out of town.'

'But some?'

'Yeah. A couple.'

'Could you describe them?'

'I dunno,' she answered dubiously. I took it for a no. 'There was an older guy, I guess.'

'How old?'

'I dunno. As old as you, maybe older.' I digested that one in silence. At thirty-three I didn't generally describe myself as old.

'Would you recognize them?'

'Uh . . .' Her voice drifted off.

'Did her regulars call her or pick her up on the street?'

'Probably picked her up, I'm not sure. She had a couple of set dates each week.'

'If we hung out on the stroll for a while and they showed up, could you pick them out?'

'Oh. Yeah, I could, I'm sure I could. I might recognize the cars too. Maybe.'

'Kat!' Charity sounded shocked.

'Lighten up, Charity. Have faith, hope, you know the routine.'

'Kat!'

I knew the routine, too. And I was hoping I wouldn't have to deck myself out in high heels, a leather mini-skirt, and a tight sweater and take a walk on the stroll, looking available and expectant. It wasn't part of the job description. Also I didn't have a leather mini-skirt. Or high heels.

'Is that what we're going to do?' Lindy looked nervous. 'Do you have a gun? Will you take it? Do you have two guns? Can I have one too?'

'Not a chance, kid,' I said grimly. 'We're not desperate and we're not crazy.'

'Thank God,' Charity said, sounding relieved but not convinced.

'Why would we need a gun?' I asked curiously.

'Somebody killed Lisa. Another girl disappeared too. There was talk that she got dusted.'

'What was her name?'

She shrugged. 'Dunno. I never knew her, just heard. Kat, you've got to find out. It's still ticking. I know it is. I can hear it in my dreams, my nightmares I mean.'

I took her by the shoulders and shook her gently. 'Lindy, stop it. Stand back, push off.' I used the same words Henley had used to me. I didn't mean to but I did. 'You're letting it get to you, letting it make you crazy. That's no way to help Lisa.'

'Yeah? I guess you're right but I can't help it. I can't.'

'What are you afraid of?' I asked, still gently.

She looked at me astounded. 'My best friend gets dusted and you ask what I'm afraid of? Isn't that enough?'

I looked at her and thought about it and, yes, I guess it was. That and the fact that she was still just a heartbeat away from life on the street. The street is never a safe place for a woman/child alone. Especially after dark. She looked young and very vulnerable.

I surprised both of us by leaning over and hugging her. She relaxed for a moment, no, a nano-second, then stiffened.

'Fuck you!' she said. 'Just fuck you.'

I sighed. We seemed to have come full circle.

'Have a nice weekend, you guys. Knock 'em dead at the horseshow, Charity, you and StarBroke. See you when you get back.'

Charity didn't say anything. Maybe she couldn't. She looked somewhat shell-shocked as Lindy kept up a steady chant of fuck you's in the background. I decided, again, that I would never have children. Babies are sweet and cute 20 percent of the time but, inevitably, grow into teenagers.

I didn't slam the front door behind them. I had that much dignity left. Not much more.

Eighteen

There are a few logical choices in country music. I tried
them first and started striking out immediately. The
Texas Saloon wasn't country anymore, it was Tex's with
pool tables and a card room. Had been for a while.
Things like that remind me I don't get out enough.

Then I tried Skip's on Auburn east of Fulton. It's a
high-tech musician's idea of died-and-gone-to-heaven. I
checked the bulletin board first: a lot of drummers looking for a band; lead guitarists on the same search; a
Christian band that wanted backup singers; a hard rock
band wanted a bass player, 'kick-ass, no wimps or whi-
ners.' There was no lead singer named Micha looking.

The gal at the desk got right into it with me: asked
around, called her agent, rattled off a bunch of bars I
should go check out, people I should talk to. No one
had heard of anything going down in the Placerville
area. It didn't help that I had no names or clues. Still,
I left with an agenda and a full dance card.

The Yellow Rose was first. It was one of the closest,
just down the road on Auburn Boulevard. I got there
shortly before nine as the band was tuning up and spoke
to the bartender, a nice gal who didn't bother to look
country. She was wearing jeans, a T-shirt, and thirty

extra pounds. There was a rose on her T-shirt and a tattoo on her hand. I ordered a draft beer.

'Has the band been playing here long?'

'Almost a year.'

'Who's the lead singer?'

'Billy.' She looked up at the stage. 'He's not here yet.' She turned, got my beer, slapped it on the bar. The tattoo was a swastika. I looked at her face. She still looked like a nice girl but now I wondered. Swastikas do that to you. She put the change for my ten on the bar and looked up again.

'There's Billy now. You want to talk to him, you're better off taking him a drink.'

'Okay, whatever he drinks.'

'He'll start with beer.'

I nodded, and she put a Bud on the bar and took more money. The beer and I walked over to say hi to Billy. He looked at me without much interest. I handed him the beer.

'I'm looking for a favor so I thought we might start off like this.'

He grinned. 'Why not? Here's to ya.' He chugged on the beer, then started tuning his guitar, a cigarette stuck between the strings at the neck of the instrument. 'What can I do for you?'

'I'm looking for a singer called Micha. She's new in town but I hear she's playing around here somewhere.'

He thought and shook his head. 'Don't ring a bell. She's not at any of the big clubs. Try some of the smaller ones out in West Sac, Elk Grove, Rio Linda, Auburn.' He ran through some names. 'Ask for Joe at Sams.' That cryptic line wound it up.

'Thanks.'

He nodded and turned away, looked at the band, then stepped up to the mike. They swung into 'On The Road Again.' I made it back to the bar before I was trampled to death on the dance floor. Barely made it. The dancers are serious here and they were out in force – in ruffled blouses and skirts, in western shirts, jeans, and belt buckles the size of small hubcaps. And boots. They were dancing, twirling, doing figure eights and loop the loops (or is that airplanes?)

'Hey, wanna dance?'

A good-looking cowboy stood in front of me, six-foot-four-inches of muscle and smile. I swallowed hard and shook my head. If this was dancing, I didn't know how to dance. I drank my beer and left.

Nashville West was next. I liked it better, felt more comfortable there. You didn't have to have a ruffly blouse and skirt to belong. You could, but you didn't *have* to, it was optional. The lounge was dark, the music loud.

The steel guitar whined and cried as I picked my way through the crowd, past the wall covered with a Budweiser sign and eight Clydesdales. Subtle. Low key. And headed for the bar. There was one stool, I grabbed it. The bartender looked at me.

'Bud Light.'

I said it without thinking. Obviously advertising works; I don't even particularly like Bud. The Clydesdales shook their harnesses at me.

The singer moaned a Merle Haggard song into the mike, 'Bottle Let Me Down.' The guy next to me nodded in agreement. I gathered the bottle had let him down too.

I drank my beer and looked around. A girl in a fluffy

pink top, a short skirt, and a bouffant hairdo out of the fifties sat next to me. She was drinking a margarita and chewing gum. A guy asked her to dance. She looked him over, snapped her gum, nodded, and stood up.

I waited for the band to break and was glad that I didn't have a bouffant hairdo or chew gum and that I did have a boyfriend.

'Wanna dance?'

Déja vu? I looked. No, it was a short chubby guy with an alligator on his shirt and a leer on his face. Nervy, it was a slow song. I shook my head. He muttered something as he walked away. I didn't think it was a compliment; I didn't care. The band took a break and I got off my stool.

'Hey, I'm looking for – '

I slid into my now familiar routine. The lead singer, a beautiful girl in tight pants, a shiny top, and a smile, listened to me. Hang 'Em High was the name of her band. I couldn't quite match her up to the name.

'No,' she said politely. 'I've never heard of her.'

She called one of the guys over and he agreed, he'd never heard of her either. I asked about Placerville. The bass player, a guy with long hair, a drooping mustache, and a bald head, overheard.

'Try the Alibi Inn. They got a good band there with a girl singer.' He spoke slowly, rationing out his words, saving them, presumably, for songs. 'I dunno, maybe new.'

I thanked them. It was the most I'd gotten so far. Then I left. My clothes and hair stank of cigarette smoke and my brain reeled with country lyrics.

I don't see me in your eyes.

I'm killing my troubles, one shot at a time.
It's all over but the crying.

To hell with it. I didn't have any answers and I was
tired. I went home; tomorrow would be soon enough.
And it required some planning. Going alone to bars in
West Sac, Rio Linda, or Elk Grove was not my first
choice. Or second, or third. This is honesty, this is reality.
These were, some of them, rough places, redneck bars.
I called Rafe. He was glad to hear from me but turned
me down. Flat.

'Can't, babe, got a hot date.'

'Bring her along.'

'To a bar like that?'

He sounded shocked. I thought that was good, very
good, coming from someone who had logged a lot of
alcohol-sogged hours in dives.

'Not for long, Rafe, just—'

'Next week, Katy. When I say hot, I mean *hot*.'

I gave up. I knew from past experience, many past
experiences actually, too many in all honesty, that there
is no point in trying to discuss anything at all with
activated male hormones. They are not rational, reasonable, or sensible.

I gave up, but not graciously.

'Well, shit!' is what I said. He grinned over the phone,
I know he did.

'Later, babe,' and he hung up. Some friend.

Okay. Plan B. I chickened out and decided to call, to
let my fingers do the walking in the safety of my living
room. I struck out some more: every place I called in
Elk Grove, West Sac, and Rio Linda. But not at the
Alibi Inn.

There I didn't even get up to the plate.

'What's the name of your band?' I hollered into the phone and noise in the mega-decibel range.

'Yeah, we got a band.'

'With a woman singer?'

'Drinks two dollars, beer a buck and a half.'

'Micha, you ever heard of her?' My voice cracked slightly under the strain of screaming.

'Band plays until one-thirty.'

He hung up. I sat there limply for a while, then decided to drive up, check it out. It wasn't just the most promising lead I had.

It was the only lead.

Nineteen

I found the Alibi Inn easily enough. I wasn't the only one. The parking lot was full: pickups, good-old-boy cars, and a sprinkling of Japanese economy models. My battered Bronco II fit right in. I squeezed in between a utility pole and a beat-up Ford truck.

The building was ancient, long and low. It squatted on the ground like a truculent old-timer. The wood outside was worn, weathered, and beaten, tired but not hopeless. Inside, in daylight, it would have looked the same, maybe a little sad. At night, with music, it was warm and lively; with a couple of beers it would look even better.

A forty-foot bar ran the length of the building with tables crowded everywhere except for the dance floor and the stage. The band was on a break and the jukebox was on. I bellied up to the bar and hollered for a beer around what looked and smelled like an unwashed, unkempt gold-miner. It was standing room only. I took my beer and leaned on one of the heavy wooden timbers that held the building together. It was crowded, noisy, and smoky and I settled in for what turned out to be a twenty-minute wait.

The band moseyed back one at a time; the singer last.

She was slim, about five-four with curly dark hair. She wore blue jeans, a white shirt with the sleeves rolled to below the elbow, a wide leather belt with a big silver buckle, and cowboy boots. She was Michaela.

I was sure. Almost. I'd be positive when I saw her eyes. The lead guitar took the mike and swung off into the set. Michaela followed. It had the crowd hooting, hollering, chugging beer, and dancing.

It had me convinced.

The last song in the set was an old one, one you don't hear much anymore. *'Don't call me Jolie,'* Micha sang, and it caught at the beer-drinking stompers. *'Don't you know my name?'* They looked at their girl-friends and wives, who were looking at them, and the guys called their girls 'sweetheart' or 'darling' or, if they were smart, by their name. See, they were saying, I know your name, I know it's not Jolie. And they moved onto the dance floor and held on cheek-to-cheek and sang along with the tear-jerk lyrics.

The song is about a woman named Leah who's with a man who calls her Jolie, only Jolie left him for another. *I'm here, I'm yours,* Leah tells him. *Love me. Her heart was faithless and mine is true.* What she doesn't say is why she's with a guy who hasn't got her name right after all these years. She should have left, like Jolie. The song ended to applause and the we'll-be-right-back-after-a-short-break routine.

I ditched my empty beer bottle on a nearby table and started for the stage, Micha was on her way out, heading toward the back and what looked like a rear exit.

'Michaela.' She stopped for a second, didn't look back, then kept on going.

'Michaela,' I caught up with her and touched her

elbow lightly. She turned then.

'My name's not Michaela.' We neither of us smiled at the echo from the song. Her eyes were big, deep, and brown: Sophie's eyes.

'It's Katy, Michaela.'

'Leave me alone.' Her voice was angry, almost desperate. 'I don't want anything to do with you.'

'Not me, family.'

'I haven't a family.' She said it bitterly.

'Not even Johnny?'

'Johnny?' Her voice caught and trembled on a note before it fell off. 'Outside. Come on.' Her hand slammed against the panic bar and we went out. The night was clear and cold. I shivered. Michaela threw her head back and breathed deeply, evenly. 'What?' she asked finally.

'It's a long story. Can I buy you breakfast after you finish?'

'No.'

'Michaela—'

'Talk,' she demanded fiercely.

Okay. I would. 'Johnny's dead.'

She collapsed on a moan as though someone had hit her in the gut. And someone had. Me. Sticks and stones will break my bones but words will never hurt me is a lie. A big lie. I kept myself from putting an arm around her but it was hard.

'How?' she whimpered finally.

'He was killed in the parking lot of the Homestead Cafe in the early morning. It was in the paper.'

She stared at me blankly. 'I don't read – ' Her voice broke. 'Oh God. Oh God. Oh God, When?' she asked in a whisper.

'Three A.M. Sunday.'

'Sunday?' she asked stupidly.

'Late Saturday night.'

She moaned again. 'Oh no, dear God, no. It can't be. Not Johnny. Not there. No. Why? Why?'

'I don't know.'

Her eyes were clear as she stared bleakly at me but there were tears in her throat, in her voice.

'Who?'

'I don't know that either. When the police figure the why, they'll probably get the who.' She leaned back against the building, head up. I could see the tears now.

'Not Johnny, oh God, not Johnny? It *can't* be.' She looked at me and I nodded. She moaned again.

'No. It can't be, it can't. I always counted on having Johnny there. We talked only a short while ago. He was going to—' She broke off and I waited.

'To what?' I asked. She moaned again, head in hands.

'It's time to come home, Michaela.'

She shook herself. 'I don't have a home, I told you.'

'Alma—'

'No.'

'Whatever happened is past. She wants to see you, to make things up, to—'

'No.'

'Michaela—'

'That's not my name, I told you!'

'Micha.'

'It's too late,' she said sadly. 'Way too late.'

The door banged open. 'Micha, we're on.'

'Yeah, okay.'

'The memorial service is—'

'It's too late, I told you.'

'For Johnny?'

'For all of us. If Johnny were alive and needed me I'd come—' her voice clouded. 'It's too late now, for him, for me.'

'Alma?'

'We went in different directions years ago.'

The door banged open again. 'Micha!' The light shafted out from the bar across her face. The noise and the smoke rolled across us.

'Micha!'

'All right; I'm coming.' She looked squarely at me. 'Go away. Leave me alone. The past is dead.'

'Not the past. Johnny.' I paused. The door was open and the light fell on both of us. Soft light, harsh words.

'Johnny wasn't a late-night person, but you are. He would have met you in the middle of the night if you asked him. Johnny would have done anything for you. Did you meet him for breakfast at the Homestead after work last Saturday?'

For a moment I thought her eyes looked stricken and afraid but the light was uncertain and she moved into the building too quickly.

'Go away!' she said fiercely, then pulled the door shut behind her.

And I did.

Twenty

The phone rang at six-thirty in the morning. Of course I was asleep. I always am at six-thirty in the morning. It was either Hank or Alma, both of whom think I'll be so happy to hear from them it doesn't matter what time they call. They're only half right.

'Hey, sweetheart.'

'Hi,' I mumbled. 'Isn't this your day off? Why are you up so early?'

'Early? It's six-thirty, Kat.' Hank was into his early morning cheer routine and it hardly seemed worth staying awake for. I yawned. 'Somebody stole Al's daughter's car. We're going out looking for it.' I yawned again. Al was another detective.

'Who'd be dumb enough to steal a cop's car's daughter?'

'Mmmm, I woke you up, didn't I, Kat?'

'Hank, it's six-thirty. *Of course you woke me up.*' In spite of myself I sounded annoyed. Which was only half right. I was annoyed but I didn't want to sound it.

'Can you get away for three days next week? We could go desert camping.'

'I don't know. Right now it doesn't look promising at all.' I yawned again, I couldn't help it. It had been two-thirty by the time I got home from Placerville last night. And I hadn't slept well.

'Anything breaking at all?'

'I found Michaela.'

'Where?'

'Singing in a bar in Placerville.'

'And?'

'And it's only the beginning, not an ending.'

'That's usually how it works.'

'Hank,' I yawned, 'I'll call you back later when I'm awake, okay?'

'All right. Watch your step.'

'Yes. You, too.'

'And think about next week.'

'Okay.' We hung up on a smile and the noises lovers make at each other. I was just starting to drift off into never-never land when the phone rang again. Ten of seven. Hank had called, so that left Alma.

'Hi, Alma.'

'Katy, dear, that's amazing! How did you do that? You detectives are something else.' There was a long admiring note in her voice. I decided not to explain. I'd tried before with no success.

'What's up, Alma?'

'It's about Johnny. And Michaela. They . . . the coroner . . . he, uh, released the . . . Johnny . . . yesterday. The memorial service is the day after tomorrow, or should it be later? Michaela, what about Michaela? Do you think – ?'

'I found her, Alma.'

'Katy, that's wonderful, dear! How is she? Where is she? Oh, I can't wait to see her! Is she all right?'

'Yes and no. I found her singing in a bar in

Placerville.' I took a deep breath and tried to think how to explain it.

'When is she coming over? Today? Oh, Katy dear, you've been splendid, just splendid!'

'It's not that simple, Alma.' Something in my voice must have tipped her off.

'No? No, of course not. Tell me.'

'She was shocked and hurt about Johnny but she didn't want to have anything to do with me. Or with you, especially you. She sounded bitter and said you'd made your decision long ago.'

'Yes,' Alma agreed sadly. 'And in many ways she's right.' I said nothing. There was nothing for me to say. 'The memorial service? Will she come to the memorial service?'

'No. She said she would have done anything for Johnny but it was too late for that now. He was dead and it didn't matter. She sounded like you, actually. She said it was too late for her too.'

Alma sighed, a sad old-lady sigh that traveled pitifully around a few blocks and then settled into a dusty corner. 'Did you ask her what she'd been doing?'

'No. I didn't get that far; she didn't let me. I was lucky to get what I did. She told me to go away, to leave her alone. She said the past was dead.'

'Ah. But it's not.'

'No, or she wouldn't be bitter about it.'

'Is she singing again tonight?'

'Yes.'

'We're going.'

I started to protest but then decided it wasn't such a bad idea. Not good, maybe, but not bad either.

'Okay, I'll pick you up at eight. Have a nap. It's going to be a long night.'

I hung up and decided to have a nap too. Right now. Why wait? Three and a half hour's sleep and I wasn't firing on all four cylinders. I was just drifting off when Xerxes thudded onto the bed, restless and hungry. I coaxed him under the covers and into my arms where he finally curled up making the cement-mixer sound of his that passes for a purr, and went to sleep. We slept until nine. Xerxes had his breakfast, then sat on the edge of the tub and washed his face while I had a bath. Then we read the paper and I had breakfast.

Alma was ready when I got there at eight. Eager. She was on the front porch pulling the door behind her as I got out of the car. I opened the door for her and climbed back in. Then, as usual, we had a fight over seat belts.

'I'm eighty-one years old and I damned – ' I winced – 'well don't have to wear a seat belt if I don't want to.'

'That's true,' I agree, 'except when you're riding with me. I'm not having a crazy old lady flying around if we hit a bump.'

'Dammit, Katy!'

But I can be stubborn. I had a good teacher, after all. I sat there with my seat belt on, my arms folded, and waited. She finally gave in and buckled up.

'And if you take off, like you did last time, I'm turning around and we come straight home. I *mean* it, Alma.'

She sniffed derisively. 'I wish you wouldn't treat me like a child, Katy.'

There was an obvious answer to that and I didn't give it. Ten points for me. She sniffed again.

'Tell me again how Michaela looks, Katy.'

I thought about it. 'Grown-up and pretty, very pretty. I remembered how beautiful her eyes were but my memory didn't do them justice. Her hair is short and curly, like a kid's.' Like Lisa's, I thought; no, shorter. 'She is slim and graceful.'

'And she sings like an angel.'

'Yes.' I wouldn't have put it that way but, yes, she did. 'The audience is putty in her hands. She plays with them.'

'Maybe she knows then.'

'Knows what?'

'The power that beauty holds – like a flame for moths. Sophie had it, but never knew it. Walter knew,' she added, 'but he sure as molasses in January didn't want her to find out.'

'I thought it was "slow as molasses in January." '

'Katy,' Alma sighed, 'pay attention, dear, do.'

I ground my teeth, down-shifted to pass a car doing forty in the slow lane, then popped the clutch slightly. I do that when I'm pissed off.

'Can't you speed up, Katy? We're only doing fifty-five.'

'Sixty,' I said, but she wasn't mollified. Alma likes to do seventy or eighty and in the fast lane, which is why she loves to drive with Rafe in the blast-away Corvette. 'Beauty?' I asked, trying to steer her back to the conversation.

'Sophie was beautiful. She didn't develop her own talents but she did her children's. Michaela has her mother's beauty. I thought maybe she would see, would find it out through her music. Did she?'

'I don't know, I couldn't tell. She knows the effect she has and how to play to it. That's different from knowing the power of beauty, I think.'

'We'll see.'

'What's the plan, Alma?'

She shrugged. 'I'm not sure, dear. We'll just play it by ear.' I shuddered. I've been in some memorable spots with Alma, 'just playing it by ear.'

'I do want to talk to her and she must, she really *must* come to the memorial service.' Alma's tone was definite.

'She's an adult, not a child. You can't make those decisions for her or tell her what to do.'

'We'll see.' I shuddered again.

Parking wasn't difficult, as it was early in the evening yet. We climbed out of the car. I was wary. Alma looked eager and excited. I took her hand.

'Go slowly, Alma. It's a lot for her. She only learned last night about Johnny.' I hoped that was true. I hoped to God she hadn't known last Saturday. 'And now both of us.' I squeezed her hand. 'It's a lot.'

'Yes, dear. I only want to love her, you know.' She said it calmly. I started to answer, then realized there was no answer. It was true, and maybe she could do it with Michaela; she had with me.

We walked in and got hit by the music. The smoke wasn't bad yet. There weren't that many people there yet. I threaded through the tables and seated Alma at one in front, not front row but close. We could see Michaela and she could see us. Her eyes widened slightly as we sat down.

'May I help you?' The cocktail waitress was in a hovering pattern near us.

I looked at Alma. 'Manhattan with two cherries, please,' she said.

'Lite beer, bottle, no glass,' I added. From the moment we walked in Alma never took her eyes off Michaela. She almost missed her chair because she wasn't watching where she was sitting.

'A voice like an angel,' she said softly to me, or to nobody in particular, I couldn't tell which.

After that we didn't talk much. We drank and listened to the music and watched Michaela. At break Michaela moved quickly off the stage. I started to get up and follow her but Alma put a hand on my arm.

'Let her be,' she said. She caught the waitress's eye and ordered another round of drinks. I shrugged. It was her party.

Michaela didn't reappear until it was time to play and then she walked stiffly, kept her eyes down, and avoided looking at us. We sat through another set, Alma sipping on her Manhattan and singing accompaniment in a rickety voice with some of the songs. She learned the words and refrains quickly. Hers was not the voice of an angel but I, fortunately, was the only one who could hear.

Michaela let her eyes drift over us, watched us covertly when she thought we weren't watching her. At the next break she scampered off again. I raised an eyebrow at Alma, who shook her head and ordered her third Manhattan. I switched to 7Up.

By the third set Michaela was looking nervous and a little jumpy. She still hadn't looked at us directly or acknowledged us in any way. Alma was stoic and calm, a Rock of Gibraltar sipping Manhattans and eating too many red dye #13 cherries. I was resigned, a little restless, more than a little curious. And sad. Seeing Michaela brought back a bunch of stuff. About when I was young. About Johnny.

The band swung into the set I'd heard the other night. *'Don't call me Jolie, don't you know my name?'* Michaela sang, only at first it came out wrong. It came out, '*Don't call me Micha.*' She looked at me then and our eyes held briefly. I wondered if it was a slip, a clue, or a cry. I don't think anyone but me noticed.

At the end of the set Michaela stood for a moment at the mike, holding it, clutching it, grabbing at straws and looking for life preservers that weren't sailing by. Then she stepped off the stage and walked over to our table. The chair scraped as she pulled it out. Otherwise it was silent. She sat down heavily, gracelessly, and looked from me to Alma.

'All right, I'm here. What do you want?' Her tone was hostile; her eyes were wary. It sounded as though her soul were bruised. I let Alma take it.

'We're family and we've lost Johnny. I've let you down, I know, but I love you. I always thought there was time, time to make things right and come together again. And then Johnny died and we lost it, the chance, the time . . .' There were tears in her eyes.

'Don't you use Johnny to get to me. Don't you dare!'

'Come to the memorial service, Michaela.'

'Where were you when I needed you?' she spat out fiercely, harshly.

'Not there, and I'm sorry. But you didn't come to me either and ask. A phone call, a note, I would have come. Your father—'

'Oh God, why Johnny? Why not him? Johnny was so good, so dear, and he—' She broke off.

'He?' I prompted. She focused on me with faraway eyes.

'My father is cold and distant. He was the wrong person to bring up children after my mother died.'

'You look so much like Sophie,' Alma said softly. Michaela flushed.

'I use her name.'

'Micha?'

'Micha Budroe.' She laughed. 'And what a clumsy mouthful that is.'

'It's a good name.' Alma nodded approvingly. 'Johnny would have liked—'

'I told you – don't use Johnny on me!' Her voice was fierce and rough. 'Oh damn, damn, damn.' She hit the table softly with each damn.

'Hey, Micha, want a drink?' the cocktail waitress called out informally across several tables.

'No. Yes. A double. Kahlua and cream.' She roughly wiped the tears from her eyes.

'Johnny talked about you both. A lot. He loved you.' She said it grudgingly, but she said it. There were tears still in Alma's eyes. 'He said Katy was a hot ticket and you were a tough old lady.'

'I'm not tough,' Alma said. I looked over at Michaela. In her eyes she pulled back.

'No phony sympathy pleas, Alma,' I said.

'No,' echoed Michaela.

The waitress bumped Michaela's drink down in front of her, spilling it slightly. I pointed at the money by my glass. She took it and then hovered.

'Guy over there wants you to sing "Your Cheatin' Heart." You know it?'

Michaela nodded abstractedly.

'Micha?'

'I know it. I'll ask the guys.'

'Okay.' She flounced off.

Michaela drank a quarter of her drink in one swallow, then wiped her mouth on the back of her hand. It was a childish and oddly touching gesture.

'You're wrong. Johnny wouldn't care whether I came to the memorial service or not. Life is for the living is what he would have said.'

'You didn't let me finish,' Alma countered. 'He would care that we were together, that we were a family again.'

Michaela stared at her for a long moment, then shoved her chair back, grabbed her drink and left. She didn't say good-bye. Alma sighed, looked around, waved at the cocktail waitress and ordered another Manhattan. I sighed too. I wanted to say good-bye to this evening but didn't bother trying. We weren't going anywhere until Alma was ready and I knew it. The realization made me bitchy.

'That's your fourth Manhattan.'

'Third.'

'Fourth, and eighth cherry. The cherries are probably worse for you than the Manhattans are.'

She shrugged. 'At my age, who cares?'

'I do. I have to put up with you.' The music started again. Just as well.

In the next set Michaela sang 'Your Cheatin' Heart' and 'Crazy.' Alma sang along, sang that she was crazy to try, or cry, or love. I sat and thought about how we were all crazy. About love. About something. After that a string on the lead guitar broke and the music stopped for a minute. Michaela tossed back the rest of her drink and walked over to our table.

'All right, I'll come.' She sounded mad. 'When is it?'

'Thursday.'

'Where?'

Alma told her.

'See you.'

Alma nodded. 'Thank you, dear.'

'It's just this, nothing more. Don't be making anything out of it.' Her voice was hostile, angry. 'And don't call me dear.'

The lead guitar finished tuning up and called her back with a musical riff. She stared at us, daring us with her eyes to say something. We didn't. She spun around on her toes and left.

'Thank you, dear,' Alma said softly into the smoky haze Michaela seemed to trail behind her like a veil.

'Let's go.'

Alma nodded, ate her last cherry and slugged the remainder of her drink down in a very un-old-ladylike fashion. She tried to snag the money I left on the table for the waitress but I caught her.

'Fifty cents would be fine, Katy.'

'No, it wouldn't. Times have changed.' She frowned. I smiled at her. 'But you were right about everything else tonight.'

Later she tried to talk me into speeding on the way home. I didn't do that either.

Twenty-One

Alma buckled up without a murmur and fell asleep as soon as the car started moving. Michaela had done that as a baby. Lullabies made her wide-eyed and wide awake with interest but a moving car lulled her to sleep. Alma leaned against the door and snored softly. I thought about Michaela.

What did I know about her? I knew the baby who fell asleep in the car, and a five-year-old with crooked teeth and carefully tied ribbons. I'd met secondhand the high school girl who was Susan's friend and the young woman who had stayed at the Weyland Home and knew Julia. And I'd talked to Micha. I knew a lot of things; I'd met a lot of people. But I didn't know Michaela.

I woke Alma up before El Dorado Hills. I had to shake her. It was the four Manhattans, no doubt.

'Hmmm. What, dear? I was just resting my eyes.' She sat up alertly and cleared her throat. 'My, those cherries leave a nasty aftertaste.'

'Would Michaela kill Johnny?'

'Why?'

'I don't know. Would she?'

Alma drummed her fingers on the armrest and thought about it. She has a remarkable ability to not get caught up in sentiment, to dispassionately consider a situation.

'I shouldn't think so. At least not the Michaela I knew as a child. Why would she want to? She loved Johnny.'

'Money.'

'Johnny's money?'

'Yes.'

'Nonsense. She's going to have her own and that's more than enough.'

'But she won't get it for two years. She'll get Johnny's money right away.' I caught a deer with wide frightened eyes in the headlights. I slowed and it stayed by the side of the road. The eyes reminded me of Michaela's the other night.

'What's two years?' At eighty-one Alma had forgotten the warped perspective of youth, where now can be a forever without end or hope.

'At twenty-one two years is a long time, especially if you're not happy.'

Alma digested that. 'Would money make her happy?'

'Probably not, but I bet music school would, and that takes money. I doubt that singing at the Alibi Inn is what she wants to do with much more of her life.'

'Kill Johnny for *money*?' Alma sounded shocked. The dispassionate mood was past.

'People do it all the time. Especially for money. And we don't know Michaela now: who she is, what winds her watch, what's important to her.'

There was a long silence.

'Phooey.'

'I don't like it either, but it's a possibility.'

'All right. She could have, Katy. You could have, I could have. You don't know.'

'Yes, you do. About some things you do. *You* couldn't have killed Johnny.'

'I could have killed the man who broke into my house the other day if I'd hit him harder with that cast-iron skillet. I was holding back,' she added parenthetically. 'It's my favorite skillet and I didn't want it all gooed up with blood and brains. I would never have felt the same about it again.'

'Alma.'

'Well, it's true. And if I'd gotten his gun,' she shook her head, 'look out.'

'It's not the same.'

'No, but now we've established that I could kill, or you could, or anyone, given the right situation.'

'That's a big given.'

'Yes, thank goodness.'

'Why would you kill Johnny? Or I? No reason.'

'I can think of reasons.'

'Do it.'

The silence got so long I checked to see if she had fallen asleep.

'All right,' she said finally. 'Let's say I catch Johnny embezzling my money and stealing my antiques. We get into a big argument and I—'

'No. You have to stick with the facts. Johnny wouldn't embezzle; he wouldn't take anything from you. And anyway, you don't have that much money and the only antique in your house is you.'

What sounded like a sullen silence greeted my reasoning.

'All right. I have Alzheimer's and I become irrational and decide to kill Johnny. I go over to the Homestead, I kill him, and I come back.'

'You don't have Alzheimer's; you can't drive; and

you're not strong enough to kill Johnny, even if you caught him off guard.'

'Yes, I am.' She argued, but it was pure orneriness. I said nothing. 'Okay, I hire a hit man.'

'A hit man? For godssakes, Alma, you don't know any hit men.'

'No, but Angelina's sons do.' She said it on a note of triumph. And she had me. I bet they did, at that. 'So there!' She let me stew for a while. 'All right, you killed him, then.'

'How?' I inquired reasonably.

'You found out that he was getting serious about this really dreadful young woman—'

'So I killed him,' I finished cheerfully. 'Better dead than wed.'

Another sullen silence.

'Okay, you didn't mean to, but you were arguing and struggling and—'

'With a knife? And I didn't get medical help or call the police?'

Alma sighed. 'You didn't do it.'

'Right. Neither did you.' I said it, but the hit man was still on my mind.

'And Michaela?' she asked softly.

'We don't know. We don't know her.'

'Oh, Katy dear, I can't think, I can't imagine that—' She stopped because she could imagine and didn't want to. I could too, and I didn't want to either.

'Can't we go faster, Katy?' Alma asked petulantly.

I smiled and nodded and stayed at the same speed. When Alma fell asleep again I turned on the radio. Hank Williams was singing 'Your Cheatin' Heart.' That was twice tonight and I hadn't heard it in at least five years. I wondered how much it took to make a heart cheat: how much money; how much love gone wrong; or honor betrayed; or passion refused; how many dreams lost?

I thought about that and thought about the people I loved, or had loved; Alma, Johnny, Michaela, and how little perhaps I knew about them after all. And I hated the questions my mind was asking. Hated the questions and me for asking them. I couldn't help it. I hated that, too.

Alma snuffled and snored and I drove. We were long out of deer country by then. I saw no more frightened eyes that night.

Twenty-Two

Charity called the next morning to say that she was coming to get the truck. 'Is your Bronco fixed yet?'

'Yes. Thanks.'

'We're leaving now. My neighbor's dropping me off.'

'Okay. Come for breakfast. I'll make waffles.'

'Belgian?'

I snorted. I bought my waffle iron at Sears ten years ago and Charity knows it.

'Real maple syrup?'

'If you bring it.' I buy something cheaper with, maybe, some real maple syrup in it, and she knows that, too.

'Make a lot of waffle batter. I'm bringing Lindy.' She sounded grim.

'Okay, fine. What's the matter? How did StarBroke do at the show?'

'He did great. He was everything I hoped for and more.' Her voice was flat, hollow sounding.

'Charity, what's the matter?' My mind raced: The other horses? Her ice cream melted? Her column was boring? Lindy?

'See you, Kat.' She hung up before I could say good-bye. My mind was still racing and the words hadn't caught up. I drank another cup of tea and then made a small vat of waffle batter. I'd never seen Lindy eat breakfast but Charity's no slouch in the waffle department. I was just finishing the paper when the front door blew open, bounced off the wall, then probably off Lindy. Someone hollered, 'Ouch!'

'Well, here we are.' Charity loomed her five-five frame over my chair, put her hands on her hips and glared.

'Hi. Welcome.' I smiled. Charity and Lindy glowered. My smile got lonely and left. 'Well, how about breakfast?' I asked brightly, still trying. 'There's juice in the fridge, coffee on the stove—'

'Tell her!' Charity hollered. I gawked in amazement. Charity never hollers, rarely loses her composure.

'Right now! Tell her!'

'Couldn't it wait until after breakfast?' I asked.

'No!' Charity hollered again.

'Okay.' I shrugged and looked at Lindy who was looking at her feet. 'Better tell me, kid. There's no way out of this but through.' She mumbled something. 'What?'

'Tell her!' Charity shrieked.

'I looked,' she mumbled again.

Huh? I didn't get it. 'Looked? At what? For what?'

'Not *looked!*' We both ignored Charity's latest shriek. Lindy finally looked directly at me.

'Not looked, hooked.' Her face was sullen and closed over. Charity was doing an angry elf dance, hopping up and down in one place. I sighed, got up and poured myself a cup of tea and Lindy a glass of juice. She said 'no' in a mad tone of voice but took it and drank it.

'Charity, simmer down. We can't talk if you're going to hop around like that.' She whipped her hair back and forth a bit – spending too much time with horses, I thought dispassionately – and finally dumped herself gracelessly into a chair.

'I couldn't believe it—'

'Hush,' I interrupted her. 'Lindy, you tell it.' A long pause. 'Lindy?'

'I did. I told you. I hooked.'

'At the horse show?' She nodded. 'Why?'

She shrugged. 'Maybe I wanted to.'

'Did you?'

'Yes. No. I was tired of her bossing me around all the time.'

'I don't boss,' Charity's voice rose in a shriek again. 'I could never be bossy, *never*. I was just explaining the right way to do things.'

'Do this, do that. Don't do this or that. You can't have a corn dog, blah, blah, blah. I'm sick of it, sick of all those stupid rules.'

'Corn dogs aren't good for you,' Charity wailed.

I stepped in. 'Yes, they are.' Startled, her eyes met mine.

'It wasn't just that. I needed the money.'

'*I* would have given you money,' Charity said in martyred tones.

'Needed money for what?' I asked, practical as always.

'For a corn dog and a 7Up.'

'Oh. I wouldn't have given you money for *that*.'

'You hooked for a corn dog and a 7UP?' I tried to keep the incredulous note out of my voice.

'For money. It was way more than that, more than a corn dog and a 7Up.' Outside a dog barked and someone slammed a gate. 'I can do what I want to.' She said it defiantly and I sighed.

'No,' I said finally, 'you can't. That was the deal.'

'The deal wasn't that I took orders from *her*.' She

made a rude gesture toward Charity with her thumb.

'The deal was that you stayed off the streets.'

'Well, I have. Almost.'

'Almost isn't good enough.'

Temper flared in her eyes. 'So what do you expect me to do?'

'Just say no, Lindy, like Mrs. Reagan says.' Charity announced this in a pious tone of voice. The dog barked again.

'Mrs. Reagan, she was a hooker?'

Lindy looked at me and I shook my head. Don't kids know anything these days? 'Of course not.'

'But she *could* say no.' Charity looked at me for confirmation.

I nodded, which made me feel a little guilty. She could, true, but only to things that weren't a temptation to her in the first place. Like cocaine. Run a line of designer clothes under her nose and she started sniffing, all right.

'So there,' said Charity, still in an infuriatingly pious tone. 'It's easy. You just say no.'

I jumped in before Lindy decked her. 'Give the kid a break. It's not that easy, changing things, changing habits, even when you want to.'

'Hah!'

'When was the last time you just said no to a dessert?'

Charity flushed and Lindy laughed, then turned it into a cough.

'Lindy made a mistake.' I looked at her. Nothing. 'So what do you say, kid?' Nothing. I waited quite a while.

'Yo, Lindy.'

'Sorry,' she muttered.

'Okay. We back on track?' Nothing. 'Hey, you guys,

this is where you just say yes.' They both muttered
at me.

Close enough.

The waffle iron was fired up, sizzling and ready to go.
I ladled in the batter. The fences were marginally
mended and it was time to eat. Charity forgot that the
waffles weren't Belgian. Lindy and I didn't care.

We pigged out.

After they left I couldn't quite decide what to do
with myself. On a whim I reached for the phone book.
Rhonda was easy to find. Only it wasn't Rhonda, or
Ronny. It was Rhoni. An affectation or a fashion statement? Maybe both? She was home and answered on
the first ring. Her voice was high, breathless, and eager.

'Hallo-o,' she crooned with a bit of a foreign accent.
Accent?

'Ronny, this is Kat Colorado. Remember me?'

'Kat?' Long pause. 'Katy?'

'Yes.'

'What do you want?' Her voice dropped an octave,
became flat and hard-edged and without an accent.

'To talk to you. May I?'

'What about?'

'I can't say over the phone.' I could, of course, but I
wanted to see her. There was silence. Curiosity and lack
of interest fought it out. Curiosity won.

'When, now?'

'Sure.' I took it as an invitation. 'Tell me how to get
to your house.'

'Apartment.' She gave me an address in Carmichael.

'I'm on my way.' And I was.

She answered the door in model type clothes,
makeup, and an attitude. She couldn't have achieved it

in the twenty minutes since we talked so it was, presumably, the way she looked all the time. She stood there, poised and posed by the door, one hand on her hip, the other on the door frame.

'May I come in?'

'Please,' she gestured gracefully.

'It's been a long time, Ronny, how are you?' She looked at me suspiciously. Probably knew I spelled her name wrong in my mind.

'Fine.'

'What do you do? School? A job?'

'I'm a model, a fashion model.'

'In Sacramento?'

She flushed.

'No, of course not. I just finished my training. You make it big time in LA, New York, Paris, Rome – ' She paused. 'Not in *Sacramento*.' No, not in Sacramento. 'I'd do anything to hit the big time. Anything. I'd die for it, kill for it.' She laughed. 'If I had the money I'd do training in Paris.' She preened and pouted. She didn't look like Paris material to me.

'Anything?'

'Anything.'

'Would you kill Johnny?'

'Johnny?'

'Johnny Benson.'

'For half a million, sure. Did he have half a million?'

'More like a quarter of a million.' I exaggerated a little.

She stared at me. 'No shit?'

'And somebody killed him.'

'No shit? What does this have to do with me?'

'Nothing yet. His sister gets it. But if something

happens to her, you get it. It was Sophie's money and she was always fond of you.'

'No shit? A quarter of a million dollars. No shit!'

'Did you know that?'

'Know what?' Her face got cunning and ferretlike. Maybe she knew it, maybe she didn't. Either way she wasn't saying, or giving it away.

'Know that you inherited after Johnny and Michaela?'

'Well, my mom told me that – uh, Sophie, uh, no. How could I have?' The cunning went away and was replaced by simple ill-disguised greed.

'Somebody could have told you.'

'Nobody did. I read—'

'Read what?'

'Nothing. How's Michaela?' There was greed now in her voice.

'Fine.' She looked disappointed. 'Hey, I'll save you a trip to Paris.'

'What do you mean?' She changed the disappointed look to a puzzle one.

'Forget modeling. You haven't got what it takes, not in looks or character.' It was a cheap shot, sophomoric even. The fact that it was true didn't make it any better.

'Get out of here, bitch.' She stood up, walked to the door and flung it open.

I left. I'd already delivered my exit line.

I thought I heard her say, 'Me next. No shit! Ha. One down, one to go,' as she slammed the door behind me. I hoped she had more class than that.

It didn't seem likely.

Twenty-Three

The memorial service was in one of the older churches
of Sacramento. Johnny would have liked that, I thought,
before I could catch myself. Odd how you think about
things like that and try to make them matter. And they
don't. Life matters.

I sat in a front row and tried to make things matter,
tried hard the way you do when someone you love has
died. Then I got restless, so I got up and walked around.
Alma followed me like an old and wrinkled-up shadow.

A lot of people came: high school friends; college
friends; neighbors; family friends; Walter, his fiancée,
and her two daughters were there, all dripping in black.
I hate seeing young girls in black. I thought I saw
Henley too, but maybe not. Maybe it was just the sight
of dark blue polyester that threw me for a moment.

There was a young man who could have been Gil; if
Gil had cut his hair, taken a two-hour shower, bought
clean clothes, shaved, and worn dark glasses. It seemed
unlikely but I wanted to check it out. I just couldn't get
over there, hemmed in as I was by well-wishers with
messages of comfort and condolence. Michaela came in
late as we were all sitting. There were no seats left and
she stood at the back, poised and ready for flight. She

was wearing faded jeans, a heavy coat, and a sad look in her eyes.

The minister hadn't known Johnny, so he spoke in platitudes, certainties, and complacent tones. It was easy to tune out, and I did. Instead I let the memories and the look and feel of Johnny fill my mind and heart. I wondered how much longer I could do that before it would fade and memories and certainties wouldn't come back when I summoned them. And I wondered how you get used to death, but I knew the answer. You don't.

Afterward the minister asked if people wanted to say something about John.

Walter stood and solemnly spoke about a father's love for his only son, a father's treasure even if he is a bit of the prodigal. And then he spoke of endings and new beginnings and how fortunate he was to be blessed in his coming marriage and two new daughters. His bride-to-be fidgeted and simpered a bit and the girls looked like the floor could open up and swallow them anytime: they were ready, impatient even. It was touching and loving, though Walter never spoke John's name; it was just, 'my son.'

Alma stood and said simply, 'I loved Johnny and I will miss him. I wish it had been me instead.' It brought the place down; snuffles and handkerchiefs appeared everywhere. After that a lot of people spoke: with love and tears and words that are only uttered in moments of life and death. I didn't; I couldn't; I don't know why. I spoke to Johnny in my heart instead.

Things were beginning to wind down when a slim woman with short, dark sculptured hair stood up. She was in her early thirties and Johnny had been right: she was beautiful – stunningly, heartbreakingly beautiful. There was a catch in her voice and she had to clear her throat twice before the words came out. Even so it was soft. I leaned forward to listen.

'I never spoke these words when John lived and I'm sorry, dear God, I'm so sorry. John, I love you,' she finished in a whisper. 'And I hope you can hear me. I'm sorry.' Her low voice broke up on a sob.

She bolted. I was right behind her.

She had a good head start on me and for a moment I thought I'd lost her. I picked her up again part way down the block, one hand on a tree, the other over her eyes. When I got closer I could see she was crying. I could hear it, too.

'Bella?'

For a moment she froze, then she started to walk away. I reached out and touched her arm gently.

'My name is Kat. I'm John's cousin. I loved him too.' She looked at me finally. Her eyes were moist and wet like delicate, controlled fountains about to spill over. Her hair was in slight disarray and charming; her makeup was flawless and her nose wasn't red. She was a work of art in motion. In spite of this perfection (Alma had taught me that you can't trust a person who looks good when crying), I believed she loved Johnny. It was her eyes: dark, lonely, and bleak.

'Then I'm sorry for both of us,' she said at last, turned, and walked away.

'Bella.' No response.

'Belinda.' Her shoulders hunched up protectively and she walked faster. I did too. 'I need to talk to you. Please.' She stopped finally and I caught up. 'John was murdered.' She looked at me expressionlessly. 'I don't want someone to get away with that, do you?'

'No, but it has nothing to do with me.'

I took a deep breath. 'A while ago you said you were sorry for things you didn't say and do. Don't let that happen now. Help me know and understand John. Help me find the person who killed him.'

'That's not your job, that's for the police.'

'I'm an investigator; it's my job. And I loved him.'

'It's not mine.'

'You loved him too.'

'Yes, but if you think that I am going to strip myself naked so that you can peer and poke around you are mistaken.' Her face was still and closed over. There was a slight breeze but it didn't ruffle her hair or expression. While I wasn't noticing, someone had composed her features and then lacquered them, her, her hair. She was safe and protected under a transparent shell. A work of art no longer in motion.

Bella reached into her purse, pulled out a bunch of keys, unlocked the car door, and climbed into a dark green, buffed out Bug. I tried the door on the passenger side, locked, so I stuck a card under the windshield wiper. She ignored it. I stood in the exhaust and watched her drive away. And memorized her license plate number.

The church was still full of people when I got back. They grabbed at me physically and emotionally until I was exhausted, until I felt shellacked as well. An older man introduced himself as a professor of John's at the veterinary school. We shook hands warmly and he told me what a fine student John had been, how promising, how hard-working. That was the John I had known, not the one having an affair with a mysterious dark-haired woman ten years older than he.

'Professor,' I interrupted his impromptu eulogy, then

bit my tongue, hoping it would be written off to grief and distraction, not to a lapse in manners. It was both, of course. 'Do you know who the dark-haired woman who spoke at the end was?'

He looked puzzled and then shook his head. 'Indeed not.'

'She was not a student in veterinary medicine?'

'No.' He was emphatic.

'Yes, you do, dear.' The professor looked irritated, his wife looked smug. Until now she had been a silent appendage at his elbow.

'I do what?'

'Know who she is.' She waited expectantly to be asked. I waited expectantly too. I could tell it was a game they played often; he put her down and she got back at him like this. It was a long wait. I got bored with the game before they did.

'Who?' I asked. They both ignored me; I wasn't in the game.

'Well,' he said impatiently.

'You *know*, dear,' she said in an infuriating patient and patronizing tone.

'Who?'

'You remember.'

'Muriel—' There was an angry note in his voice.

'It's the young woman at the gallery,' she said hastily. She'd played it as far as it was going to go. 'Remember the opening last month? She was one of the artists, I'm sure she was.'

'Ah.' He nodded his head ponderously, dignified and in control again. 'Quite right, she was.'

'Do you remember her name?' But they didn't. 'Or the name of the gallery?'

The professor looked blank. 'Nouveau,' the wife said

triumphantly as she put her hand on his elbow and steered him off.

'In Davis?' I called after them. She didn't turn around, it would have spoiled her exit, but I thought she nodded. I was still thinking about it when Alma grabbed me by the arm and yanked on me. It amazes me the power she has. Soaking wet she doesn't weigh ninety-five pounds and her arms look like shriveled-up carrots.

'Come, Katy.'

'Why?' I asked, coming.

'Come!' She hauled me across the floor. 'Michaela needs you.'

Alma was right. Michaela needed me, needed a rescue of some kind. An airlift helicopter would have been ideal. Walter had backed her into a corner and was patting her arm, smiling benignly, and talking a mile a minute. It looked like it was all he could do not to pinch her cheek but maybe he'd already done that. The fiancée and kids flanked him and neatly hemmed Michaela in. She was white-faced and silent.

'Hello, Walter,' I said, cutting through the rear guard and standing next to Michaela, one shoulder in front of her. She sighed and slipped a hand into mine. I remembered suddenly how she'd done that as a child. Her hand was still and cold. I squeezed it but it didn't squeeze back. She sighed again.

'Are you all right?' I asked her. She shook her head. Walter beamed paternally on us. For some reason I was included.

'I wanted to introduce Micha—'

'*Don't* call me that!'

He cleared his throat, 'Uh, Michaela, to my fiancée

and express our earnest desire and dearest wish—' He paused. The fiancée made a face and didn't look like any of her desires or wishes included Michaela, not even in a passing thought. Walter glanced at her and she slapped a smile across her face. It was an insult. Michaela's fingers tightened on mine.

'Our dearest wish is,' Walter continued, 'that you come to our wedding. You are part of the family. My daughter,' he said emotionally. 'And now that John is—' He broke off and brushed his hand across his eyes, although I didn't see any tears. The fiancée murmured sympathetically and tucked her hand into his elbow. He put his hand on hers.

'Thank you, dear.' They looked sweetly into each other's eyes. I gagged slightly. 'You will come?' he asked Michaela, tearing himself away from the fiancée's hot moist eyes.

'I'm sorry,' she said formally. 'I don't believe I'm free.'

'But I haven't mentioned the time.' He looked bewildered. Michaela turned even whiter.

'It's her music schedule,' I ad-libbed. 'She's booked solid for the next six weeks.' Michaela nodded mutely.

'I want my money,' she said in a whisper, 'and I want it now.' Walter looked pained. The fiancée was clearly embarrassed that anyone could be so ill-bred. I thought Michaela was gutsy as hell. She dropped my hand and said in a stronger voice, 'Now.'

'Of course, my dear. We can talk about this later, surely? And in a civilized fashion.'

'No.' Michaela shook her head. 'Now, I want it now.' There was a mulish expression on her face that I recognized from years ago. Evidently Walter did too. His brow furrowed up like a field plowed by a drunken farmer. 'Now.' Her voice was getting quite loud, quite uncivilized. I had to work hard not to smile.

'But my dear—'

'Don't call me *that* either.' Walter looked helpless. I stepped in and was civilized. 'I will call you tomorrow. We will set up a business appointment.'

'Fine,' said Walter, hearty and relieved.

'No,' said Michaela. I kicked her. 'All right,' she agreed, after a perceptible pause.

The rear guard was getting restless. Out of the corner of my eye I saw Alma closing in. Walter saw it too. He nodded formally to us. 'Well, my dear?' he addressed the fiancée. She was tight-lipped and frozen and it seemed to worry him. 'We really must be going.'

They started off but weren't fast enough. Alma snagged them. It was like watching a small shark move in on large, stupid, helpless fish.

'So,' she announced, 'it takes a death to bring you into the family. That is a pretty sorry state of affairs and a sad cattle of fish.'

Walter looked puzzled. 'Kettle,' I explained. The fiancée looked impatient and embarrassed.

'Come, dear,' she said, pulling on Walter's arm.

'I'm Alma Flaherty, Sophie's aunt. Who the hell are you?'

The fiancée looked like she'd swallowed a frog. I swallowed a grin. Walter started to sputter and Michaela started drifting away. I drifted with her.

'You had no right to interfere!' She was haughty and in control again, had forgotten already that I'd rescued her, that she'd held my hand like a small and frightened child.

'What did you expect him to do, hand over a suitcase of old bills in small denominations? Pull stocks and securities out of his hip pocket? Give him a break. I expect there are legal formalities to be observed as well.'

'I want my money and I want it now.'

'I'm sure something can be worked out so that you can draw on it immediately. Walter will undoubtedly know—'

She snorted. 'I don't trust him.'

'He *is* your father, Michaela. Whatever your differences in the past I hardly think—'

'You! You don't know *anything*.'

'All right.' I shrugged. 'Deal with the cotrustee then.'

'You! You're probably in it with them.'

'In what?' I inquired reasonably.

'To see that I don't get my money.'

I shook my head. 'I'm on your side. I always have been, yours and Johnny's.'

'You were a lot of help to Johnny, weren't you? A lot. Where is he?' There were tears in her eyes. 'He's dead. That's where. Yeah, you were a lot of help, a lot.'

Alma walked up in time to hear the last part. She looked at Michaela steadily for a long, silent moment, then slapped her face. 'I should wash your mouth out with soap, young lady.'

The color rushed into Michaela's cheeks. 'Go to hell. I don't need you, either of you.' She spun on her toe and ran off. I watched in silence before I turned to Alma.

'She said some stupid things. All right. Her only brother was murdered and she saw her estranged father for the first time in four years. That's her excuse. What's yours?'

There were tears in Alma's eyes. 'Oh, Katy, this temper of mine will be the death of me. When will I learn?'

I didn't answer. At Alma's eighty-one I didn't have a

lot of hope: old dogs, new tricks, and her temper didn't add up to anything very promising.

It was time to move on. I did.

Twenty-Four

It was dark when the phone rang. Other than that I was clueless. I finally found the clock on the floor where I'd inadvertently knocked it off the nightstand the evening before. I do that a lot. It had stopped again. No help there. I found the phone on about the fifth ring.

'Katy?' I didn't recognize the voice. 'Katy, are you there? It's Micha.' I still didn't recognize the voice. 'Katy!' She was crying. 'Katy!'

'I'm here, Micha.'

'Katy, don't be mad at me. I'm sorry for earlier. Please help me. Please. You will, won't you?'

'What is it, Michaela?'

'Won't you?'

'Yes.'

'Oh, thank God!'

'What's the matter?'

'Someone just called me. He said all these awful things, he said—'

'Slow down.' She was working herself up to an hysterical high. 'Take a deep breath.'

'Katy!'

'Do it!' She did. 'All right?'

'Sort of.' She sobbed a long breath.

'What time did he call?'

'Just now, ten minutes ago. I took the phone off the hook and sat here shaking for a while trying to figure out what to do.'

'Did you recognize the voice?'

'No.'

'What did it sound like?'

'Deep. It was a nice voice saying all these awful, awful things.'

'What did he say?'

'He called me a whore and a slut and said nobody wanted my kind around. He said it was a good thing when I left town before and that I should've stayed gone. He said,' her voice trembled, 'that if I wanted to stay healthy I should get the hell out of town again. He sounded like he meant it, too. Katy, I'm scared.' The hysterical note was back again. 'What should I do? Should I call the police?'

'It won't do any good. There's nothing for them to go on in an anonymous phone call.'

She sobbed in the background. 'Oh God, Katy. I hear a noise! Someone's in the house.'

'Are you alone?'

'Yes.'

'What kind of noise?'

'A creak.'

'Does your house creak?'

'Yes. Oh God, I hear it again!'

'Are the doors locked?' She moaned. I took it for a yes. 'Did you hear any sound of a break-in?'

'N-n-no.'

'Are you in bed?'

'Yes.'

'Get up, get dressed. Leave the phone off the hook. I'll be here.'

'Oh God, I can't, I can't. I'm too scared.'

'Don't be so gutless, Michaela. You're a woman, not a slug.'

She started crying and the telephone crashed down. I waited, listening to muffled noises in the background.

'Okay,' she sobbed. 'I'm dressed.'

'Do you have your car keys?'

'They're in the other room.'

'You're going to come over here. Can you make it on your own or shall I come get you?' She sobbed. 'You're all right, Micha. This guy threatened you. Now he's going to give you time to get out, not move in on you right away. That's the MO.'

'Oh.' She blurted the word out on a gasp of relief. 'Do you really think so?'

'Yes.' I said it but I didn't believe it, not necessarily. I couldn't know. I could guess, I could hope, but I couldn't know.

'Really?'

'Yes.' I was lying; fortunately I was the only one who knew it. 'Can you drive or shall I come for you?'

'I can do it,' she said bravely.

'Good girl.' I gave her directions. 'It will take you about forty minutes from where you are. I'll be waiting.'

'Okay.' Her voice fluttered and scampered about like a dry leaf in a fall gutter.

'Michaela.'

'Yes.'

'Don't turn any lights on. Can you see your car from the house?'

'Yes.'

'Watch it and the street for five minutes. Time it. If you see anyone or anything out of the ordinary call the police and stay put. Okay?'

'Okay.'

'Do you have anything you can use as a weapon?'

'No. Yes, a stick.'

'Heavy, solid?'

'Yes.'

'Jab with it, don't swing. To the belly. Kick knees and groin. Hold your keys in your hand. You can go for eyes and the hollow of the throat with them. Do you understand?'

'Yes. I'm scared.'

'I'm giving you information and that is your protection. Use it. You are not ignorant and helpless. You are not a victim.'

'No-o-o.'

She sounded doubtful and I wasn't reassured. 'Tell me what you're going to do.'

'I watch the car and street for five minutes. Then I leave and drive to your house.'

'Don't carry anything but your keys and the stick.'

'My purse?'

'No. Leave your hands free to fight if you need to. Got it?'

'Yes.'

'Fight if you have to. Scream. I don't think you'll have to. Hang up now. I'll see you soon.' She sobbed again and then hung up.

I got up, got dressed, and built up the fire in the wood stove. Then I waited. I hate to wait and I don't do it well. Time stalled around like an old car, starting, stopping, lugging along. I paced. I made hot chocolate with marshmallows, a childhood favorite of Michaela's. I waited. The marshmallows were melted, gooey and perfect, so I ate them. Then I waited some more. Xerxes yawned, washed his face, and wondered why I was up so early. Me too. I also wondered, and not for the first time, why I wasn't in a different line of work.

I heard an engine gunning and gravel flying as a car pulled into the driveway. I was sure two wheels had been on the ground coming around the corner. Reasonably sure. Michaela half fell in as I opened the door. 'I did it,' she cried. 'I did it. They didn't get me.'

I smiled. 'Come in where it's warm.'

'I was scared, real scared, but they didn't get me.'

'No.'

It wasn't over yet, of course. I knew it, even if she didn't. She picked up Xerxes and hugged him. He got grim-faced and outraged but was too dignified to hiss. I went into the kitchen, dropped some more marshmallows into the cocoa, and turned the burner on. Michaela followed me.

'Owwwww!' She dropped Xerxes; he disappeared. 'Your cat clawed me.'

'He doesn't like to be hugged by strangers.'

'Oh. Is that cocoa? May I have some?'

She ate a marshmallow out of the pan, grabbing it with her fingers and licking the white goo off. I dropped some more in. I let her drink her first cup of cocoa before I started. I waited because I knew I wasn't going to like myself a whole lot. It's not nice to jump on people when they're vulnerable. Not nice, but a good way to get information.

'Tell me from the beginning, Michaela.'

'What?' She made her eyes go wide and innocent and

fished the last marshmallow out of her cup with her fingers. 'May I have more?' I nodded. She busied herself at the stove.

'This guy threatened you for a reason. He knows it, so do you. If you want my help I need to know it too. What did you do four years ago that was so bad someone would threaten your life?' Her face went white and still. It was like watching time lapse photography of ice forming on a pond. And I knew she wasn't going to tell me.

'Nothing. I made a mistake like a lot of girls and got pregnant. I didn't want to marry the boy and I didn't want to have the baby.' She smiled bitterly. 'I didn't get married but I did have the baby. I put it up for adoption. That's all.'

I looked at her steadily. She fidgeted in her chair, then got up and went back to the stove. I watched her pop the last marshmallow into her mouth and pour the rest of the chocolate into her cup.

'That's all. Really, that's all.'

She was a lousy liar and she knew I knew it as she licked her fingers and smiled absently at me. Xerxes hopped into my lap. Michaela started to reach for him but stopped when he bared his teeth at her. She'd rattled his dignity and cage.

'What did you and Johnny talk about over breakfast that night?'

'After breakfast; I didn't eat. I—' Her cup slipped and almost fell out of her hands, making a cocoa splash trail down the front of her sweater. Her eyes went from innocent to frightened. They stayed wide. 'What night? What do you mean?'

'The night Johnny was killed.'

'I didn't. How could I? I—' She paused and glared at me. 'You're trying to trick me. First you help me, then you trick me. I don't get it,' she whispered.

I shook my head. 'I'm trying to help you. What are you trying to hide?'

'Nothing.'

'You were with Johnny that night.' She made an abrupt gesture of denial. 'It's too late. You told me already. Tell me the rest of it now.'

'Goddamn it, Katy. Goddamn it all to hell.'

She started to cry. I waited patiently. Finally she wiped her nose on the back of her hand and looked at me.

'If it weren't for me, Katy, maybe he'd be alive still. He met me because I asked him to. I insisted. I said I was desperate and I was, I am. He wanted to do it another time, Sunday brunch maybe. You remember how he hated to stay up late but would get up early in the morning? I said no, I couldn't wait. I begged him.

'So he came. Of course he did. I knew he would. He always came when I needed him. Oh, if only I hadn't he'd be alive now. I killed him, Katy, I killed him!' The words fought with each other, tumbled and bounced and rolled out of her mouth like Demosthenes' pebbles.

'I killed him.' I looked at her steadily, not saying anything. 'I killed him as surely as if I pulled the trigger.'

'He was stabbed, Micha.' She waved her hand, dismissing it as an unimportant technicality.

'It doesn't matter. I killed him.'

'Why were you so desperate?'

'The band. Money. There's this guy – money. Oh, everything,' she sobbed.

'The band?'

185

'Yes, it's all right for now, it's a living, but it's nothing, nowhere really. And the music. Oh, Katy! Broken hearts, cheatin' hearts, barroom brawls, smoking, drinking, drugs. Oh Katy, it's not *me!* It's not what I want.'

She sounded like a spoiled child but I recognized it as a cry from the heart and I remembered crying like that. When you're young you think it's only right that you get what you want. When you're older you learn how difficult that is to achieve.

'The guy?'

'What guy?'

'The one you mentioned.'

'Oh.' Her face flushed, then got pale. 'In the band. He won't leave me alone. I *hate* it. I hate *him*.'

'Tell him to get lost.'

'I do but it doesn't work. He said if I didn't sleep with him he'd get me fired and put the word out so no one else around would hire me. Katy, I didn't know what to do.' There were tears in her eyes. 'I don't know how to get them to leave me alone,' she whispered. 'I only know how to run away.'

'And for that you needed Johnny's help?'

She nodded. 'I needed money,' she said simply.

'Johnny's money?'

'Yes.'

'What were you going to run away to?'

'I wanted to go to music school. I'm an artist. I mean I know I can be, I just need the training, the chance.'

'And the money.'

'Yes, the money.'

'Johnny's dead. It's yours now.'

'Don't look at me like that. I didn't kill him. You

186

don't think – Katy, I didn't! I *wouldn't!*'

'How many times did you just tell me you did?'

'Yes, but I didn't mean I *really* killed him. I meant I never should have gotten him to meet me late at night at a horrible place like the Homestead. If only I could have been patient.' She wrung her hands. 'How can you say that? I would never hurt Johnny. Never. I loved him.'

'You were at the crime scene, you benefit from his death, you could easily get a knife. That's what cops look for. So far you're batting a thousand.'

She burst into tears.

Twenty-Five

'Katy accused *me* of killing Johnny.' Michaela looked at Alma and her eyes filled with tears as she filled her mouth with sausage, eggs, and cornbread at breakfast the next day.

'I asked you.'

Michaela looked sad as she chewed and swallowed. 'Is there any more cornbread?'

Alma nodded and pointed to the stove. 'Did you kill Johnny?'

Michaela shook her head in a matter-of-fact-way. 'Of course not. Don't be ridiculous.' That quiet voice was more convincing than her tears and hysteria had been.

'You were desperate.'

'I didn't have to kill for the money. Johnny was going to give it to me.' I wondered about that. John was generous but also convinced that people should earn things, not be handed them. 'Not give, lend, and just until I was twenty-three and got my own money. He said he would regard it as a short-term, high-yield investment. For a little help he said he would get years of pleasure of listening to my music. Years.' Her eyes filled with tears.

'Only it didn't work out that way.' She buttered a

188

huge chunk of cornbread. 'I was going to pay him interest and everything.' The cornbread started to disappear.

'Did you meet him in the restaurant?'

She nodded, her mouth full. 'I was late and he'd already had breakfast. He was just drinking coffee.'

'What time was it?'

'I don't know, I didn't look. Two-fifteen maybe. I came as soon as the band finished playing.'

'Did you sit down?'

'I started to. Johnny asked me if I wanted breakfast but I didn't, not even coffee. It was loud and crowded and noisy there. Drunks. Drunks from bars trying to sober up before going home. I'd had enough of that for one evening and asked him if we could sit in the car and talk. So he paid the bill and we did.'

'And?'

'And I told you the rest.'

'How long did you talk?'

'I don't know, a half hour maybe. We would have talked longer but it was really cold. And I was tired too.'

'So you left?' She nodded.

'Johnny walked me to my car, made sure I locked the doors, then went back to his car – well, Alma's car I guess.' I nodded. 'I saw him get in and close the door. Then I drove off.'

'Did he lock his doors?'

'I don't know.' She sighed. 'Don't make me talk about it any more, Katy. I don't want to.' A yawn, a stretch. 'Alma, can I eat the rest of the cornbread? Please,' she added. I got up.

Alma nodded absently. 'What are you going to do now, Katy?'

'Go over to Michaela's and pick up clothes and probably whatever she needs for the next few days. It's probably just a nut but—'

I didn't finish my sentence. Nobody else did either.

In the daylight Michaela's house was quiet, serene, and unthreatening. Still, neither of us felt disposed to linger. She packed quickly and efficiently and was almost done when the phone rang.

'Shall I get it?' I asked.

'Oh, no.' She shook her head, nonchalant in the morning sunshine, and picked it up. She listened and then beckoned me, face drawn and pinched, eyes full of frightened thoughts. Wordlessly she handed me the receiver. I didn't recognize the voice but the words were familiar and the meaning unmistakable.

'I'm going to get you. Wherever you go I'll find you. I'll get you. I'm watching you all the time. Like now. I know just where you are. Always. You're scum and I'm going to get you: at home, at work, at that PI's. Wherever you go I'll find you and when I do –'

He started to recite what he would do when he found Michaela. Rape and sexual abuse were at the top of the list. I broke the connection, listened for a dial tone and left the receiver off the hook.

'Are you packed?' She didn't answer, couldn't. I looked at the suitcase; it looked packed. It would have to do. I closed it.

'Come on.' She sat there staring insensibly, like a small animal frozen into immobility by a predator.

'Micha.' I put my hands under her arms and yanked her to her feet, grabbed the suitcase, and propelled her out the door and into the car.

'Where are we going? It doesn't matter, you know. He's going to get me so I might as well just sit here and wait. Wait right here.' Her voice was thick and dead, like gravy that's been left on a plate overnight.

'I didn't know you were so spineless, were such a quitter.' She started to cry. 'What happened to beating out the bad guys?'

'You're being mean to me. I'm scared, terrified, and all you can do is be mean.'

'There's a difference between being scared and being a victim. You can be scared and fight back.'

'I can't.'

'Start learning or you may not live long enough to go to music school.'

'I – want – to – run – away,' she sobbed.

'You can't run forever.'

'He said he'd get me at work.'

'Yes. You're too vulnerable there. Call in sick or scared or whatever you want to do, you're not going. Is there someone who can stand in for you?'

'Yes.'

'Good. We'll arrange it.' I pulled over to a gas station with a phone booth and climbed out, ignoring Michaela's nervous questions. It took me two phone calls and less than a minute.

'Where are we going?'

'Sunrise Mall.'

'My life is in danger and all you can think of is shopping,' she wailed.

'When the going gets tough, the tough—'

'They *don't*, they don't go shopping.'

'They don't whine either.'

She subsided into sullen silence that lasted until I

parked and we got out. We ambled through the mall and in and out of stores until I was satisfied.

'You're not buying anything, are you? You're not even looking at anything.'

'No,' I agreed.

'So what are we doing here?'

I ignored the question and headed for Sears. I'd told Rafe to be at the south exit just outside the tool section. 'I'm going to walk you past an exit. When I point it out, use it. Don't say good-bye or ask questions, just go. There will be a tall, blond man in a black Corvette waiting outside for you. His name is Rafe and he's a friend of mine. He's taking you out to Charity's ranch; she's another friend. You'll be safer there than at my house. Call the stand-in from Charity's. I'll get your things to you later. Now. That door to your right.'

I took a left and headed for power tools. I hadn't found the radial saw of my dreams before I saw Michaela head out the door. A black car pulled up. I sighed in relief and lost interest in angle, power, and operational ease. Just in time. A salesman was headed in my direction with a fixed and determined look in his eyes.

I made tracks.

I went out to the Alibi Inn in Placerville that night on a whim and with a warning. I had no way of knowing if Michaela had said something to her stand-in. I hoped so. If not, I would. And I wanted to look around.

The place was the same: loud, packed, full of people and drunken Friday night energy. The band sounded commonplace without Michaela's voice to lift it above the humdrum. I got a beer and leaned on a post. It was standing room only.

'Damn good band, huh?' A guy in jeans and a western shirt smiled at me. I nodded but didn't smile. 'They never used to draw a crowd here, now they pack 'em in. It's the singer, she's dynamite.' He paused and I nodded, not doing much to keep up my end of the conversation. 'You like her?' I nodded. 'She's been with them for three months now.'

'*This* girl?' I was surprised into asking.

'Yeah. Wanna dance?'

'No. Thanks,' I added, but it was too late.

'Yeah. Me either.' He walked off moving his shoulders aggressively. I looked at the stand-in. She didn't look like Micha, or sound like Micha, but it was close enough for that guy. For him and a lot of other people probably. She was small and dark-haired. The set ended and I moved up toward the stage.

The closer I got the more the resemblance dimmed. She looked thirty-five and hard, was still pretty but it wouldn't last long. High on her right cheekbone two little blue tears were tattooed. If she was sad it was bone deep, not running on the surface.

'My name's Kat. I'm a friend of Micha's.'

'Yeah. So?' She spoke like she had an axe to grind and figured I had one too.

'Did she tell you what this was all about?' The singer shook her head. Dammit, Micha! I thought.

'Hey, Glory, let's go,' a guy in leathers commanded as he jerked his head at her. 'We got time to do a number.'

'I got to go.'

'Glory.'

She turned around. 'Gloria to you.'

'Gloria. Someone threatened Micha, threatened her life. I don't think you should go outside. Stay in here around other people.'

Leather heard me and laughed. 'Ain't nothing going to happen to her. That's why she got me.'

'Yeah. That's why I got Hughie. He's one mean son of a bitch.'

He winked at me. I shrugged and walked off. I'd said what I'd come to say. At the front door I stopped and looked around. There were a lot of regulars; I recognized some of them already. Nothing sinister. People looked like they were having a good time. I walked out into the cold night air.

The stars were close and sparkly, the way they get on cold, clear nights. The air was frosty enough to hurt when I sucked it in, then blew it out in puffs. The gunshot was a surprise, I guess it always is. It made a loud pop in the night and the dark. It sounded close but it's hard to tell, tough to call.

I waited for a moment to see if there would be more shots. Nothing. My breath made little clouds in the air. The silence was oppressive and ominous as I slipped into the shadows and around to the side of the building where Micha took her breaks and Glory and Hughie were doing a number.

Glory was crumpled on the ground. There was blood on her chest and blood in the blue tears on her cheek. Her eyes were closed. Hughie was holding her hands and moaning. His eyes looked stoned: grief or drugs, I couldn't tell.

'Ain't nothing gonna happen to her. That's why she got me,' he moaned.

'It was a gun, Hughie. Everybody's a tough guy with a gun. An eight-year-old could take you with a gun.' I knelt over Glory, then stood up. 'She's alive, she needs help.'

'Ain't nothing gonna happen—'

The door stood open and a young kid, twenty-one and change, walked out.

'Oh, Jesus!' His face went white.

'Call an ambulance,' I said, 'and the cops.'

He turned and ran back inside. There was nothing for me here. And I needed to know that Michaela was all right.

'Ain't nothing gonna happen to her. That's why she got me,' Hughie said over and over.

It sounded like a chant, a religious incantation, but it was to a God I didn't know. I don't think Hughie did either.

Twenty-Six

I stopped at a gas station to call. A young feminine voice I didn't recognize answered on the second ring. It sounded like a woman's dormitory in the background. The woman's voice said hello and giggled. I asked for Charity. Then there was a wait.

'Yes?'

'Charity, is Michaela all right?'

'Hi, Kat, fine. We all are.'

'Any phone calls? Anybody you don't know coming around?'

'No, nothing, and the dogs are out so we'd know.' There was a crash and laughter in the background.

'What's going on?'

'Some of Lindy's friends are here.'

I thought that one over. There was another muffled crash in the background. 'You're having a slumber party for teenage hookers?'

'And Michaela.'

'How is it going?'

'Fine. Well, we ran out of popcorn, ice cream, juice, and granola bars; I confiscated some drugs, and their language—! My goodness, Kat, where do they learn those words?'

'On the street. For an advice columnist you live a sheltered life.'

'That's *why* I'm an advice columnist, so I'm at a desk instead of on the street. No!' she yelled. 'You absolutely can, I mean may, not. Put that away.'

'What?'

'Rum. They wanted to put rum in their Cokes.' She sounded distracted. 'Kat, I've got to go.' Her voice faded out.

'I called with bad news, Charity.'

'What?' Her voice was back, sharp and anxious.

'Someone shot Michaela's stand-in.'

'Oh, dear God!'

'For Michaela's safety we need to assume it was someone after her, not the stand-in. And I'm certain it was. Don't tell her unless you have to, unless she starts to get stupid or reckless, but watch carefully. Everything, everyone. Call the police if anything unusual happens. Don't wait; it can take forever to get out there to your place.'

'Okay.' Her voice was small and scared.

'Do you want me to get Rafe to come over?'

'With all these girls?' She sounded outraged.

'Charity, they're children. Rafe's a responsible adult; well, an adult, and a gentleman.'

'I'm not worried about him. It's about the girls. I'm trying to raise their consciousness and I can't do that with a man around.'

I didn't say what I was thinking, that life seemed more important than consciousness right now. I didn't say anything at all for a bit; it was tough. 'Mmmm, is Ripper loose?' I was on a roll with good ideas.

'No, do you think—?'

197

'Yes. I do. Introduce him to the girls so they *know*. That will keep them in and everyone else out.'

'All right.'

Ripper is an incredibly vicious dog (named after Jack) who thinks Charity is his angel and everyone else, from day-old foals to doddering senior folks, is a sworn enemy whom it is his, Ripper's, appointed duty to decimate and render into mincemeat. He is on a steel chain fastened to a metal rod driven six feet into the ground. Even that doesn't seem quite enough to most of us.

Charity is the only one who can control him. She thinks he's cute, and he slobbers and drools all over her in fawning adoration. Everyone in the neighborhood has been trying to feed him poisoned meat or 'accidentally' shoot him for years.

'Do you want to come out, Kat?'

I shuddered at the thought. 'Not tonight, not as long as you're okay.'

'We're fine.'

There was a thump in the background, a crash, a bang, a shriek, an answering shriek from Charity, and the line went dead. I went home.

The phone machine was all aglow and excited with six calls. I built up the fire, the coals banked from this morning, and then punched the play button on my way to the kitchen and a sandwich.

'Hellooo, this is Betty from Multiscore Insurance. I'm wondering if you know . . .' I rooted through the refrigerator and came up with stale bread, cheese, a slightly wilted tomato, and an avocado that looked okay on the outside but turned out to be dead on the inside. I hoped there was another jar of mayo in the cupboard.

Betty finished her pitch on how I could score with

Multiscore and I started digging through the cupboards, found a quart jar of mayonnaise and dusted it off. I was careful not to look at the expiration date in case it would spoil my appetite.

There were several business calls, one from Alma, one from a friend in Oklahoma who wanted to know how I was and could they stay with me while they went to Disneyland? (Disneyland is over four hundred miles from me. How can people be so ignorant about California geography? There is more to this state than Los Angeles and San Francisco but you cannot prove it by the population of the greater US.) I popped the stale bread into the toaster.

The call that caught my attention was the one that began with, 'Well, bitch...' I stuck the knife in the mayonnaise jar and walked over to the answering machine. The voice was low, throaty, familiar. Sexy, too, and that made it even more ugly and scary.

'Are you listening, bitch? Are you listening good? That little slut singer didn't listen good, did she, not good enough. And now she can't listen no more. Something bad happened to her, just like I said it would if she didn't go away. Now I'm telling you. I'll get you, too, any time I want to, bitch. Any time. Don't get no ideas about investigating the slut's death. She's gone and good riddance. You're the next if you don't leave it be, bitch. I mean it. And it won't be easy, neither. Not like the singer bitch. Here's what I'm going to do to you...'

His voice got soft and warm and he described in loving detail how he would violate my mind and body. 'This is a warning. Be good or I'll be seeing you, bitch.'

He laughed and it was familiar. I knew that laugh. I

made my mind go blank and waited for the realization. When it came, it scared me. It wasn't the laugh in particular I knew but the one in general. It was the kind that happens in horror movies when people are still in control but right on the edge. And then they hear that laugh. The edge dissolves and they go over.

I made myself go back into the kitchen, make and eat my sandwich. Then I played the last message again. Friday, ten-thirty P.M., the machine told me, minutes after Glory was shot. I popped the tape out, labeled it, filed it. Then I poured myself a glass of wine and considered, considered going to get Ranger, Johnny's dog, considered going to bed with my gun under my pillow. I didn't consider giving up. Not yet, not much anyway.

It was only a threat, a phone threat, and there's something very cowardly about an anonymous phone call. Cowardly but not unreal, I reminded myself. There was Glory with her red and blue blood tattoo tears. I hoped she was still alive. I wasn't convinced of it.

I was well through my first glass of wine and into second stage considerations when I heard the yowl. It sounded like a vampire-cat-from-hell cry. I didn't like it.

It's rare that Xerxes needs my help in anything but I went out to see. I took my gun, my new one, a .380 automatic. Nothing. An almost full moon hung halfway up the western sky. The old man winked and smiled. There was green cheese stuck between his teeth. I called Xerxes. Nothing. I shivered. I should have put on a sweater. And shoes. God knows Xerxes wouldn't come until he was ready. Cat timetables have nothing to do with people concepts.

I shivered again. The grass was wet and my socks were soaked. The gun dug into my waist. The man in the moon wasn't winking anymore. His eyes were closed, his face was shuttered and cold. How can the moon look like it has no heart and be a symbol for lovers?

I decided to take a quick look out back in the grape arbor. In the summer the patio was green and cool under a leaf canopy. Now the bare branches of the grapevines stood out in stark relief against the moonlit sky. Shadows played dark and shiftily in the moonlight like indecipherable paleolithic reminders. I stubbed a wet, cold toe on the uneven brick walkway and swore. Xerxes favorite bench in a warm, sheltered spot was empty.

Enough. A potbellied stove, a glass of wine, and a pillow were calling me by name. It was a quiet, insistent, commonsense chorus. Only a fool would ignore the call. I wasn't a fool and my cold, stubbed toe ached.

I almost tripped over the warm wet thing. I bumped it with my foot first but I couldn't tell what it was. My feet were so cold they were numb, dopey, and dead.

So was the warm wet thing.

It had fur, big bulging eyes, and it was lying in a puddle of thick dark oil. When it had been alive it was Xerxes. I reached out a hand to touch it; it wasn't stiff yet. My mind clouded over. The moon shone bright and still. Over lovers and corpses.

'What happened, Xerx?' I whispered. 'Why? Why? Oh, God.' I started to stroke him but I couldn't bear the feel of his still body, cooling and unresponsive. 'Why?' His mouth was open, his tongue protruding slightly, his body unmarked. I wondered about the oil. He wore a bib of it on his front, like a sweet and tidy little kitten. I stuck my finger into the puddle. Not oil, blood. His throat had been cut.

My mind reeled about like a drunk on a merry-go-round. It stopped reeling finally but it didn't start making sense. There was no music playing, just a hoarse rasping sound, my breath I realized after a while.

'Xerx,' I whispered in the moonlight. 'I got you into this somehow and I'm sorry.'

But sorry didn't cut it, not for me, not for Xerxes. I rocked back on my heels and looked at the blood, looked at the not so warm, wet thing that had been Xerxes and would never again bump his head under my hand to be scratched, or sit on top of the refrigerator and talk to me while I made dinner, or catch butterflies in the sunshine.

And I remembered Hughie moaning over Glory and saying, 'Ain't nothing gonna happen to her. That's why she got me.'

But it hadn't worked out that way: not for Glory, not for Xerxes. The moon shone over lovers and corpses. I was scared, scared like Michaela had been the night before, only she had me to talk her out of it. I got up finally, the gun in my hand now.

The house was warm but it didn't make a difference. I was cold still. I headed for the phone and punched buttons, slowly, dully, methodically.

'Hank?'

'Kat! I was going to call you later. What's up, sweetheart?'

'Hank –' I heard my voice fade.

'Kat, are you all right?'

'No. No, I'm not.'

'What's the matter?'

'Hank, you said if I ever needed you, you'd come. I need you.' My voice faded again. I couldn't control it.

It was like a radio station getting too far away and drifting out.

'Kat, what is it?'

'I need you.' It came out in a whisper.

'Are you hurt?'

'No. Yes, inside. And I'm afraid.' There was a long silence. The phone felt too heavy and I wondered if I could hold it. I felt like crying. The silence went on.

'Hank?' The fear messed up my vowels.

'I'm coming, Kat. I need to figure it out is all.' Another pause. 'I'll square it at work and be on the road by midnight. I'll be there tomorrow by mid-afternoon.'

'No.' The fear was messing up my consonants now too. The 'n' was in triplicate. 'Take the plane, it's faster. The first plane you can. I'll sit right here by the phone. Call and tell me what time. I'll come and get you. I can drive,' my voice faltered. 'No, I'll leave when you call and wait at the airport. I'll – ' I stopped. I didn't know what I'd do. My kitty was dead; I hadn't protected him, and it was my fault. He had me and I wasn't there. Oh God, there was just no telling.

'Kat, call Charity.'

'I can't.'

'Rafe? Alma?'

'I can't.'

My kitty was dead. The lovely grape arbor wasn't safe. There was no place to go, no safe place.

'What happened, Kat?'

'Not now, I'll tell you when you get here.' I was still whispering.

'All right. Sit tight, I'll call you right back with plane times. Hang on, sweetheart.'

'Yes,' I said.

The receiver slipped from my hand. It took me a long time to pick it up and put it back on the phone. I sat there for a while, my mind messed up over the dead ones: Johnny, Lisa, Xerxes. And the dead dreams. Johnny would never be a vet, or Lisa a high school graduate. Xerxes would never again catch a fat little mouse. Even Glory had had dreams, one more number, one more song.

The music had stopped.

Xerxes was outside in the cold and the damp and the moonlight. I shivered. I was still wearing wet socks. Suddenly I couldn't bear it that Xerxes was in the cold. It was stupid, I knew it, but I couldn't bear it.

I picked up my gun and went out to get him. On the way I hoped that, somehow, I'd been mistaken about what I'd seen. That was stupid, too. My mind was messed up. My guard was down.

And that was stupidest of all.

As I stood over Xerxes I heard a noise behind me. Something had stepped on a branch. Not something, someone. And it wasn't a cat. The cat was dead. The cat's body had been warm, its throat slit. There was someone out there with a knife and a taste for warm blood. Gun in hand, I started to turn. Something caught me first, flung me around. The bat hit me in the belly and, as I doubled over, across my chest.

There was pain, a lot of it. That was all right, it brought my brain back into focus. I was alive; it was important to stay that way. Then it was like being shoved out of a lighted room and into a dark closet.

The door slammed shut and it was black. Black and dreamless. I slid into it.

Twenty-Seven

When I woke up everything was white. I'm a detective so the white told me something. It couldn't be heaven, my record wasn't that good (and surely heaven smelled better?). That left a laboratory or a hospital. A nurse bustled by and settled the issue.

'Is she awake? Can I see her? Is she all right? Hey! Yo! Hey, Kat, are you there?'

'Timmy?'

'Yeah. They don't want to let me in, but I just wanted to see that you were okay. I won't bug you. I promised them I wouldn't.'

'You're not bugging me. Come on in.'

I looked around for buttons to push so I could find out where I was and what I was doing here. My chest hurt, my brain was clogged up with day-old oatmeal, my memory function was on the fritz. And I couldn't find the call button. I considered getting out of bed and hollering down the hall, but I was wearing one of those hospital gowns which embarrass you and everyone else. I could handle it, but Timmy was young and impressionable.

'You scared me, Kat.'

Shit! It was worse than I thought. I tried to remember and couldn't.

'I did? Timmy, what did I do?'

'You were just lying there in the rain, and,' his eyes filled with tears, 'Xerxes was too.' It came back then. Damn, damn, damn. 'Kat, Xerxes is—'

I looked at him bleakly. 'I know.'

'I was afraid you were dead, like, like Xerxes. You were so cold and just lay there. And there was blood too, I think?' I nodded. 'I wasn't *afraid* afraid, just afraid for you.'

'Yes.' I nodded. 'But you were brave.' He shrugged, then shivered a little. 'What did you do?'

'I ran home. Mom and dad were out but I called nine-one-one just like they told me. You told me too, Kat.'

'Yes.' It hurt to nod my head so I was yessing.

'I should have called from your house. It would have been faster.' He looked at me. 'It was the blood,' he added simply.

'No, you did right. Always go to a safe place to get help.' He looked relieved.

'They came real fast. I made them tell me where you'd be so I could come see you the next day. Today,' he corrected. I looked out of the window. The rain had stopped but the sky was gray and cloudy.

'Kat?' He sounded anxious.

I looked at him and smiled. 'You did a real good job. Thanks, Timmy.' He smiled back shyly. 'Why did you come over last night?'

'I don't know.' His forehead wrinkled up. 'I just suddenly thought I heard Xerxes, or thought he might need me or, I dunno . . .'

'Ms. Colorado?' A nurse stuck her head in and half smiled at me, half frowned at Timmy. 'You're awake? Good. Your husband's here.' She frowned wholeheartedly at Timmy. 'Your visitors should be limited. We suggest only your immediate family.' Timmy started in on a stutter.

'He's family,' I said. 'What husband?' I started to ask but stopped myself in time. She sensed it and glared at both of us, then trotted out, white starch muttering darkly.

'Husband?' Timmy and I said at the same time in the silence of the hospital room. The door banged open and Hank walked in. My head reverberated with the door.

'Kat—' He reached out and hugged me, kissed me, made my head swim and hurt and made me feel better at the same time.

'Are you my husband?'

His face went blank, then cleared. 'They didn't want to let me in. Sweetheart—' He broke off and kissed me again. 'Goddamn it, Kat, can't you stay out of trouble for a minute?'

I sighed. 'Aren't husbands nicer? Whatever happened to, "Hi dear, how are you?" or "Good to see you." How about, "Hi honey, I'm home?" That's pretty popular too.' Timmy giggled.

'This is not a joke, Kat.'

'No,' I agreed. 'It's not.' Hank's handsome face had a hard set-in-concrete look. 'Timmy's been telling me what happened. I don't remember very well.'

'You know about Xerxes?' I nodded and looked away. More bits of things were drifting back. I wished they wouldn't.

'I found him, then I came inside to call you. I lost it. I'm sorry. I don't know what—' Hank sat on the bed and put his arms around me. 'I'm okay now, I think. Mad, sad, but okay. I don't know why I lost it.' I paused.

'Anyway, I couldn't stand the thought of Xerxes alone and cold in the rain. I know it's stupid but—'

Timmy, white-faced, shook his head. 'It's not stupid, Kat. It's not!' I smiled at him. It was feeble, like I felt.

'Then I don't remember.'

'Someone hit you in the stomach and on the chest – hard enough to knock the wind out of you, apparently hard enough so you lost consciousness. There's a bump on your head, too, but you probably got that when you fell. You were suffering from cold, exposure, and shock by the time they got you in here.'

I looked at Hank in admiration. 'You got a doctor to tell you all that?' He flushed.

'A nurse.'

Timmy and I both giggled.

'You smooth-talking, good-looking, son of a—'

The door blew open and the parade started. Alma was first, then Charity, Lindy, Rafe, and a couple of girls in hot pants, boots, and goosebumps. It was February, after all. They were carrying flowers, candy, and balloons. Rafe had a kazoo and was playing either 'For She's a Jolly Good Fellow' or 'Hail to the Chief.' It was hard to tell. They covered me with kisses, flowers, and chocolates. Someone popped a balloon.

'Hi,' I started to say, but then decided to eat a chewy nut chocolate instead. I was starved. A nurse walked in, disapproval written large on the billboard that had been her face. I chewed faster and swallowed. 'All family,' I assured her.

She didn't call me a liar, but that's what she was thinking. Her eyes roamed the room and settled on the obvious, the girls in hot pants. A logical choice, I admit. She raised her eyebrows at me. I smiled.

'They are not family. They are—' She hesitated.

'Trying out for their school play,' I finished. 'What is it this year, girls, *All's Well That Ends Well*?'

The girls were clearly clueless but they nodded brightly, earrings bobbing and jingling. Rafe started to play either 'Row, Row, Row Your Boat' or 'When the Saints Come Marching In'. Alma tapped her foot and had a chocolate. So did Timmy. So did I. The doctor walked in. I offered her one too.

'Your visitors should be limited. Perhaps just family for now.' She smiled.

'My husband and my son,' I said. Hank glowered and Timmy grinned. Hank hates it when I fib. Too bad, he started it. 'My grandmother.' Alma knodded, her mouth full of chocolate.

'My sister, her husband, and their girls.' Charity blanched at her sudden acquisitions and Rafe started on what might have been 'Here Comes the Bride.' The girls giggled and started punching Rafe and calling him Daddy. He stopped playing and told them to shut up and shape up. It was a touching family scene. The doctor stepped gracefully into a conversational pause.

'How do you feel?'

'My head hurts, I'm bruised and hungry, otherwise fine.'

'The X rays show nothing. Everything else is okay and your color is good. You might as well go home. You should rest,' she added, looking doubtful. I nodded agreeably. She continued to look dubious and then left.

'I brought you some clothes, Kat.' It was like Charity to remember that. I was grateful and said so. 'Let's go, guys. C'mon, Timmy, we'll give you a ride.'

'See you back at the house, Kat.' That was Rafe.

'No.' Charity was firm. 'She needs rest. Tomorrow maybe.' I nodded, grateful again. The room emptied out. I ate another chocolate and leaned back into Hank's arms.

'Want one?' I asked.

'No.'

Hank hates it when I eat meals out of order, especially when it's dessert first. I ate another candy, a mocha cream. He didn't seem to notice and that made me notice.

'Hank?'

He kissed me. 'I didn't tell you everything, sweetheart.'

His fingers played gently up and down my arm, giving me the shivers and making me want to go home. I bit into a caramel marshmallow chew.

'When they found you someone had painted a red slash on your throat. It was cat blood.'

I gagged and threw up on his lap.

Twenty-Eight

I started to put my hand to my throat, then stopped. 'Is it still there?'

'What?'

'The slash mark.' He shook his head. 'Was it Xerxes's blood?'

'Yes.' He stood up, wet a washcloth and washed my face. Then he cleaned up his lap.

'I'm sorry.' He looked puzzled. 'About throwing up on you.'

His face cleared. 'Kat, people I've liked a whole lot less have done a whole lot worse. Get dressed, sweetheart, let's go home.'

'Xerxes?'

'I buried him.'

'Where?'

'Under the apple tree.' I nodded dumbly. It had been one of his favorite sitting and climbing spots. It was a good place. Except that when you're dead there's no such thing as a good place.

Hank was driving my Bronco. I didn't bother to ask him how he'd gotten to town and found out I was in the hospital. He'd tell me later and right now I didn't care. I turned the heater all the way up, until Hank was

211

steaming, but I still couldn't get warm. I sat as close as I could to him and damned bucket seats. He held my hand on his knee and played with my fingers.

'What happens when you lose your nerve, Hank?'

His fingers stopped playing with mine and tightened.

'Sometimes you get over it, sometimes you don't.'

'Does it happen to everyone?'

'I don't know, Kat. No, probably not. Not everyone faces the kind of situation you're talking about. The ones who do? It's different. I know a woman who was in a car accident at twenty-two. She's thirty-five now and hasn't driven since that day; I don't think she ever will. People fall off the side of a mountain, break half the bones in their bodies, then haul out the ropes and pitons as soon as they're on their feet again.

'I've seen cops who were shot get out of the hospital, put on a uniform and go back to work; I've seen cops who couldn't do it, who quit, or retired.'

I shivered, cold still. The sweat stood out on Hank's forehead.

'The extremes, concentration camps and torture, will break most of us. The rest,' he shrugged, 'you do the best you can. You get help when you need it, and you don't blame yourself for needing it or asking for it.'

'I should have—'

'No, Kat.'

'Hank, I was so scared.'

'Yes. You should have been; it was a frightening situation. Bravery is not in not being afraid, but in action in spite of the fear.'

'I didn't. I wasn't.'

'You called me. You left the hospital. You're picking up the threads of your life. Don't be so hard on yourself,

Kat. You're trying to be a tough again.'

I chewed on that for a while.

'And you're mad at yourself for coming to me for help.'

I sighed. He was right. I'd been alone and independent for too long. It was hard for me to lean on Hank, hard for me to believe he'd be there for me to lean on even though he'd never disappointed me.

'That's what friends are for, Kat.' I sighed. 'And I'm more than a friend.' I sighed again. 'You—'

'Oh, can it, Hank,' I said crankily. 'This is beginning to sound like a cross between a pep rally and a Sunday school lecture.'

He grinned at me. 'See, you're feeling better already.'

'I am not,' I said, still contrary. 'And I'm hungry.'

'Is there any food at home?'

I thought about it and didn't know, couldn't remember.

'Probably not,' he said philosophically. 'Why should today be different from any other day? Is the Pasta Palace open for lunch?'

'I think so.' My stomach gurgled. 'Let's see.'

The Pasta Palace is one of our favorite restaurants. It's in Rancho Cordova, sort of on the way home. The food is cheap and wonderful and the decor, like the name, is hideous. The first thing you see when you walk in is a huge collage made of dried beans spellings out Pasta Palace. Palace is spelled with two l's.

On the back wall is a framed picture made of spaghetti dried on a tomato soup-colored cardboard background. Violent red and green candles left over from Christmas are stuck in long-neck Coors and Bud bottles. There is a picture of Marco Polo and one of Venice,

California. It is a safe bet that the Pasta Pallace has been entirely untouched by fashion, the Yuppie influence, or modern trends in the restaurant business.

We seated ourselves. A Chinese waiter named Segovia brought us a basket of hot garlic bread and took our order. The butter dripped on my fingers. I licked them and ordered with my mouth full. A carafe of harsh red wine followed the garlic bread. I wanted to talk about Johnny but Hank wouldn't let me until I finished two pieces of garlic bread, my salad, and a glass of wine. Wise move.

'I'm spinning my wheels, Hank. Nothing's happening.' He raised an eyebrow at me. 'I know a lot more than I did but nothing's adding up.'

'Let's hear it.'

'There's Gil Jones, the animal rights activist. Let's start with him. He's about as unattractive a person as you can imagine. He's obsessed with animal rights and peaceful humane treatment of animals but is irrational, vicious, and violent in his words and sentiments to people who oppose him.

'He didn't like Johnny and is the first to admit it, even goes so far as to say that he is glad John is dead. He's definitely got a few screws loose and one wheel on the curb,' I said, cheerfully mixing metaphors that were dubious at best, and pausing for a bite of linguine with clam sauce.

'He is capable of destructive behavior directed against material objects: buildings, lab equipment, and facilities. So he is capable of violence. Murder? I don't know. I find the combination of violence, irrationality, and obsession disturbing.'

Hank nodded. 'Rightly so.'

'I considered Johnny's roommate, Ned, but I can't get too excited about it. He was a little jealous of John, of his talent and money and the fact that Sally, his girlfriend, was somewhat sweet on John. Tough on a friendship, maybe, but it hardly seems enough to murder for. Ditto Sally, only she had even less of a reason. She was mildly jealous of Bella, the new woman in Johnny's life.'

I shoved my plate over to Hank for him to finish and ate a ravioli off his. 'The possibility exists but hardly the probability.'

'Given the assumption that everyone is acting rationally and sensibly.'

'Yes.'

'Frequently an erroneous assumption.'

'Yes.'

'Bella.' I thought about it. 'She is intriguing and mysterious, probably ten years older than Johnny. She is also beautiful, exotic, and an artist. Ned and Sally both said Johnny was wild for her. They also thought she had a husband or a steady boyfriend, as she refused to meet John in the evening or at her place, and would only see him occasionally for short periods of time. Love triangles are loaded with possibilities, possibilities both interesting and unpredictable.' I had a sip of wine.

'So are drugs.' Hank looked at me. 'They found drugs in Alma's car. I don't believe it was Johnny but,' I finished lamely, 'they were there.'

The waiter appeared, took our empty plates and asked about dessert. Hank had coffee and I finished the rest of the wine.

'Walter is my favorite candidate,' I said, the wine sharp and bitter on my tongue and the regret bittersweet in my mouth. 'Hands down. There he was in charge of a large, no doubt tempting, trust fund. Who's to say that, like little Jack Horner, he didn't stick in a thumb and pull out a plum?'

'And?'

'No. He checked out with the cotrustee, a banker, and with the police. Although—'

Hank laughed. 'Give it up, Kat. Your prejudice is getting in the way.'

'Mmmm.'

He was right, but it was a hard one to let go. I hadn't thought much of Walter for years; that made him an easy designated choice for bad guy. Too easy. I sighed. It was a less than professional approach and that made me feel a little testy.

'Does he benefit from John's death in any way?'

'No.'

'And if Michaela dies?'

'Still no.'

'No motive, Kat.'

'I *know.*'

The only thing that makes me crabbier than the realization of my professional shortcomings is having someone point them out so reasonably, helpfully, and politely. Hank grinned and I stuck my tongue out at him just as the waiter appeared. He looked at me with Chinese/Italian inscrutability which, as we all know, is a cover-up for disdain, and poured Hank some more coffee. I stuck my tongue out at his retreating back.

'I don't think you've lost your nerve, Kat.'

I caught my breath. 'It doesn't take a lot of guts to stick your tongue out at someone.'

'No,' he agreed.

'So?'

'Nerve is a state of mind, not a random physical act.'

He smiled at me. The waiter slapped the bill on the table and Hank paid it. We usually go Dutch, or take turns, but my purse was at home, at least I hoped it was. It was another one of the things I couldn't quite remember.

In the car I ate chocolates as Hank drove.

'There's one thing I haven't told you yet,' I said finally, still not telling him.

'What?' he asked. I hesitated a long time and Hank looked at me. 'Don't tell me, then,' he said reasonably.

'It's prejudice getting in my way again.' Hank didn't say anything. 'About Michaela.' We stopped at a red light, then turned left when it changed. 'She met Johnny at the Homestead the night he was killed. They sat and talked in Alma's car. She was, is, desperate for a new life, for money to go to music school.' I stopped and took a deep breath.

'She said Johnny agreed to lend it to her, then she left. She didn't know anything was wrong until I told her.' I could hear the pleading note in my voice begging Hank to believe me, begging *me* to believe me.

'A possible suspect is placed at the crime scene. She has a strong motive and the weapon is a readily available one.' His voice was cold and dispassionate.

'Yes,' I agreed miserably.

'All it means is that she could have done it, Kat, not that she did do it.'

'Alma and I argue over it. She claims we're all capable of killing anyone.'

'Of killing, yes, I agree. Anyone? No, I don't think so.'

It was comfort, but small comfort, cold comfort.

'I haven't told the police.'

Hank didn't look surprised. 'The more they know, the more likely it is the homicide will be solved. Give them some credit, Kat.' I didn't say anything. 'You want it cleared up, don't you, even if Michaela is responsible?'

I didn't answer, I didn't know. And I didn't feel comfortable with that knowledge.

I woke up the next morning with Hank's arm around me and a dull ache in my chest from the thumping I'd taken two days before. My body hurt and the morning was grey, cold, and foggy but my nerve felt fine. I smiled, yawned, and stretched. Hank tightened his hold on me and kissed my ear.

'Why would someone threaten Michaela?' I asked. He kissed my mouth. 'Or try to kill her?' He kissed my eyes and mouth. I gave up. I couldn't see. I couldn't talk. Michaela would have to wait.

It was late by the time we got up but not too late to have breakfast; we decided on omelettes and hash browns.

'Kat, I wish you wouldn't do that.' The disapproval was heavy in Hank's voice. I licked my fingers.

'Do what?' I asked, but I knew.

'Eat chocolates before breakfast. You'll ruin your appetite and they're not good for you.' I laughed. Hank is such a mom sometimes.

'Just one more.' He frowned. I ate a mint and then put the box away. 'Hmmm. Don't make me a big omelette, I'm not that hungry.' He glared at me and I grinned. 'Just kidding. I'll eat all my hash browns, too.'

'I'm not telling you what to do, Kat.' He put his arms around me.

'Yes, you are.' And there was more to come, I knew it.

218

'Fly back with me today. There are things I have to finish up, but next week I can take some time off. We'll drive back.'

I shook my head. 'I can't leave now, not in the middle of things. And Michaela—' I broke off. I wasn't sure what to say about it but something had to be done.

'It's not safe, sweetheart.' I looked at him and tightened up inside. We'd had this discussion before.

'Life isn't safe,' I answered in a reasonable tone. 'Statistically, either one of us is more likely to get scrambled on the freeway than anything else.'

He shook his head. 'Maybe, but right now you're dealing with a psychotic, a person who has already attempted murder' – I saw Glory's blood-filled tears in my mind again – 'who draws on you in cat blood and who has called both you and Michaela with threats. Not just simple death threats but threats of torture and mutilation.'

Hank looked at me steadily. 'You're leaving that out of your statistical calculations.'

I shivered. He was right, I was.

'Fly to Vegas with me. Next week we'll come back. I'll stay for—'

'I can't, Hank.' He let go of me and turned away. 'When you fall off a horse you have to get back on and ride before the fear takes over. And you have to do it alone. No one can do it for you.' He didn't turn.

I put my arms around him and rested my head on his back. His belly, under my hands, was tight with tension. 'I'm on my guard now and I won't take any chances. I'll be all right.'

'It's crazy, Kat.'

'No. It's not. You're the one who told me that bravery

219

is action in spite of reasonable fear. I want to be a brave person, Hank, someone who looks life in the eyes and doesn't back off from what she sees.'

'I hate it when you do this,' he said despairingly.

'But it's why you love me.'

'Yes.'

We made omelettes. I ate all of mine but couldn't quite finish the hash browns, so Hank did. At the airport we kissed for a long time. Fortunately you get to do that at airports. Hank made me promise I'd pick up Ranger, Johnny's dog, and wear my gun.

I didn't have any problem with that at all.

Twenty-Nine

Ranger was excited to see me and to be leaving the place that, without Johnny, wasn't home. I didn't blame him. Life had been pretty bleak since Johnny died. I was uneasy about having a pet after what happened to Xerxes, but Ranger was an Australian shepherd and tough. He cocked one blue and then one brown eye at me and allowed as how he could take care of it. We headed home that evening.

I picked it up a block away.

I would have noticed even if I hadn't been on guard – it was a tough one to miss. My place was lit up like a Taco Bell at Christmas, every light in the house and yard on. I parked at the end of the block, took my .380 from my purse and stuck it in my waistband, shoved my purse under the seat and the car keys in my pocket. Ranger and I walked it from there. The gun was in my hand.

Ranger followed obediently at my heels and whined nervously now and then. We could hear the music from some distance away. I couldn't recognize it but that had nothing to do with volume. Ranger whined again. It wasn't until we were almost there that I saw Charity's BMW half hidden in the shadows of the driveway. I stuck the gun back in my waistband and walked up the steps.

The front door was partly open, testimony to someone's fearlessness, carelessness, or nonchalance about my heating bills. Maybe all three. The music grated on me but the open front door put me in a bad mood. Ranger went bounding into the house, tail high and wagging, and I clomped along feeling glum and mad.

'Hey,' someone yelled, 'a dog!' The kitchen was full of people. There were only four, true, but they were the kind of people who constitute a large crowd: Charity, Lindy, and the two teenage hookers who, by now, had traded in hot pants for jeans. One of them was taking something out of the oven. She backed into me and stepped on my foot. Hard.

'Excuse me, am I in the way?' I asked sarcastically.

'No, Kat. Of course not. Come on in, it's okay.'

The girls nodded. I stared at them. Sarcasm was obviously too subtle a verbal tool. I turned off the radio and opened my mouth to be less subtle.

'Would you like a cookie?' A sweet-faced girl held out a spatula with a steaming cookie on it.

'We found the dough in the fridge, Kat,' Lindy said. '*They* wanted to eat it raw but I said we had to bake them first, right?'

Wrong. I'd rather eat raw cookie dough any day.

'We came over to check on you and make sure you were all right.' Charity looked at me anxiously and I nodded halfheartedly.

'We brought stuff for sandwiches. Would you like one?' I shook my head. 'Okay, just as well, I guess. There's not a lot left.' I looked at the debris on the kitchen table. There had been bread, cheese, salami, pickle, onions and olives. There were two olives, a pickle, and a pile of onions left. I ate a cookie. I ate two cookies.

'Good, huh? Trinka baked them.' I said hi to Trinka who smiled back. Then I looked at the other girl.

'That's Sasha.'

I said hi to her too, had another cookie, and wondered if hookers always had names that end in a vowel.

'Where's Michaela?'

'At the ranch.'

'Alone?'

'Rafe and Ripper are out there. She didn't want to be around people, she's all right.' Probably, but it worried me a little just the same.

'Have you found out anything more about Lisa?' Lindy asked.

'No.'

'Or Johnny?' Charity chimed in.

'No.'

'Did Hank leave?'

'Yes.' I ate a bite of cookie and then gave it to Ranger.

'Kat, why are you in such a bad mood?'

'My cat's dead, I just got out of the hospital, and I've got a lot of things on my mind.'

'That's why we came by,' Lindy said, 'to cheer you up.'

'And,' I continued relentlessly, 'my house is full of teenagers, the food is all gone, and my hopes of a peaceful evening are history.'

The room was silent. I started to feel bad. I was being a grouch and taking it out on friends.

Trinka cleared her throat. 'She's probably sad because she looks so crummy.' Lindy and Sasha nodded wisely.

'Yeah,' they agreed.

'You know, you always feel better if you look good. Did you really take your boyfriend to the airport looking like that?' Trinka spoke the words as though she couldn't quite believe it, not even stretching her imagination.

'What's the matter with the way I look?' I asked before I could catch myself. Besides the gun, of course, as guns are not a fashion accessory. Even Charity looked at me in astonishment.

'Kat, I thought you *knew* and just didn't care. You mean you don't *know*?' I looked at myself. I was wearing a flannel shirt over a turtleneck tucked into belted worn jeans and boots. I thought I looked fine. I was afraid to say so.

'We'll teach you how to dress better.' Sasha smiled shyly at me.

'Thanks, but hot pants are not for me.'

'Oh, that.' She dismissed them with a wave of her hand. 'That's just for work.'

'I do *not* need a bunch of teenager hookers teaching me how to dress.'

I reached for another cookie, then stopped myself. Ranger looked longingly at the plate and panted slightly.

'Why not?'

'Yes, you do.'

'It couldn't hurt,' they chorused at me.

To hell with it. Ranger and I had another cookie. 'Listen, you guys, thanks for coming by and for making me cookies and everything but now—' I yawned. When Hank was here I ate well and lost sleep. On balance I had no complaints. 'Now, I'm afraid it's my bedtime.'

'Okay, girls, let's clean up.'

'I'll do it tomorrow.' They looked at me dubiously. 'Really.'

'Kat, come out to the ranch with us, it's safer.'

'I'm safe. I've got deadbolt locks, Ranger, and a gun. Don't worry, Charity.'

'I do.'

'Don't.'

'Where am I going to sleep, Kat?' Lindy asked.

'I don't know. Ask Charity.'

'No. I mean where am I going to sleep here? I'm going to stay with you. You need someone.'

'No, it's not safe,' I started to say. Charity looked at me with her see-I-told-you-so look. Damn. 'It's not safe for Lindy when I'm not here,' I amended.

'I'll go with you,' she said.

I shook my head. 'I'm working tomorrow and I've got a full day.'

'Where, Kat?'

'Lindy, I mean it, it's not all that safe. I say this because I care about you.'

'She's safer here than she has been for months on the streets.'

I was on shaky ground arguing with that one so I didn't. I sighed and gave up.

'Where, Kat?'

'In my office. There's a sofa bed in there.' The girls bounced out of the kitchen to scope it.

'Charity, talk to Michaela. There's something she's not telling. Something big.'

'There's something everyone's not telling,' Trinka said, walking back into the kitchen. 'Me.' She looked at Sasha and Lindy. They nodded. 'Them.' She looked at me. 'You. Charity. Everyone.'

'And it doesn't follow that it should be told, Kat,' Charity said.

It was a good exit line. Unfortunately they didn't

leave for another twenty minutes.

I was up early. It wasn't too wet so Ranger and I went for a mile run. I was ready to stop then even if he wasn't. Back home I made coffee and phone calls. Alma and Henley were both in and would see me. Alma sounded delighted; Henley, resigned. Close enough.

Lindy strolled into the kitchen at ten in tousled, kittenish disarray. I looked up from coffee and the paper to answer her good morning.

'You're up early.'

'I am, huh?' She yawned and stretched, then nearly tripped over Ranger. 'Charity's been trying to get us up at seven. "Early to bed, early to rise," all that kind of crap. I'm not used to it. None of us are.'

'Is.'

'Huh?' I didn't answer. 'Anyways we're not used to it. Night work, you know. Most nights I work from seven to twelve or one. On a good night, though, the tricks just keep on coming.' She winked and leered. It didn't make her look knowledgeable or sophisticated, but like a third-grader trying on her mommy's clothes and high heels. It made me sad; I tried hard not to show it.

'Coming and coming,' she said, sitting down at the table across from me. 'Coming.' She shrugged. 'Course some nights you can't get going, not to save your life. Then we quit early.'

'And do what?'

'We might go out for something to eat if we got the money. If not,' she shrugged, 'we get us a bag of cookies and a quart of milk. One of the girls has a good collection of fashion magazines. We look at them and talk and stuff. Sometimes we do drugs, too.'

'What?'

'Dope and lines, coke or speed. Speed's cheaper and it lasts longer. Some of the girls do crack. Not me. I tried it and I liked the rush but not the crash. Total downer, total. Going up, coming down.' She hummed a song I didn't recognize.

'Coming, going,' she sang in a sultry parody of a nightclub singer. 'Too damn fucking much coming and going in my life.' The jump was from fifteen to forty in a sentence and a heartbeat. 'Is that coffee?' she asked, and continued before I could answer. 'Can I have some?' I nodded.

She poured half a cup of coffee and dumped in sugar and milk to fill the cup. I watched, puzzled.

'Do you like coffee, Lindy?'

'Not really.'

'Why do you drink it?'

'I don't know. It's there. It's hot. It's – I don't know. I'm used to doing what I don't like, I guess. It's no big deal.'

'There's milk, juice, tea, and cocoa.'

'Could I have cocoa? Please,' she added.

'Chocolate and marshmallows in the cupboard behind you. Milk in the fridge.' I went back to my paper.

'Can I have cookies for breakfast?'

'Sure. Not too many, though. I'm taking you over to Alma's later on and she'll feed you.'

'Can I have the comics?' I pushed them over. She didn't pick them up. 'Kat, how come you're not shocked?'

I looked up. 'You want me to be?'

'Well, I dunno. Yeah, I guess. Most people are.'

'At what? You're a hooker. Hookers turn tricks. Most hookers are dumb enough to do drugs. Dumb enough or don't care enough,' I amended. 'So you fit right in with ninety-nine percent of hookers. Big deal. Yesterday's news.' She stared at me.

'You want to shock me, do something different.' Her lips pulled back in a snarl. I shook my head at her and the snarl went into suspended animation.

'I'm not finished yet. You're starting to, not shock me, that's the wrong word, surprise me. You've been off the streets for almost a week now. You're working things out with Charity. You've even got some of your friends thinking about it.'

The suspended animation stayed, the snarl disappeared. 'I wasn't sure you could do it. I hoped you could but I wasn't sure. I'm still not.' I got up and walked over to the stove. 'Cocoa?'

'Yes.' She pushed the word out of frozen lips.

'You've got people pulling for you, Lindy. Me. Charity. There will be others. But it's still your decision – you have to make the move. People can help you; they can't do it for you.' I made cocoa for her, poured more coffee for me. 'I believe in you, believe you can do it.'

'You ever get high, Kat?'

'I drink.'

'Drugs?'

'No, I don't do illegal stuff.'

'You drive too fast.'

'I don't do illegal drugs,' I amended. 'I don't do legal drugs either. I don't like what drugs do to your body.' I looked at the clock. 'We've got to get going.' Lindy slugged down the rest of her cocoa. 'Do you have clean clothes to wear? I've got a flannel shirt you can borrow.'

Lindy turned around to stare at me, then laughed. 'I could like you. Maybe.'

'Yeah? Work on it, kid.'

'I could like you, but not your flannel shirts.' I shrugged. One out of two was not so bad.

It was later, in the car, that I brought up Lisa.

'The cops don't know who did it, but they know something.'

'What?'

'In the last nine months at least three girls have been killed in the Sacramento area. They're all young; they're all prostitutes; they're all small, dark-haired women.'

The silence stretched out over a mile or so. 'Some kind of a crazy guy?'

'Yes, I would think so.'

'It didn't have anything to do with Lisa as a person?'

'No.'

'He just killed her because of the way she looked? He killed her and she didn't even *matter* to him?'

'No.'

She started crying.

'At least it could have mattered to him who she was, a jealous boyfriend, something. At least it could have *mattered*.'

'It didn't matter. She didn't matter. She was just a young, dark-haired prostitute.'

'It *matters*. Lisa *matters*. She does!'

'Not to him, but to you. To other people, too. And to the police. You matter, too, Lindy, but on the streets you don't matter much.'

She shrugged it off. 'I'm blond. I'm okay.'

'You don't think there's a crazy out there somewhere who has it in for blondes?'

She stared at me for a long time. 'I don't know. Is there?'

'I don't know either. Probably.' That silence went most of the way to Alma's.

'Alma is your grandmother?'

'Adopted grandmother. I was like you, a kid nobody wanted. Alma took me in.'

'Everybody matters, Kat, don't they?'

'Yes.'

I dropped Lindy off with a quick introduction. They could figure it out and I was late for my meeting with Henley.

Thirty

Henley was growling on the phone when I got there. He waved me into a chair, finished talking, and slammed the phone down.

'Yeah?' he growled at me.

'I'm late. Sorry.'

He shrugged. 'You come here to get information or give it?'

'Both.'

'Start.'

I started. 'I found Michaela Benson.' He opened his mouth to comment but I kept on going. 'She's going by the name of Micha Budroe, is living in West Sac,' I gave him the address, 'and working, singing, in Placerville at a place called the Alibi Inn.' He grunted. It sounded more good-humored than the previous ones, but hard to tell.

'When did you find her?'

'Just before the memorial service.' He looked pissed. 'Henley, I've been busy, it slipped my mind.' He looked pissed and unconvinced.

'I can find her at this address?'

'No.' He rumbled his shoulders and a brief shower of dandruff and gray hair dazzled me.

'What the—'

'I'm telling you,' I explained patiently. 'Give me a chance.' The shoulders and dandruff shower subsided. 'Michaela received several threatening phone calls. Not vague threats, specific. Against her life. She was too frightened to stay alone. She stayed with me for the night and then I took her out to a friend's ranch in Wilton.' He looked at me, pencil in hand, and I rattled off the pertinent information.

'Call first,' I said, thinking about Lindy and the girls. 'They're out working the horses a lot. And stuff,' I finished lamely.

He nodded, like he'd let so much else slide, why not this, too? It worked for me.

'The night of the second death threat Michaela didn't go to work. She got another singer to stand in for her. The stand-in was shot.' Henley snapped to attention.

'The Alibi Inn, Placerville?' I nodded. 'You were there at the time of the shooting?'

'I was just leaving.'

'But you saw what was going on?'

'No. I arrived on the scene after it was all over. Once help was on the way I left. I could see it was a police matter and naturally I didn't want to interfere.' I said it piously, a shade too piously, I think. Henley snorted again.

'Did you talk to the girl?'

'Before.'

'Why?'

'To warn her, just in case.'

'And?'

'And she shrugged it off. The boyfriend, in leathers, laughed at me, said he could take care of her.'

I'd had the last laugh but it hadn't made me feel good, hadn't made me feel like laughing.

'Leathers?'

'Hell's Angels insignia on the jacket.'

'You see anything?'

'I heard one shot. I looked around and didn't see anything.'

'Didn't wait for the Placerville cops either.'

I sighed. 'Give me a break, Henley. I'm here and I don't have to be.'

He scratched his right temple and dislodged a large fleck of dandruff that landed in his eyebrow. I waited hopefully for an acknowledgment or thank you. It didn't come. Surprise.

'Someone seems to be serious about trying to kill Michaela. Anonymous phone calls and death threats are one thing, shootings are another. Unless someone has it in for Gloria. Interesting coincidence though.'

Henley ignored my speculation. 'The girl's dead?'

'I don't know. It rated three column inches the next day in the paper and I haven't seen anything since then. The hospital wouldn't give me the time of day and I didn't want to call the cops. Let me know when you find out, will you?'

Henley grunted and made another note on the pad in front of him. 'What else you got for me?'

'Someone jumped me, too.'

His head snapped up in another impressive dandruff shower. Didn't he watch TV, read magazines? Hadn't he ever heard of medicated shampoos? Was his wife oblivious? Were his children tongue-tied? I wondered, I didn't ask.

'Kat?' There was a note of concern in his voice. I

think it was concern. I debated it for a moment. 'Kat?'

'Yes.'

'What happened?' He almost reached a hand out to pat my arm but stopped himself. Cops are tough.

'I was at home and heard what sounded like a cat scream. When I went out to investigate I didn't find anything at first, then I saw my cat. Somebody had cut his throat.' I felt my eyes start to tear up but I blinked it down. 'I lost it, Bill,' I said softly.

He nodded. 'It happens.' There was no judgment, no put-down in his voice, just acknowledgment. 'What did you do?'

'I stumbled inside and called my boyfriend. He's a cop in Vegas.' Henley nodded like it made sense to him. It sounded dumb to me, but that was today, and in the daylight talking to a cop. That night was something else again.

'Then I went outside again. I couldn't stand it that Xerxes, my cat,' I explained, and he nodded, 'was out there cold and alone in the rain. It was stupid, I know. Lame,' I added.

'It happens,' he said, still no judgment in his voice.

'The guy came up behind me. I heard him, but not in time. I swung around and he nailed me. Put me in the hospital overnight. My twelve-year-old neighbor found me.'

'Good.'

'Yes.'

'There's more.' He made it a statement, not a question.

'There was a slash mark across my throat drawn in fresh cat blood.' My voice shook. I heard it but I couldn't stop it. He thought it over.

'You see your attacker?'

'No.'

'You all right now?'

'Yes.'

'You need help with anything?'

'No.' He nodded. 'Thanks for asking.'

He nodded again. 'I got something for you.' I raised my eyebrows. 'Gil Jones, the animal rights activist?'

'Mr. Charm.'

'Yeah. His real name is—'

'Sam Spade.'

Henley snorted. 'Easy, Kat. You skate on thin ice too often.' He paused. 'Gilmer Caldwell. Jones is an alias.'

'*Come on*. Nobody would use Jones as an alias. It's too obvious. Even Gil can't be that stupid.'

Henley shrugged. 'Your average criminal has an eighth grade education. Caldwell has a record, too.'

'What?'

'Drugs, burglary, receiving stolen property, vandalism. Crimes against property, not people.'

'So?'

'So, chances are he's not our boy; chances are he hasn't changed his MO overnight.'

'We don't know,' I said, hating to let Gil off the hook.

'No, I'm guessing. An educated guess, Kat.'

'Okay,' I agreed, but reluctantly. 'Now what?'

'You haven't told me everything.'

'I spilled my guts, Bill.'

I looked him straight in the eye and blacked out my knowledge of Michaela's breakfast meeting with Johnny. White out, not black out. E-Z erase cover-up.

'Yeah, right,' he said after a pause that was too long.

'Right,' I said, definitively. 'I gave you a lot of stuff

and all you tell me is that Jones is an alias. Big deal.'

Henley grunted. I ignored it. Cops always get more information than they give. 'Do you know about Bella?' I asked after a moment.

'Bella?' he echoed in a low key.

'Bella,' I said.

He waited for me to continue. 'Spit it out, Kat,' he said finally.

'I heard about her from both Ned and Sally, John's roommate and his girlfriend. She came to the memorial service, cried, said she loved Johnny. Word has it that she's an artist, maybe in Davis. I didn't get a last name.'

He looked disgusted. 'You know how many artists there are in Davis?' he asked sourly. 'They're probably a dime a dozen.'

I ignored the interruption. 'She was driving a dark green Bug, California plates, license number—' I rattled it off.

He grinned. 'Nice work, Kat.'

I looked pointedly at the computer. 'Well?'

He grinned again, then flipped it on, waited for it to boot up, and entered the information he needed. 'Belinda?' He looked at me. I nodded.

'Bella is a nickname.'

'Doveccio. Davis address.' He wrote it down, letting me see, and the conversation died.

'What about Johnny?' I asked finally.

'It's still under investigation, Kat.'

I sighed. That's what cops say when either they don't have anything, or they do and you're not going to get it.

'You still working the drug angle?'

'Not heavy. We didn't find anything in his apartment, his life-style, or in what his friends and associates said to corroborate it. Maybe it was something new for him, or it involved a friend. Maybe we find out, maybe we don't.'

'That's a lot of maybes.'

'Yeah. I'm interested in Michaela. She's the one who benefits.'

'Why would she kill Johnny? Money?' I shook my head. 'She gets her half in two years and it's more than enough. And either one of them would have helped the other if they needed it.'

'Maybe.'

'For God's sake, Henley.' All my earlier rapport with him was evaporating rapidly. 'A woman doesn't kill the brother she loves for a few bucks. Catch a clue.'

'No? People kill for money all the time. Last week a gas station attendant was dusted for sixty-two dollars. Sixty-two dollars. Here we're talking thousands, not just a few bucks.'

I shook my head. 'Not Michaela.'

Henley leaned forward. 'John wouldn't do drugs, Michaela wouldn't kill. That's what you're starting with, Kat. A good investigator doesn't operate that way. She might end up there, conclusions based on facts, but she doesn't start there.' I flushed.

'You know that, I know I don't need to tell you this. We none of us see straight on things close to us, and family's the closest of all. Let us take care of it. We want to see this case closed as much as you do.' I started to get up. He put his hand out.

'Don't take it wrong, Kat. Somebody killed my cousin, they wouldn't put me on the case. Personal feelings cloud your professional judgment. And nothing's more personal than family.'

'Why would someone want to kill Michaela?'

He shrugged. 'You tell me. What were the threatening phone calls about?'

'A man called her a slut and a whore, said it was a good thing when she left town before and that she should've stayed away. He threatened her life if she didn't leave again.'

'Why'd she leave before?'

'Teenage pregnancy. Her dad was ashamed of the situation.'

'So she left, had the baby, and came back?'

'No. That was four years ago. She's only been back for a month or so.'

'She put the baby up for adoption?' I nodded. 'None of that sounds like a reason for threats against her life. There an old boyfriend in the picture?'

'I don't know. There's a lot she's not telling me.' For sure. 'You lean on her, see what you get.'

'No problem.'

'Johnny's dead and someone's trying to kill Michaela.'

'You don't know that.'

'You think Gloria was the target, or Hughie, her boyfriend?'

'I don't know yet. I'll look into it. You said the guy was wearing an Angel's jacket. Could be drugs, could be a lot of things.'

'Superficially Michaela and Gloria look alike. They're both small, dark-haired women. At a distance, at night, it would be easy to mistake one for the other.'

'Could be.' He was noncommittal.

'Henley, for godsakes, it's too much of a coincidence. There's got to be a connection.'

'Maybe, but maybe not. Don't ever assume anything, Kat.'

He was right, of course. I left, and I left in a bad mood. By the time I got to the car I realized I'd forgotten to ask about Lisa and the serial killings. It made my bad mood worse.

I was one hell of an investigator, that's for sure.

Thirty-One

Michaela was waiting for me when I got back to Alma's. She was neatly dressed, her eyes all large and full of unspoken thoughts and hopes. She was edgy as hell. We had a two o'clock appointment with Walter Benson.

'We're meeting at my office?' It was more of a confirmation than a question. That's what we'd previously agreed on.

'No.' She surprised me.

'Where?'

'At his office.'

'Why?'

'I don't know. I guess he – it just seemed to – I don't know.' Her voice trailed off.

'You let him call the shots?'

'Yes, I guess I did,' she agreed miserably. 'I didn't mean to, but I did.'

'We're meeting on his ground; that's to his advantage.'

'I know, I *know*. Don't be such a jerk about it.'

'I'm not being a jerk, Michaela, I'm pointing out how things work. You're the one who said you didn't trust him.'

'I don't.'

'Call him up. Reschedule the meeting and have him

come here. Or meet with the cotrustee.'

'No, I can't, I – oh hell, let's just go and get it over with.'

It was not a pleasant ride. Michaela glowered and refused to talk so I listened to a country music station. Occasionally she snarled about my choice of music. I told her to go to hell and wondered why I hadn't come clean with Henley. She was making family loyalty a lot less appealing.

The closer we got to Marysville the more she fidgeted. As we came over the bridge into town she was biting her nails, chewing on her lips, and mumbling to herself.

'Want to talk about it?'

'No. I just want to get my money and get out of here. Let's do this fast.'

'It's your party.' I parked and we walked into the office. Walter was working at his desk in three-piece-suited calm and splendor.

'Good afternoon.' He stood, smiling, and walked around to meet us, his hands out as though he wanted to clasp Michaela's shoulders and kiss her.

'Don't touch me,' she hissed. He was taken aback. Me too. 'This is just a business deal, nothing else. I want my money. I want it now and then I want to get out of here.'

She was barely polite, very goal oriented. Walter cleared his throat and turned to me, holding out a hand. I took it and returned his good afternoon. His handshake was warm, firm, and reassuring. He held my hand just a moment too long.

'Please. Sit down.' He waved in friendly fashion at the chairs placed before his desk.

'No,' Michaela snarled. I sighed and sat down.

Michaela seemed a little old for adolescent rebellion, and surely the bitterness of a decision she disagreed with four years ago would have faded by now.

Walter sat next to me. It was obviously a concession; he looked as though he would have been more comfortable behind his desk. I probably looked as though I would have been more comfortable almost anywhere else. Which, God knows, was true.

'Lighten up, Michaela,' I said. 'Our business will run more easily if you rely more on impersonal formalities and less on personal animosities.'

Walter smiled tentatively. 'Thank you, Katy. May I offer you a cup of coffee?' His look included us both.

'Yes.'

'No.'

We spoke at the same time. She was the no, of course. Walter and I got our coffee and Michaela stared sullenly at the ceiling.

'I want my money,' she said when we were settled. 'I want it now.'

'My dear—'

'*Don't* call me that, I told you.'

Walter's face got rigid and cold. I didn't blame him for losing patience.

'Very well, let us begin. John is dead and you are his beneficiary. The money, however, does not immediately come to you.'

She opened her mouth to protest and he raised a hand. It almost looked as though he were going to slap her; she winced slightly and then subsided.

'Fortunately, the money was in a living trust and the will does not have to go through probate. Probate would have delayed proceedings for six months to a year.' Michaela's eyes got wide. 'As I said, that is not the case.

Nevertheless there are legal procedures and formalities to be observed. It is not just a question of take-the-money-and-run.'

Walter stretched a tight, thin-lipped smile across his mouth. It didn't fool me into thinking he was having fun. Michaela didn't look fooled either.

She made a low, whimpering sound. 'I want my money.'

'I understand; it is legally yours but not yet available to you.'

'I want a full accounting of all the funds, mine, Johnny's, everything.'

Walter's thin smile tightened, then faded. 'I do not have that information at my fingertips, but you will, of course, be provided with it. This week is very busy for me but—'

'Now!' Michaela demanded. I looked at his computer and wondered why he didn't give her the same stuff he gave the police.

'I will be available next week. As you may remember, I am getting married this weekend, Sunday, in fact. Saturday is the rehearsal and dinner and the rest of the week is taken up with preparations. I am sorry, but your affairs will have to wait.'

She whimpered again. 'I want my money.' The broken record.

'I should be glad to advance you what you need out of my personal funds since the principal is presently unavailable to you.' He took a checkbook and pen out of his inner pocket and held it poised.

'Your money? Oh no!' She said it with loathing.

'For goodness sakes, Michaela, take it. Take what you can get. Go for a thousand.'

'I do not have a thousand immediately available,'

Walter said stiffly. 'Would five hundred do?'

'No! I won't take anything of his. *Anything!*'

I shrugged. 'Shall we say next week, then? Ten o'clock Monday morning at my office?' Walter nodded and made a note of it.

'I want my money Monday. I want it!'

Michaela's voice was shrill and unpleasant. I didn't meet Walter's eyes. I didn't want to share that thought with him. It was getting harder and harder to remember that I was on Michaela's side.

The ride home was sullen and silent on Michaela's part, merely silent on mine. I didn't see any point in starting a conversation and I couldn't wait to get rid of her. I dropped her off at Alma's and headed for the freeway and Davis.

Bella lived in an older part of town, near D and 6th not far from the high school, that had charming two- and three-bedroom houses and neat well-kept lawns and yards. The street was lined with trees, their branches thin and stark now, but in the summer it would be cool and green. I found her house – brick painted over in white with a shingle roof and red trim – without any trouble.

It was meticulous and ordinary, which surprised me. I guess I imagined that artists lived in houses very different from the rest of us. Or maybe, because their inside perception is so different, the outside is ordinary, banal. No doubt the totality balances out.

There were no cars in the driveway, no trikes or trucks on the front walk. A poinsettia, obviously planted outside after Christmas, struggled along in a dispirited way. I walked up to the front door and knocked. Several times. It didn't surprise me that there was no answer.

There was no name on the front mailbox either. I knocked again and walked around a bit. It was closed up and contained. A grandmotherly lady of sixty-five or so flounced out of the house next door, wiped her hands on her apron, and looked at me pointedly. Gray Panther crime alert.

'Hi.' I waved. 'I can't believe I missed Bella. She said to meet her here in the morning or,' I shuffled through some papers in my purse, 'darn, I lost the address. I'm pretty sure it was in Davis, though. The gallery, I think? I'm from out of town and—' I broke off, trying to look lost and a little helpless. I don't do it very well so she didn't buy it immediately, but she bought it. Eventually.

'Probably the gallery. She works there four afternoons a week.'

'The gallery. I thought that was it. Do you have the name?'

'Nouveau,' she said kindly, 'though I think that's a silly name, too foreign sounding. What's the matter with American anyway? Would you like a cookie? I've got to take a batch out of the oven.'

'Oh, no thank—'

'It's no trouble. You just come on over and have a few. Take some to Bella, too. That girl doesn't eat enough to keep a bird alive. I'm worried about her. We need to get a little meat on her bones.' I followed along, ready to talk if not to eat.

'I'm Rosa, by the way.' She smiled at me.

'Kate.' I went for conservative.

'You look like a Kate.' She nodded in approval and I tried to smile like a Kate. Rosa pulled open the oven door and began flipping cookies around with dual spatula action. 'Milk with cookies, or coffee?'

'Coffee, please.' I took a bite of a cookie. They were better than Alma's. I was impressed. She smiled angelically at me.

'I have the recipe all printed up. You can have it; everyone wants it after tasting just one,' she said proudly. I thanked her. What with Hank and teenage hookers dropping in, it couldn't hurt.

'I've been a little worried about Bella.' I took a sip of coffee and considered what would say nothing much and yet encourage Rosa to talk. 'She doesn't seem herself lately.'

Rosa shook her head sadly. 'No, she doesn't. Have another cookie, dear.' I didn't want another cookie, I wanted information. She watched me expectantly. I took a cookie and nibbled at it.

'Maybe it was that guy—' I broke off. I still didn't know Bella's marital status.

'Oh, *him*.' Rosa was disgusted. 'I never did like him and I told her so. Although,' she paused appreciatively, 'that boy could eat. It was something to watch.' There was a note of awe in her voice. 'A regular eating machine, he was.' She shook her head.

'But he didn't do right by her, I know he didn't. Hah! Always flexing his muscles and roaring up in that fancy expensive sports car. His beauty was only skin deep,' she said darkly. 'Skin deep.'

'Fancy car?'

'One of them foreign jobbies.' The word foreign was loaded with disdain. 'The one that sounds like porch.'

'Porsche?'

'Yes.' She looked at me, uncertain whether to be pleased that I knew the car or dismayed that I knew a foreign word.

'Muscles?'

'He was into weight lifting, body building.' She snorted. 'Vanity, I call it. Why didn't he get a real job: building bridges or farming or something, if he wanted muscles?'

I held myself back. There was no reason to interrupt her flow by pointing out that Davis doesn't need bridges and farmland is fast disappearing.

'What does he do?'

'Do? Heavens, who knows? He didn't seem to *do* anything except run around looking pretty and fancying himself. All hours of the day and night *he'd* come over and *she'd* let him in. I don't know,' she said. 'I just don't know.'

I didn't either. 'I thought from something Bella said that that was pretty much off.'

She shrugged. 'I guess, I don't know. He hasn't been around much lately, well, not at all lately that I've seen, and not much for a month or so before that. She said she got tired of his jealous rages. That's why he was always coming by at all times of the day and night, you know. It was to check up on her. Imagine!' she sputtered and poured us both more coffee. 'Have another cookie, dear.'

'Oh, I couldn't, I'm stuffed.' Which was true, they were very filling cookies.

'I *insist*,' she said and was silent. I took one. It was the price I was paying for this conversation.

'Anyway,' she resumed, garrulous again now that my mouth was full, '*my* mister is not the jealous type, no siree, and it's not because he don't love me. He does and that's a fact. Me *and* my cooking,' she added with a smile. 'No, it's because he trusts me. And what's the good of a relationship what's not built on love and trust? And what's the good of men who can't trust, I ask you?'

I couldn't answer, my mouth was full. She answered for us and I nodded in agreement. 'No blame good, no blame good at all.' So much for muscle porch.

'Was there someone new, do you think?' I swallowed hastily. 'I kind of got the impression there was.'

'I think so,' she nodded. 'Bella wasn't around as much as she used to be and I thought I saw someone come by now and again. An older car, I think, and an odd color, maybe turquoise. I didn't get a good look at him. Of course I would never want to *pry.*'

'Of course,' I agreed.

'Have another cookie, dear.'

'I can't.'

And it was the truth. One more and I'd burst. This would have to be enough information for today.

'Here, take these with you for Bella.' She handed me a foil-wrapped plate she'd made up. 'And come back anytime. Monday, Wednesday, and Friday are baking days. The mister, he loves to eat.' Good thing, I thought as I thanked her. I wondered what size the mister was.

It wasn't hard finding the gallery, on 2nd between D and E, and it didn't take me long to find a parking place. I forgot the cookies, though, and had to go back for them.

Bella welcomed me warmly, salesperson to customer, as I walked in, then looked at my face more closely. Her forehead furrowed up in a puzzled, frowning way. The puzzlement deepened as her eyes traveled from my face to the cookies and back again. I held them out to her. She shook her head.

'No strychnine,' I announced, 'no arsenic, no drug overdose. Just cookies, Rosa's.'

'Oh,' she said, her frown deepening, her eyes clearing, 'it's you.'

'Yes,' I agreed, and put the cookies down on the counter in front of her.

'You've been snooping around.'

'Yes.'

'Shit.'

The word sounded funny coming from such an elegant, ladylike person. She ripped the foil back, took a cookie and began eating it thoughtfully.

'I don't suppose you'd just get the fuck out?' That sounded even worse.

'No.'

'It would take more than asking?'

'Yes,' I agreed.

'How much more?' I shrugged. She put the cookie down and reached under the counter. 'Maybe this?' I looked down the barrel of a gun.

Thirty-Two

Her voice was calm and detached, her hand was shaking. Her finger was on the trigger.

'Maybe this?' she repeated.

Maybe that. There is nothing like looking down a gun barrel at close range. The only thing worse is knowing that the person holding it is scared and that she probably doesn't know anything about guns.

'Put it down, Bella.' I kept the panic out of my voice, kept it quiet and cool.

'Why? I like it, I like the power. It lets me tell you to get the fuck out of here.' She waved the gun slightly. 'You seem to have trouble hearing my words. This speaks a little louder, doesn't it?' It did, but I didn't tell her so.

She smiled. It wasn't a smile that used up her mouth, just borrowed the corners and twisted them around in a nasty, ugly way. I didn't like it. I hadn't liked her lacquered look either but I liked it a whole lot better than this.

'So, why don't you just get the fuck out of here? And don't come back. Not to here, not to my home, not to anywhere.'

'Put it down. You don't know how to use it.'

'You just pull the trigger,' she said softly, and then that smile again.

'Not with the safety catch on.'

The smile faded from the corners in. Revolvers don't have a safety; I knew that, she obviously didn't. She looked down. With the side of my hand I slammed her wrist. Hard. The gun hit the counter and went skittering off onto the floor. I picked it up, swung the cylinder out, and dumped the bullets into my hand.

'Damn you. Goddamn you!'

I dropped the bullets into my pocket. 'It was a bluff, anyway, wasn't it?' She stared at me, tears in her eyes. 'You wouldn't have used it.' I dumped the gun into my other pocket.

Her eyes dropped. 'No. It's here because, because sometimes we work late at night. There's a lot of valuable stuff here.'

'Don't pull out a gun you're not prepared to use.'

'Oh, fuck off.' She made a rude noise and gesture at me.

'Why do you swear so much?' I was curious.

She looked at me in disbelief. 'What does that have to do with anything?'

'Things count. Words, too. You're too smart to misuse them the way you do.'

'Oh, fuck off,' she said again, sounding disgusted. It seemed like a good time to change the subject.

'May I see some of your paintings?'

'I'm not a painter.'

'What then?'

'I sculpt.'

She stopped. I waited. Then she pointed to a corner of the gallery. Ledges and tiers were draped in dark blue velvet. Small figures rested, danced, almost flew about on them. I caught my breath and walked over. They were beautiful; alive with whatever it is that makes the difference between art and representation. It's not technique, I've seen children do it. I don't know what it is, but it's something inside.

'You can do this and you need a gun to make you feel powerful?' I turned to her and she started to cry. 'Let's go get a cup of coffee.' She shook her head. 'We're going to talk. I'm not leaving until we do.'

'Please, just leave me alone.'

'No. People count, too. Johnny counted.' She started to cry again. 'Let's go.'

She sighed. 'All right.' She leaned over behind the counter.

'Hold it,' I said. Even to me my voice sounded hard and mean.

'What?'

'Walk out here. I'll get whatever you need.'

'It's all right.' She spread her hands out helplessly. 'I was just trying to scare you off before. I wouldn't *really* have shot you.'

I shook my head. 'Do it. I don't like to get caught on the same stunt more than once a day.'

'It's all right,' she said again, but she came out. I got her stuff and it was all right. Still, it made me feel better. Of course, I'm one who closes the barn door after the horse gets out.

'Where? This is your town.'

'This way. We can walk, it's only a few blocks.' She took me to Baker's Square, nice, predictable, impersonal. It surprised me.

'There are other places, nice places, a croissant shop

where I go, a cafe—' She broke off. 'But I might know someone there.' She said it simply, not to insult but to explain. I nodded. We were seated by a bustling, efficient little person in tan and brick plaid who took our order.

Then we sat in silence. I decided to wait it out. I looked at the tall woman sitting next to us, early fifties and weighing in at two-eighty easy, wearing a brown flowered muu-muu and Swedish clogs. She was moving her lips as she read *The Wall Street Journal* and rocking around and around in a circular motion. I see stuff like this that I can hardly believe; it happens all the time.

'Do I have to drag it out of you?' I said at last.

'No,' she said, resigned and sad sounding. 'I'll tell you. I met John a couple of months ago. I was in a bad relationship at the time.'

'Muscle Porsche?'

She smiled. 'His name is Stan but that does sum him up rather. Anyway, I was on campus helping with the layout of an exhibition and I saw John. His face had very interesting angles – the shadows, the play of light.' Her eyes got faraway. 'I turned around and ran after him, asked him if he would model for me. It sounds very forward, I know, but I didn't mean it that way. He didn't take it that way, either. He was a good person.'

'Yes.' Was can be such a sad verb. I tried not to think about it.

'He didn't really want to, he said he was busy all the time, but he agreed to meet me at the gallery the next day for coffee and to see my work. He was intrigued by me,' she said simply and without vanity, just as her due, 'interested.'

I nodded. It didn't surprise me. The waitress refilled

our teapots with hot water and Bella punched her teabag around with her spoon. Then she picked at her three-layer carrot cake with whipped frosting on the excessive side of excess. I looked at my apple bran muffin and indulged in regret. And waited.

'He was impressed with my work.'

'Yes.' That didn't surprise me either.

'I got him to agree, although reluctantly, that he would at least pose for some sketches. And that's how it started. He fell in love with me; he couldn't help it. I'm older, an artist, sophisticated. I don't think he'd known anyone like me before.'

'No.' I didn't think so either. Marysville wasn't full of people like her, and veterinary classes probably weren't either.

'I couldn't resist the angles, the beauty. I never can,' she said miserably. 'Never. Even when it's mad, when it's stupid. Like Stan.' She said the words helplessly. 'I loved to look at his body, to touch it, to create from it, so I was his lover. He's a jerk, jealous and violent. Even as I loved his body I hated him.

'You asked why I needed a gun with the power in me, but sometimes I don't know whether I possess it, or it possesses me. I wonder if, in the Middle Ages, some of those witches who were burned weren't artists, or at least people with that kind of perception, people who were possessed with something, though it wasn't witchcraft. That's how I feel.' I nodded.

'John was a good, kind, healthy person, just the kind of person who should work with people or animals. He loved living things. I don't; that's not the part I care about. It's beauty that I love, that I crave. And that's gotten me into trouble.'

'Yes. I can see where it would.'

'Like Stan.'

'Yes.'

'Like Johnny, too, but in a different way. It's easy for me to love beauty and hard for me to love people. Still, I never knowingly hurt anyone. Not like Stan who loves to hurt. He was the kind of child monster who would stick pins in bugs and pull their legs and wings off. Slowly. Sadistically. Butterflies would be the worst,' she shivered, 'because they're so beautiful.

'John was like a moth, a beautiful night moth, and I was his flame. But I didn't want to burn him, to hurt him. Truly I didn't.'

She looked at me, looked as though she wanted me to believe her, and I did.

'We had an affair. I even came to love him in my way, but still that's all it was, an affair. He couldn't understand that. He wanted to marry me, to live happily ever after. Like in a fairy tale,' she said incredulously. I nodded. It sounded like Johnny.

'I didn't even want to be seen publicly with him that much. I have a position, a standing in the community, and I didn't care to compromise that. He was twenty-two and just a student. He couldn't understand that either.'

No. He couldn't have. Johnny was black-and-white and fierce in his loyalties. Things were all or nothing for him.

'And I'm an artist, off an edge. I couldn't marry a plain down-to-earth vet.' There was horror in her voice. 'And that was the most important thing he couldn't understand. Instead he just tried to make everything into a story with a fairy tale ending. Life isn't that way.'

No. And John's ending had been far from fairy tale.

'So that's it.' She drank her tea and picked at her carrot cake.

'Bella, where were you on the night that John died?'

She stared at me. 'Oh, *please*.' She looked disgusted. 'Get real, for godssake.'

'It's just routine.' I winced inside at the cliché. 'Where were you?'

She sighed and rested her hand in her chin. 'At home,' she said at last.

'Alone?'

'No.' She flushed. 'I, uh, Stan was there. He just dropped by. If he'd called I would have told him no, but he didn't. He came by and I couldn't resist, couldn't send him away. You see?' she said miserably. 'You see how it is?'

I nodded but I didn't see. And I thought she was weak. I didn't say so; I tried not to let it show in my eyes.

'What time did he come over?'

'Ten.' She flushed again.

Ten o'clock on a Saturday night and Stan hadn't gotten laid yet so he came by for a sure thing. Maybe Bella needed a gun after all. She needed something.

'You were together all night?'

'No. He left about one-thirty. I remember because we were watching a movie. He wanted to see the end. Then he left to catch last call at some place.'

'A bar, you mean?'

'Yes.'

'Which one?'

'I don't know.'

'You didn't want to go?'

'I wasn't invited.'

Last call, last chance. Muscles and a Porsche – it was within the realm of possibility that Stan could score again.

'What movie?'

'Huh?'

'What movie did you watch that night?'

'I, uh, I don't remember. It was an old one.'

'Who was in it?'

'I don't remember.'

'How old?'

'I don't know.'

'What was it about?'

She stared belligerently at me. 'Fuck off. I don't remember. I don't care. And that's that.'

'All right.' I paused. 'Who would want to kill John, Bella?'

'I don't know.' Her face softened.

'Like you said, he was a good person, kind, loving, caring. Who would want to kill him? And why?'

'I don't know. I really don't. I would tell you if I had a clue. He's the kind of person who should live. Why? I don't know that either. If it had been Stan—' she broke off and shrugged. 'Well, I could have understood that.'

'How jealous, possessive, and violent is Stan?'

'No,' she said. 'It wasn't like that. 'Don't start with it. Don't. Anyway, it was over between us. He knew that.'

'Did he? He came back. You let him in. That's what you call "over"?'

'That was just – it didn't *really* count. He knew, I knew – it was over.' Okay, it was over. They understood it and the fact that I couldn't was my problem, my limitation.

'How jealous, possessive, and violent is Stan?'

'Stop it! I told you, I *told* you. Now leave it alone. I *mean* it. I want to go, let's get out of here.'

I picked up the check, paid it at the front desk. Then we walked back to the gallery. The silence was heavy.

'Don't come in,' she said when we got there. 'I don't want you to.'

'All right.'

'May I have my gun back?'

I gave her the gun but I kept the bullets. She didn't thank me. I didn't thank her either.

There didn't seem to be a lot to be thankful for.

Thirty-Three

I went to the office, not home. There were a few things, still, that I needed to take care of. Then I called Michaela at Charity's ranch. Not being in much of a mood to speak with her, I dispensed with the preliminaries.

'Have you ever received anything in writing from your father, the cotrustee, a lawyer, anybody, with regard to your inheritance?'

'No.' She sounded about as thrilled to be talking to me as I was to her.

'Nothing?'

'No.'

'Ever?'

'No.'

'Do you know the name of the cotrustee?'

'Everett.'

'First or last name?'

'Last. Dave Everett.'

It rang a bell. I couldn't tell which one or why. 'What bank?'

'Harding Savings and Loan.'

'How did you find that out?'

'Johnny mentioned it. Also I asked my—' She broke off. 'I asked Walter.'

'Have you met Everett, or heard from him, or one of his representatives?'

'No. What are you getting at, Katy?'

'Nothing. It's routine.'

'So, when do I get my money?'

'I don't know, I'm working on it.'

I said good-bye before she could get started and hung up. My next call was to Henley. We skipped the preliminaries too. Cops are good at that.

'What do you know about Benson and Everett?'

'Who the hell is Everett?'

'The cotrustee.'

'What do you mean, what do I know?'

'Could we start with the night Johnny was killed?'

'Benson checked out okay for that night. His fiancée was with him and vouched for it.'

'They were together all night?' I was surprised. In this day, when everyone did it, they didn't seem the type.

'They were on a camping trip with others in their church. There was a men's cabin, a women's cabin, and a children's cabin.' He rustled papers. 'Just short of twenty people vouch for him.' That covered it all right.

'What about Everett?'

'What about him?' Henley asked it in the tone that, roughly translated, means: Who gives a shit? Although that might have been a little too polite for his tone.

'What was he doing?'

'The officer that spoke with him, Kat,' he said in a patient, almost condescending tone, 'interviewed him with regard to the disposition of financial matters. He is a bank manager and a cotrustee. He does not stand to gain in any way from the death of any party involved. For his services he is paid a nominal sum to execute

260

the provisions of,' another pause, more paper shuffling, 'the late Sophia Budroe Benson's will.'

'And the financial accounting. Did you go over it thoroughly?'

He sighed. 'We went over it enough to see it was on the up and up. We didn't do a fine points accounting or a financial analysis, but we didn't miss anything big either. What tree you barking up?' His tone implied that, whatever it was, it was the wrong one.

'Just checking.'

'Yeah. That it? I'm busy.'

I let him go. Something was still nagging at me and I couldn't figure out what, or why. I dropped it and went back to work on a case I had outstanding. I didn't get it for another two hours. Even then it didn't hit me, it just trickled in.

Everett. It was a familiar name.

I kept working on the other case but in the back of my mind I played with it, bounced it around, looked at it from different angles and tried to come up with the connection. When I finally did it was no big deal, but it was something. I looked through my files, found what I wanted then reached for the phone. Ted Kramer owed me a favor.

'Kramer Construction.'

'Ted, it's Kat.'

'Hey, how are you?'

'Curious.'

He laughed. 'Yeah, what's new? Not that.'

'Remember the deal you were trying to put together about six months ago and asked me to look into? You needed a financial backer and/or partner and were considering working with a guy named Dave Everett.'

'I remember.'

'Did you?'

'No.'

'How come?'

'Partly it was the stuff you turned up. You remember the details now? I don't.'

'He skated pretty close to a Chapter Eleven a few years ago. Apparently the only thing that saved him was a last-minute undercover bail-out. Since then, nothing. His bank, as I remember, was involved with a lot higher proportion of questionable deals than most banks are. Most banks, not necessarily savings and loans. No solid black marks, but a lot of gray area.'

'Yeah. I don't go for that. Like I said, it was partly that and also that I had other options. I found someone else and the deal went through fine. I did okay.'

'What's the scuttlebutt on Everett? Is he working with any other contractor or developer?'

'Not that I heard.'

'Would you have?'

'Hard to say. Not necessarily, but likely. I'll ask around, let you know.'

'Thanks, Ted.'

'You bet.'

Now that I was wondering about Everett I might as well wonder about Walter too. I'd run a quick check on him a few days ago and hadn't come up with anything unexpected. He was well respected in both his business and personal affairs, had a loyal group of clients, worked hard for them, and made them, and himself, money. His personal life seemed to be above reproach, his fiancée the only woman his name had been seriously associated with in years. Both were active in church affairs.

Most people would have had enough there to drop it. Most people have that much sense.

I picked up the phone again. This time I didn't have to look up the number, Judy is one of my favorite people. We hardly ever see each other but we go back to where you can count on. She caught the phone on the first ring, dropped it, and then said hello in a terse, tight tone.

'Hey, hot dog.'

'Kat! What's up?'

'I can't believe I caught you.' Sometimes it takes days talking to her answering machine to catch up with Judy.

'Me either.'

'Still working eighty-hour weeks?'

'Yeah.' Judy's a minor genius as a financial consultant and, while I've never figured out what that is precisely, she works long hours and makes the big bucks.

'Can I dump some more on you?'

'Dump away,' she said cheerfully.

'Walter Benson is a stockbroker in Marysville. I want everything you can dig up: business, personal, rumor – ugly or benign. Everything.'

'You got it.'

'Thanks.'

'Priority?'

'Yes.'

'Time frame?'

'Yesterday.'

She laughed. 'Same old Kat.'

'Mmmmm.'

'I'll get back to you.'

'I owe you. Lunch? Dinner?' We both laughed. Except for power lunches it had been two years since anyone had seen Judy slow up enough to sit down to eat.

It was a day before she got back to me but it was worth it. She found me at home; it was late.

'He's a Boy Scout, Kat.'

'Oh.'

She laughed at my disappointment. 'Honest, loyal, and true. Helps little old ladies across streets, buys Girl Scout cookies, gives to charity. Hey, he's got a long list of virtues. He's also probably boring as shit, but then you can't have everything.'

'Mmmmm. Thanks, Jude.'

She laughed at the obvious disappointment in my voice. 'That was then.' Ha. I held my breath and started to feel more cheerful. 'And then there's now.' My breath came out in a whoosh. She laughed again.

'Dirt?'

'I wouldn't go that far.'

'But something.'

'Definitely.'

'Spill it.' I walked myself and the phone into the kitchen and poured a glass of wine. Might as well celebrate and toast the possibilities.

'He's still a good boy on the outside but recently questions, like little bubbles, have been surfacing and popping.' I frowned and jammed the cork back into the wine bottle.

'Nice image, Jude. What does it mean?'

'I'm not sure. I don't have enough information and the relevant information may not even be available. However, lately his name has been coupled with one or two questionable financial transactions. That never used to happen.'

'Questionable how?'

'He's on the right side of the law, no problem, but apparently he talks with, and the presumption is, deals with, people who aren't always so scrupulous. Word was around for a while that he was involved in a pyramid investment.'

I whistled.

'Yeah. Well, that rumor died pretty much but it left suspicions. And a bad taste in some folks' mouths. A pyramid investment is a big jump off the straight and narrow for Mr. Clean.'

I whistled again. 'Anything else?'

'There was talk for a while that he, along with a couple of developers, were trying to gobble up some land cheap. The land was zoned agricultural but apparently they had – had bought, most likely – guarantees that it would be rezoned into residential. As far as I know nothing came of that either.'

'How much capital outlay are we talking here?'

'Hard to say. Some of these deals are made on surprisingly little cash. He'd need something though, for sure. Actually,' she paused for a moment, 'although he does well enough in his business, I wouldn't have thought he had the kind of money you need to play with the big boys.'

'Or the guts.'

'Hmmm. Hard to call, that one. Sometimes these quiet little mousy guys are surprisingly aggressive. You can't tell, you don't know.'

That's true. About money, about murder. The Can't-Tell-Don't-Know List is a long one.

'Good work, Jude. And thanks.'

'My pleasure. When are you going to give me some

money to play with? I'll get you into the big time.'

'You and the lottery.'

'Stick with me, I'm a sure thing.'

She was right, I knew. 'The problem is finding the money. Some days I look for quarters in the bottom of my purse.' She laughed. 'Lunch?'

'Sure.'

'Call me.' We were just about to hang up. 'Hey, Judy.'

'Yes.'

'How difficult is it to keep two sets of books?'

'Piece of cake.'

'Is it tough to spot?'

'A good job would take some unraveling, yes, but you can always do it. It just takes time. Time and the right check. There are accountants and firms that specialize in that sort of thing, but basically anytime you give anyone access to all the information they can figure it out. The fraudulent system breaks down when you ask for verification to support the bogus figures, because there is no verification.

'Actually the small-time scam doesn't generally get caught there. More likely they overreach and then face a cash-flow problem that brings the whole house of cards tumbling down.' I digested that one. 'Is this connected with our erstwhile Boy Scout?' she asked.

'I wonder. He and a banker with less than a spotless record are cotrustees of a sizable trust fund.'

'How sizable?'

'I'm not sure. In the neighbourhood of a couple hundred thousand.' She whistled. 'Maybe more.'

'That could be tempting, even to a Boy Scout. It's tough for some people to keep their hands out of the candy.'

'Especially someone else's.'

'Especially that,' she agreed. 'Let me know what you turn up, Kat. I'm curious now.'

I promised. I thought it would be an easy promise to keep.

I don't always call them right.

Thirty-Four

I wrestled with my conscience for a while. In retrospect it was clear that it was not long enough, not hard enough. So it goes. In retrospect everything is clear; that's why old folks are wise.

After my conversation with Judy I'd started adding things up: the money, Walter's delaying tactics, Everett's financial history, Walter's wheeling and dealing, the Saturday night wedding rehearsal dinner.

So it happened that Saturday night at seven-thirty I was parked outside of Walter's office in Marysville. I never was one to double-check my addition. I had my tools with me. I never was one to overload on common sense.

Even so, I hate it when I talk myself into committing a felony, which is what burglary is. I had enough on Walter, I hoped, to be safe. Mainly I didn't plan to get caught; I figured everyone was at the rehearsal dinner. Planning is everything.

Walter's office is on a quiet street not far from the center of town in a once charming little house that had been tarted up and converted to an office building he shared with a lawyer and an insurance broker. Nice company he kept. The front lawn and porch were

brightly lit but the back was dark, as was the street. I
parked in an especially dark patch half a block down
and walked quickly back, slipping around the side to
the back of the house and avoiding the well-lit area.

Four steps led up to the back door and what had
once, I was fairly sure, been the kitchen. Two locks
greeted me, one of them a dead bolt, the other a simple
latch. The dead bolt wasn't thrown and the latch the
kind you could pop with a credit card. I didn't see any
sign of an alarm system. People are too trusting. Thirty
seconds and I was in the house; a few seconds more
brought me to Walter's office.

The office was a corner room with windows on two
sides. There were venetian blinds and curtains. The
blinds were down but not closed. I closed them and the
curtains both, then played my pencil flashlight around
the room. The filing cabinet was the logical place to
start. I headed for the B's. Bingo. Sophia Budroe
Benson was a section, not a file. I skipped over Will
and went for Trust Fund and Investments, pulled them
both, first upending a file to hold my place. I opened
them on the floor in the well of Walter's desk. The light
was contained there, which made it easier to read and
harder to see from the outside.

Nothing was out of line. It was simple, straight-
forward, and aboveboard. No shocks, no surprises, no
nothing. Undoubtedly this was what the police had seen.
I put them back and started working my way through
the rest. And thinking. Walter was not an imaginative
man. What kind of a name or code would he use?

A phone rang in the other room, its tone shrill and
insistent. Startled, I almost slammed the drawer on my
fingers. I stood for a moment, frozen in place, adrenaline

pumping through my body making me flushed, nervy, and wary.

'Damn, damn, damn,' I swore softly and unimaginatively. 'Damn, damn, *goddamn*.' A change in pace.

Why would there be calls coming in at almost eight on a Saturday evening? Did the lawyer or insurance broker keep evening hours on a Saturday? After eight rings it stopped. A wrong number? Had someone seen the light, seen me enter, reported me? The phone started again, then broke off abruptly. Was I okay or busted?

I waited, suspended in time and adrenaline, for five minutes. Nothing. I put my hope on a wrong number. Quickly I finished with the files, then started on Walter's desk. With the exception of a mail order catalogue with men's golfing clothes there was nothing unexpected. I thought Walter would look good in lime green. Definitely different.

The computer was last chance/last hope. I flipped it on, cursed the dull amber light, turned my flashlight off. It took forever to boot up. I jumped into List Files right away. It was a long list, a lot of files. I scrolled through them quickly and, when nothing caught my eye, went back to the beginning and started over.

I tried not to think about the phone or how long I'd been here. I tried not to think about doing a stretch for burglary. How long would it be, I wondered. If you could kill a man and be out in seven or eight years surely it couldn't be longer than that? Five years, six at most, I told myself, but I didn't feel cheered. Would Hank wait for me?

I made a mental note on several files that looked promising and started pulling them up. Nothing.

Nothing. Nothing. Back to List Files. Outside a car door slammed. Noise carries faster and is louder in darkness and fear but it was still too close. Voices now.

I started to exit the computer. Footsteps on the wooden stairs. The computer was taking forever. A key in the lock. I hit the Off button and slid into the boot of Walter's desk, pulling the chair in a bit as the light flashed on in the hall.

'Oooo, this is nice. Which one is yours?'

'Over here.' The door slammed.

'Say, you do all right for yourself, don't you?' He laughed. 'You lawyers. You got money when the rest of us is stone broke.'

I groaned inside. A horny lawyer and a bimbo. What luck, what timing. Above me something hummed. Hummed?

'I want to look around. Can I?'

'Sure.'

Hummed? The computer? Dear God, hadn't I hit the Off button hard enough? I started to inch out. Her voice got closer. I froze. The light clicked on.

'Oh, this is nice too.'

Hank wouldn't wait for me. Five years was too long. He'd visit me for a year or two, then get tired of it, find someone else. Maybe he'd write postcards for a few years after that but . . .

Damn. I loosened my jacket so I could reach my .380 if I had to. Prison food was probably terrible too.

'It's almost nicer than your office.' Her voice was close, too close.

'No. It doesn't have a couch.'

She giggled.

'Come and get your drink.' The light snapped off,

the footsteps high-heeled click-clicked down the hall. I started breathing again, slid out quickly, hit the Off button on the computer and waited for my brain to stop atrophying and start working.

Could I leave without being heard or seen? Should I sit it out? I hadn't found what I'd come for yet.

'Where's the bathroom?' the bimbo asked, and footsteps pattered in the hall. That answered my first question. I slid under the desk and stopped breathing again.

'Charlie! You devil. Black underwear, who would have thought it?' She giggled and I sighed. On top of everything else I was going to have to listen to this.

'C'mere, you.' Hmmm. That was sweet, touching, and romantic. Charlie had a way with words all right.

'Mmmmm.' Bimbo began murmuring and cooing. Charlie apparently had a way with something other than words. In my mind I started scrolling through the files again, looking, wondering. Still nothing. The murmuring turned into moans. I stuck my fingers in my ears.

Of course the file didn't have to be here, it could be at Walter's house. My heart sank. I considered the possibility dispassionately. No, probably not, everything seemed to be here. I'd noticed Walter's income tax file, for instance.

There was some screaming in the background. I jammed my fingers in harder until my ears hurt. There was something about illicit love. You probably had to scream to feel you were geting full value. The screams died down to moans and then drifted off. Tentatively I took my fingers out of my ears. Low murmuring, that was safe enough. Something was nagging, niggling at me.

What? It stayed on the edge of my consciousness and

kicked the curb, scuffed its shoes, and thumbed its nose at me. The harder I tried to grab it, the more it thumbed and eluded me. I started scrolling through the files again. I didn't think it was there. The files in the cabinet? But that had seemed less promising than the computer stuff.

The murmuring got louder. Bimbo giggled. 'Well, hey, aren't you something.' *Shit*, were they starting up again? 'Oooo, do that some more.' She really started squealing. Charlie could follow directions all right. I sighed and stuck my fingers back in my ears, then mentally looked around Walter's study: desk, chairs, side table, filing cabinet, large bookcase with professional books and software storage area.

That was it. I almost whooped. I took my fingers out of my ears and leaned out to look at the bookcase.

'Oooo, oooo, oooo.' It sounded like an air raid siren in the background. I stuck my fingers back in my ears. In Walter's desk I'd seen a floppy disc, unmarked, unlabeled. It was the only out-of-place thing in the otherwise pristine, meticulous, and ordered office. My bets were on it; I took my money out and plunked it down. Then I took my fingers out of my ears. Silence. Thank goodness.

Get up, I willed them. Get dressed. Go away.

'Have you ever done it on that big desk in there?' Bimbo asked. I blanched. *What* big desk? *This* one? My blood ran cold, then gave up and stopped running. I shifted so I could feel the comforting bulge of the .380 in the small of my back.

'No. Do you want to?'

Are you crazy? I shouted at them in my mind. It's Saturday night, party night. Go out and have fun, save some for tomorrow. Pace yourself!

'Sure.'

He laughed. 'It would drive Walter crazy if he knew.'

Oh God, it was *this* desk.

She giggled. 'A fuddy-duddy, huh?'

No. I spoke up for Walter. Let's have a little respect here, for a man's desk, his office.

'You hungry? Let's go get some dinner.'

Yes. Good idea, I agreed with Charlie. You're probably starving, all that exercise. And you need to keep your strength up. Protein, carbohydrates, go for it. Jump into those devilish little black shorts, those clickety-click heels—

'Mmmmm,' she murmured. Shameless hussy.

'C'mon, baby, let's get up.'

'Oh, all right.'

I sighed with relief. Hurry, I urged them on, move it, shake a leg. There were bathroom sounds, clothes rustling sounds, finally the lights went off and the door clicked and latched. I sat there, limp, exhausted, soaked with sweat. I felt like they'd been there for hours. I looked at my watch: eight-thirty. Forty minutes. Time crawls when you're sweating bullets.

I clambered out from under the desk and stretched. I found the floppy without turning the light on, then flipped on the computer, waited for it to boot up, slid the floppy in and scanned. It was all there. And the software was compatible with what I had. Bull's-eye.

In the floppy disc storage I found an unused disc. I hoped it was formatted and ready to go. The prompt blinked invitingly. The monitor announced it was ready to go when I was: press any key. I was ready. I pressed a key. I made a copy. Then I was ready to get the hell out of there. I exited the computer, replaced the floppy in Walter's desk, straightened the desk chair and looked around. I wanted to leave the office exactly as I found it.

I was almost to the back door before I remembered. Damn. I was getting sloppy. Back in Walter's office I opened the curtains and adjusted the blinds. That would have been a certain giveaway first thing tomorrow, a dark, closed office in the morning light. I looked around again, satisfied, and then left.

The Bronco waited serenely where I had parked it and fired right up. Time to get out of there. I was hungry but I didn't want to stop, not in Marysville. I drank the rest of a Pepsi that I'd started earlier. It was flat and tepid. I didn't care. As I drove I peeled the surgical gloves off my hands and tossed them into the glove compartment along with the break-in tools I hadn't needed to use.

I was high. On the radio the Beach Boys sang about how they got around. I was sure I had Walter, coming, going, and sitting duck. This floppy was the second set, the real set, of books on the investments made with Sophie's money. James Brown shouted that he felt good. Me too. I thought about stopping in Citrus Heights for a pizza. I was starving but I didn't, I wanted to get home to my computer and Walter's floppy disc.

Ranger was glad to see me although he would have been a lot happier with pizza. Too bad. Besides, he won't eat green peppers even though I've pointed out their enviable vitamin/mineral content.

I headed for my study and the computer, shedding my jacket on the way. I flipped the computer on and put the .380 on my desk, the floppy in the computer. It *was* all there. Walter had siphoned off most of the money into what I was sure would turn out to be an insider trading deal. There was no other way I knew of to realize the kind of profit I was looking at. I'd call Judy tomorrow. Between us we'd nail that one down.

It looked like there was something in the neighborhood of a hundred and seventy-five thousand. That was what Michaela and Johnny knew about and, God knows, that was a nice chunk of change. But that was just the beginning.

Sophie had inherited forty acres of what was then part of her father's walnut orchard. It hadn't been worth a whole lot then. Now? With the possible exception of Barstow, real estate in California is money, big money. And that area has some of the best agricultural land in the country. A lot of it is already developed; a lot more is going to be. Using the land as collateral Walter had raised another two hundred and fifty grand. He was playing with the big boys, running with the big dogs. So it was big bucks, big time.

Big enough to take risks for. Big enough to kill for.

At my feet Ranger started growling, then furiously barking. Someone banged on the door. I stuck the .380 in my waistband and stood up.

Thirty-Five

The pounding continued. A few thumps, too, as though someone was kicking the door.

'Hey, wake up, Kat. Are you there? It's me, Lindy. Kat? Hey, Kat!'

I opened the door in the middle of the final hey. She grinned at me.

'Hi.'

Her grin faded as she saw the gun stuck in my jeans. Her eyes went wide in the way a little kid's eyes do: frightened, innocent, and intrigued at the same time. It reminded me that she was still a child, sort of.

'Lindy,' I turned and looked at the clock. 'It's almost nine thirty and a bit late for visiting. How did you get here?'

'I hitched.' I frowned. 'Hey, no "Hi, how are you?," no "Hey, what's doing?" '

'Lindy.' I said it firmly.

'Kat.' She looked at me and smiled. 'No hi?'

'Hi.'

Her smiled widened. 'I missed you.' I stared at her. Sure she did. 'Well, sort of. Charity and I had another fight and I figured you'd be better.'

I sighed, not knowing whether to lecture her on

running away from problems instead of meeting them, or just be glad she'd come to me instead of hitting the streets again. I was tired, my brain was still spinning with Walter's financial artistry, my reaction time was slow.

'Do you always wear a gun just hanging out around the house?' She reached out to touch it and I stepped back.

'Aren't you going to ask me in?' I nodded and she came in. 'Hi, Ranger.'

Ranger wagged. I shut the door behind her, turned the dead bolt and watched Lindy and Ranger playing tag around the front room. They subsided finally into a heap of giggles and wags on the rug. I still hadn't decided what to do.

'Kat, do you think I could have a snack?'

'Sure. I don't know what there is but help yourself.'

'Are you busy?' I nodded. 'Go ahead. I can manage.'

I went back and sat in front of the computer, listened to cupboard doors banging and drawers rattling and tried to concentrate.

'I'm going to make tuna fish sandwiches,' she hollered. 'Do you want one?'

'No, thanks.'

'Did you eat dinner?'

I thought about it. After that night in Walter's office dinner seemed so far away. 'No,' I said at last.

'I'll make you one.' I shrugged and tried again to concentrate.

'Do you want to eat in here or in there?'

I gave up, got up, and walked into the kitchen. The sandwiches looked really good, for tuna fish.

'You're still wearing your gun, Kat.'

Lindy wiped a glob of mayonnaise off her chin. I just stopped myself in time from telling her not to talk with her mouth full.

'It's been that kind of a week, Lindy.'

'What kind?'

'The kind where you want to wear your gun.'

That brought us full circle. She looked at me and dropped it.

'Is there anything for dessert?'

'Apples.'

'Ugh.' She started rummaging through the cupboards. 'Hey, I found some cookies.'

'Go for it.'

I couldn't remember buying them, which meant they were months old. What the heck, they were undoubtedly packed with preservatives.

'Ugh, they're Fig Newtons.'

'Good for you.'

She tossed them down in disgust, then went back and ripped open the package. 'Oh well, better than nothing.'

'Lindy, I don't mean to be rude but right now it's awkward having you around here, I'm going to take you over to Alma's.'

'Why?'

'I just told you.'

She stared at me. 'That's not really it.'

'It is, yes.'

'No, you're mad. I know you are. I fucked up and now you're sending me away. I can never, *never* do *anything* right. Don't send me away, Kat. Please. *Please!* Give me another chance.' She was on the edge of tears. I felt like a jerk.

'Listen to me!' I yelled and then sighed. Teenagers.

What a situation. What timing. 'Lindy, I'm not sending you away and I'm not mad. It's just for tonight. Okay? Trust me?' I put my arm around her shoulder and gave her a squeeze. 'Okay?'

'Are you sure?'

'I'm sure.'

'Really?'

'Really.'

'Okay, I guess.'

'Great.' I didn't want to give her time to think about it. 'Grab your jacket and scoot out the back door. The car's in the driveway.'

For once she did what she was told without a lot of lip. I found my keys, stuck the gun under my jacket and called the dog. We left, latching the door behind us.

'Kat?'

'Hmmm?'

'Can Ranger come?'

'Sure.' I whistled. We all climbed into the Bronco.

'Something's wrong, isn't it?'

'Hmmm?'

'Kat!' Lindy sounded annoyed. 'You're not paying attention. Something's wrong, I know it is. You don't usually wear a gun, do you?'

'No.'

'Can I help?'

'No. Thanks,' I added. 'Things are a little messed up right now but they'll straighten out in a day or two.'

'But, Kat, I *want* to help.' She sounded surprised at herself. I was a little surprised too.

I made myself relax, look at her, smile. 'Thanks, kid, but not this time. Not right now.'

She looked at me, puzzled. 'Friends help, that's what you told me.'

I nodded. 'But not with this, not right now.'

I tuned out then, listened to the sound of the tires on the freeway and tried vainly to sort things out in my mind. Vaguely I heard Lindy talking to Ranger and the thump of the dog's tail, soothing sounds. Since I hadn't called Alma I ran up with Lindy to say hello. I didn't linger.

'Lindy, do you want Ranger to stay here?'

Her eyes brightened. Then she shook her head. 'No. He better go with you.' I nodded, too tired to discuss it. The trip home was fast. It was late. I was speeding. Ranger was nervous and jumpy. It was a relief to get home; all I wanted to do was go to bed.

In the driveway Ranger started whining and fussing. He wouldn't go for his evening run around the yard but kept circling me, tripping me up, until finally I snapped crossly at him. He started growling as we walked in the house and I flipped on the lights. Walter stood there smiling at me. Other things have pleased me more, a lot more. I found it difficult to smile back so I didn't.

'Eleven's a little late for a social call, isn't it?'

'It's not a social call.'

'How did you get in?'

'The bedroom window. You just reach through the hole in the screen, unlatch it, and push it up.'

Damn! Hank was going to be pissed. I promised him I'd fix it first thing.

'Let's go in the kitchen. I need some coffee.'

Walter looked hesitant but he followed me. Ranger too. He was still growling. I made coffee.

'You haven't been playing fair, Katy.' His voice had a cold, ugly note to it. Too bad. It takes a lot more than that to scare me. I poured two coffees.

'You should have. You really should have.' Walter

pulled out a gun and pointed it at me. His hand was almost steady. That did it; that scared me. I decided not to show it.

'Oh?'

'Yes.'

I threw a mug of coffee in his face. He screamed in a high shrill way, like an old woman. Maybe scalding coffee does that to you. The gun clattered to the floor and his hands clawed at his face and eyes. I kicked his right kneecap; it was a well-timed and lethal kick. He went down, still screaming. In the background Ranger started barking hysterically. I leaned over to pick up Walter's gun.

'Leave it there.'

The gun was still within reach. I turned slightly. *Shit!* This was the third time in a week I'd looked down a gun barrel. It was not the kind of activity I wanted to turn into a habit. I straightened up.

'Call your dog off.' I didn't. 'You take care of it or I will.' He waved his gun. I took care of it. Ranger stood by me, quiet and alert, quivering and only occasionally growling.

'I should have known you couldn't handle this on your own, Walter.' He kicked him in the butt. 'Get up, pull yourself together.'

Walter stood, then went to the sink to wash his face. He was limping and pink, nothing too serious.

'Dave Everett?' I asked.

'The same.'

'You guys always make social calls with guns?'

'This is not a social call.'

'What is it?' It was a little late in the game to play stupid but I tried it anyway.

'We figured you to be on to us,' Everett said.

'Coffee, anyone?' I asked and started for the stove.

'Stay away from there,' Walter squeaked. Big deal. Everett backed him up with the gun. Okay, I stayed away. Later for coffee.

'On to what?' I asked. I remembered then that my computer was on. I could live with the Pacific Gas and Electric bill; it was going to be harder to explain Walter's records on the screen. In fact, I was beginning to think that this was going to be an all-around tough situation to talk myself out of.

'Can it. We know you were at the office tonight.'

'I was here all evening with Lindy.'

Everett shook his head. 'It won't work.'

Still, he looked a little shaken. Not that it mattered; they'd already told me too much. And if I knew it, they sure as hell did.

'We played Trivial Pursuit. You're jumping to some odd conclusions.'

There was a moment of silence. Walter broke it.

'We figured it out, Katy. You see, I forgot and left my marriage license at the office. That's why I went back there tonight; I knew I had a lot to do in the morning.' Walter sounded kind of vague and disconnected. He kept rubbing his knee and touching his face gently.

'When I opened my desk drawer I noticed that one stack of things, the stack with the floppy disc with the records you were looking for, was a little out of place. Not much,' he said, complimenting me. 'Hardly anyone would have noticed it. Even I wouldn't have been sure if there hadn't been something else, if you hadn't turned the porch light off. It's always on, you see. Always. It's on a photoelectric cell.'

I groaned inside. The bimbo. I had more than one thing to thank her for now. First an evening's worth of entertainment and now a second feature.

'Stupid, Kat.'

'I guess, but it wasn't me.' So much for grammar. Everett picked up Walter's gun and handed it to him.

'Sit down,' he said to me. No 'please.' So much for manners.

'Can you manage her?'

'I can do it.' Everett stared at him and Walter looked flushed and pained. 'I can *do* it, I told you.'

'Okay, I'm going to snoop around.'

He headed for my study and I wondered how long I had to come up with something resourceful. I knew how long it would take for Everett to figure out what was on the computer screen.

'Well, well, well.' Everett came back to the kitchen. 'Check out the computer, Walter.'

'That's it,' Walter agreed when he returned, a little white-faced and shaken.

'On to what?' Everett mimicked me. 'We played Trivial Pursuit *all* evening.' He spit into the sink. 'Yeah, right.' He spit again. It was gross and disgusting; so was he. I had always thought bankers were more high-toned.

'I underestimated you guys,' I said. Everett snorted. 'That was a nice setup you had going there. Who did it?'

Walter preened as Everett jerked a thumb in his direction. I tried to imagine him in a three-piece suit running a bank. It was hard. Of course it was a savings and loan in Marysville. That made it easier. He left the room to snoop again.

'A nice little scam, Walter,' I said. Walter looked pained.

'It wasn't a scam at all. I had absolutely no intention of defrauding my children. None. In fact, they stood to gain handsomely from my speculative ventures.'

'Inside trading, I believe it's called.' He squirmed a bit at that. Walter seemed unenthusiastic about the truth-in-packaging concept. 'I bet they didn't stand to gain nearly as handsomely as you. And of course if you had lost, it would have been their loss, not yours. Always a comforting thought,' but he didn't look comforted.

'I wanted to buy a house for my wife.' Greed, such a character builder. 'She's used to the finer things. I wanted her to be happy. And the girls,' he added.

'So you bought their happiness with Johnny and Michaela's.'

'No,' he said patiently, 'of course not. I just borrowed their money for a while. Just borrowed. It's almost done now; it's almost back in legitimate accounts for them. And we all made a little something on it.'

'Johnny will never spend it.'

'Damn the boy!' Walter flushed, at the epithet, I imagine. 'Why did he have to be so headstrong? He wouldn't listen to reason; he wanted the money immediately on his birthday. I couldn't do it then, not without losing everything. *Everything*,' he emphasized. 'I never wanted to do it that way. He made me.'

'You killed Johnny, then planted drugs in his car to make it look drug related.'

'No, no, he had an accident.'

'That's not what they call stab wounds to the chest in my part of town.' I stretched and started to get up.

'No, no.' Walter waved the gun in my direction. I sat back down again.

'You tried to scare me off with the shots at my car, the threats, and the death of my cat.' I kept my voice level; it was an effort. 'Who did you get to threaten Alma? And Michaela? Was it Everett?' Walter gave no indication of having heard me.'

'And then Michaela wanted *her* money right away.' He shook his head sadly. 'I just needed a little time, then it was theirs. All they had to do was wait but they wouldn't. So impatient. Children should listen to their father.'

Walter didn't sound too tightly wrapped. What the hell. I didn't care about his life, his health, but I cared about mine; I played along. 'So you threatened her with anonymous phone calls to get her to leave town, and when that didn't work, tried to kill her. Only you got the stand-in singer instead.'

'I never wanted to handle things like this,' he said. 'It's so untidy, so distasteful.' I thought those adjectives were a little underweight for describing the murder and attempted murder of your children, but I kept quiet. 'I'm a conservative businessman,' he explained. Walter, the reluctant murderer. It almost broke my heart. Not quite.

My phone rang ten or eleven times. No one answered. Everett came back into the kitchen. The phone stopped at last.

'Told her everything, did you?' he asked harshly. 'I thought you had more sense than you do, Walter, a lot more, or I never would have gotten into this.' He slammed a clenched fist on the counter.

'C'mon, let's get the hell out of here. We've been here too long already. We need to take care of her and get moving.'

I needed more time, a lot more.
I had two cards left. I played one of them.

Thirty-Six

I leaned back in my chair and stretched, looking considerably more relaxed than I felt.

'Move it, bitch.' Bitch. I recognized the vocabulary and voice of the anonymous phone calls. 'Your time's up; your number's up.'

'Walter didn't tell you about the land, did he?'

'Move it.' Everett waved the gun. 'What land?' Walter started spluttering.

'Johnny and Michaela's mother inherited forty acres of her father's walnut orchards. You know what land is going for now. Walter raised a bundle on the land. You never heard about that, did you? You were never going to see the return on it, either. That was Walter's bonus.'

There was a long, ugly silence and then Everett turned to Walter. 'Is it true?'

'No,' Walter said.

'I've got proof in the other room.'

'Well, yes and no,' Walter temporized. 'I wasn't sure I could pull it off, so I didn't want to mention it.'

'It was going to be a surprise,' I explained helpfully, 'only he's lying. He was sure; he pulled it off. The proof's in the other room.'

'You sneaky little son of a bitch,' Everett said. I

nodded. That pretty much squared with my estimation of Walter. 'Holding out on me. Fifty-fifty you said. Together all the way, you said. I got involved with murder, put my position at the bank and in the community at risk so some little, fucking, slimy weasel—' He broke off and shook his head.

'I'll make it up to you,' Walter said. There was a pleading note in his voice.

'Damn right you will, and then some. I ought to let you have it right now.' He advanced on Walter, who blanched but stood his ground. 'So you won't forget, so you'll remember exactly who your partner is. I ought to, I ought to, yeah.'

'Come on, Dave. We can talk this out.'

'Talk. Ha.'

He snorted and then raised his hand and slapped Walter open-handed and full in the face. On top of the coffee burn it must have hurt like hell. Walter screamed in his high, shrill way, went reeling back, fell over a kitchen chair, and slid along the counter knocking over the glass jars that were my canisters.

There was rice, pasta, beans, and glass everywhere. He lay there on the floor, in foodstuffs and glass, as Everett kicked him in the chest, shoulders, and gut. Walter had his face protected and was crying and snuffling. It was not a reaction calculated to bring out the best in a bully like Everett. And it didn't.

'Sneaky little son of a bitch.' Everett kicked viciously. 'I ought to bust you three ways before Christmas.'

Walter, understandably, didn't jump right on the idea. He lay and moaned. And whimpered. Ranger fidgeted uneasily at my side. Everett stepped back, crunching on wide egg noodles and large shells. His back was to me.

It was time to play my other card.

'Hold it right there, Everett. I've got a gun.'

I silently thanked all the grade B movies I'd ever watched for that bit of dialogue. He froze, unsure but unwilling to risk it.

'Walter?' he croaked. Walter patted his face gently, winced, looked up from the floor at me, then at Everett, and nodded.

'Yes, she does.'

There was a note of satisfaction in his voice, as though he'd switched sides and was rooting for me. I didn't bank on it.

'Move very slowly or I shoot.' Another acknowledgement to B-grade dialogue. 'Lower your hands to your sides, drop the gun, slide it back with your foot. Don't turn around.'

'I'll shoot you, too, Walter, if you move,' I added pleasantly. Walter froze, started to pat his face again and stopped himself. Everett did as he was told. I reached down and picked up the .45. It was too much gun for him. Too much for anyone. I stuck it in my waistband and sighed with relief.

And that was a miscalculation; it wasn't over yet.

Behind me the back door scraped and opened. A cold gust of air blew in the room and bounced kittenishly around. I shivered.

'Oh, my God,' a voice whispered. 'Kat, it's me, Lindy. I'm here, I came back.'

Damn. Damn. Damn!

'I borrowed Alma's car (read: took without permission, I thought bitterly) and came back to help you. I thought you might need me.' She said it bravely, her voice getting stronger.

'I couldn't keep running away. You got me off the street and told me it was time for me to stop running, to face my problems, to deal with them. So I did,' she said simply. 'Even though I was scared I came back to help you because you helped me. I wanted to be your friend like you've been mine.'

I groaned. Everett laughed.

'Kat, did I do something wrong?' Her voice was hurt, vulnerable.

I groaned again, I couldn't help it.

'Kat?'

'No, Lindy, but now what I need most is for you to call the police. Leave the way you came in. Go to the neighbor's. Call nine-one-one. Tell them what you've seen. Don't come back here, I don't want you around these guys. Do you understand?'

'Yes.' Her voice was soft. She stood right behind me and I could feel her breath in my hair.

'Go.'

She hesitated and then the phone began to ring, clamoring, insistent, rude, commonsensical. It broke the tension and built it. We all stood, frozen like little children playing Mother May I?, waiting for someone to say the right words. Lindy broke first.

'Shall I get it?' Her breath played again in my hair and then moved.

'No!'

I took my eyes off Everett for a moment. It was a mistake, an easy one to make but stupid nonetheless.

His arm snaked out, fastened on Lindy, coiled her in; he pinned her arms against her side and held her. And grinned. The phone shrilled on for another seven or eight endless rings. The balance had shifted; we all knew it. The silence was heavy, broken now by Lindy's shallow, rapid breathing.

'Well, well, well,' Everett said at last. 'You've got the guns, I've got the girl. Wanna trade?' Lindy moaned. Her eyes started to roll up and Everett shook her harshly. 'Well?'

I nodded. 'The girl leaves first, then you get the guns.'

He laughed. 'I don't think so.' Lindy moaned again. 'Get up, Walter.'

'I wouldn't,' I said pleasantly.

'Do it.'

Everett's voice was harsh, commanding. Walter weighed his options and started to get up. The bullet went into the cupboard behind him. Damn. First my canisters, now my cupboards. After this I was going to be even less motivated to cook than I usually am.

'I shot to miss,' I said, still pleasantly. 'I won't bother with a warning next time.' Walter's red face went white and frozen. Lindy started crying, dime-size silent tears rolling down her cheeks. How did she do that?

'Let the girl go.'

'Fuck I will.' I looked at him and nodded slowly, reflectively. 'I could snap her neck in seconds,' he said. I nodded again.

'You could,' I agreed. Lindy's tears went from dime-size to quarter-size. 'But you won't.'

'Fuck I won't.'

'You're dead then.' I was low-voiced and agreeable. Lindy stared at me in astonishment.

'Kat!' She started to wail.

I shook my head. 'Shut up, Lindy.'

The wail broke off and the tears resumed. She looked

at me as though I were a cross between Lizzie Borden and Lucrezia Borgia.

'You won't risk the girl's life.'

'Just watch me.' I didn't look at Lindy. 'Without a gun we're both dead. You know it, I know it. Let's not bother with games.'

'I'd let the girl go.'

'No,' I said. 'You wouldn't.'

He laughed. 'Well, ain't you a firecracker?'

I didn't say anything.

'I guess it's a Mexican standoff then.'

'I can wait it out.' The phone started to ring. 'That's Alma. She's worried about the girl. When we don't answer this time she'll call the police.'

I said it with confidence and authority. Anyone who didn't know Alma might have believed me. I was hoping to God she didn't head out here with a cast-iron skillet in one hand and a fireplace poker in the other. The phone stopped ringing.

'And I've got an ace in the hole.' They all stared at me. 'The dog.'

Everett's grip on Lindy tightened. She gasped.

'I'm about to sic him on you, Dave.' Ranger growled and stiffened at my knee. Right on cue. Everett flexed his arms, Lindy still in them. 'You can try and use the girl but it won't work. Say something to Ranger, Lindy.'

'Hey, Ranger,' Lindy bleated out. Ranger wagged his tail and whined in a high, excited tone.

'She's a friend – he won't hurt her. Kiss those calves good-bye, Dave. Huh, Ranger?'

Ranger growled low in his throat; it was ugly and menacing. I smiled. The phone started ringing again. Lindy lunged forward and I yelled, 'Get 'em, Ranger.'

Everett fumbled it. He didn't know whether to hold onto Lindy, to protect himself from the dog, or to try to do both. A row of snarling, advancing dog teeth doesn't give you a lot of time to consider the possibilities. He flung Lindy into Ranger's path. She stumbled and then they both tangled up and rolled. Lindy half stood, half ricocheted off a wall.

The phone stopped ringing, knocked off the hook. The receiver hung limply, swinging, bouncing off the wall slightly. I couldn't hear the bounces over the dog snarls. Everett had a kitchen chair and was trying to hold off Ranger. It was, for the moment, working.

'Lindy, get out! Scram! Fly!' She nodded, white-faced, and, limping slightly, started out the back door.

'Fly!' I shrieked at her. Her body shuddered, almost convulsed, and she picked up the pace considerably, scrambling out the door and disappearing. Thank God. 'Call the police,' I yelled at her and at the phone. 'Nine-one-one!' The receiver swung listlessly back and forth.

'Call off your dog or he's dead.'

Everett was tired of playing a lion tamer. And he didn't have to anymore. He had a .25 automatic in one hand and the chair in the other. Shit! I should have checked him out; he was carrying two guns.

'Now!'

I did. Ranger retreated, snarling and growling, to my side. 'Let's go,' I said to the dog and started backing up.

'Hold it!'

Everett growled out the words. Then Ranger growled. He did it better than Dave, much more convincing. I shook my head and kept on moving. He waved his gun at me. I wasn't so reckless, I kept mine pointed at him and it was bigger. Not that it mattered much. A well placed shot from a .25 will do the job.

Ranger and I were still backing up; the dog was still growling. Walter started making noises, whining and climbing out of pasta and glass noises, sliding on bean noises. Ranger swung around and started growling at him too.

I think he did. I was watching Everett, not Ranger or Walter – Everett and the gun. We had too many fronts to cover, Ranger and I. We were overextended.

'Keep moving and I shoot.'

'Me too,' I said agreeably. 'Let's go, Ranger.' I was backing up faster now. It was all going to plan. Everett waved his gun; I kept mine pointed. Only amateurs wave their guns. I smiled grimly, then I fell over Ranger. Wrong plan. Only amateurs fall over their partners.

I held onto the gun but it didn't matter; Everett's foot was on my wrist. Ranger was right beside me, growling, snarling, doing his Hound of the Baskervilles routine and waiting for instructions.

'Get him out before I blow his head off!'

'Outside, Ranger,' I said firmly. I didn't want my dog blown away on top of me. His eyes, one blue, one brown, pleaded with me for permission to attack. 'Out!' He went.

Two down, one to go. Now I only had myself to worry about. I tried to feel cheerful about it but it was tough. Everett reached down and pulled the .45 out of my waistband. Bummer. I hated to see it go.

He tromped on my wrist hard enough to hurt like hell and make my fingers go limp. Then he laughed. Sadistic bastard. Everett seemed like the kind of guy to get a big kick out of things like that. At the office he probably buys Girl Scout cookies and gives to the

United Way. At home he tromps and laughs.

He wasn't getting my vote for Mr. Sensitivity. I was firm on it.

'Get up, Ms. PI.' He laughed again. I got up with what dignity, minimal, I could muster. The phone was beeping at us in the background. Walter limped over.

'We've got to get out of here, Dave.' He said it in a worried and fussy tone as though they were going to be late for a bank committee meeting. 'The cops . . . whoever was on the phone . . . we've got to get out of here.'

'Yeah, I know.'

'What about the girl? She can identify us.'

'Huh?' He was someplace else.

'The girl, she can—'

Everett waved it away. 'Forget it, forget her. She's just a runaway or a hooker. And who's going to believe the word of a hooker over a banker and a broker? Kids don't notice much anyway. She probably can't tell the cops anything. *If* she goes to the cops. Which she won't, she's a hooker.'

I kept my face blank. Walter didn't look convinced.

'Let's go. Shake a leg, Walter.' Everett handed him my .380. Walter recoiled.

'I don't want it.' He put his hands behind his back. I nodded approvingly. Good man to have on your side in a pinch. 'Cover her,' Everett snarled. Walter did, but reluctantly.

'Hold your hands out,' Everett growled at me, reaching into his pocket. I did it but without enthusiasm. When he snapped the cuffs on I felt even less enthusiastic. At least my hands were cuffed in front, not in back. In tight situations your perspective changes. A blessing is a blessing, however small, and you count it.

'Now what?' Walter's voice croaked.

'We dump her.'

'We?'

His voice stopped croaking and got high and funny. What did his fiancée see in him, I wondered. Maybe he was great in bed? I tried to imagine it but I couldn't. I didn't think it was my imagination that was flawed.

'We?' he whined again.

'Me.' Everett sounded disgusted. 'I do the dirty work so you can keep your pretty little white hands clean, right?' Walter nodded, even though it wasn't the way he would have phrased it, I could tell. 'And for this we split it fifty-fifty.'

'Right, Dave.' Walter sounded manly and hearty again.

'Right.' Dave looked disgusted. 'Just remember, Walter, you're in it up to your neck. Fifty-fifty.'

'Murder in the first degree,' I explained helpfully, 'two counts; attempted murder, two counts; embezzlement, manipulating bank records, insider trading,' I was ticking them off on the fingers of my handcuffed hands. 'I bet you can plea bargain the obscene phone calls, though. That ought to take a week or two off your time.'

'*Two* counts of murder?' Walter bleated.

'Johnny and the girl in Placerville, Michaela's stand-in. Last word I got she wasn't going to make it. Her boyfriend's a Hell's Angel and they've got friends in the slammer, lots of them. I bet they look you boys up, pay you a social call. That ought to be fun,' I said brightly.

Walter looked like a big kid with a red face who couldn't decide whether he was going to cry or puke.

'Three,' Everett said.

'Three what?' Walter bleated.

'Three counts of murder.' He nodded at me. 'Her too, and that's why we're not going to the slammer.'

Another conflict for Walter. He didn't know whether to be worried at how the numbers were adding up or relieved that he wasn't going to the slammer. Relief won.

For him, not me.

I was starting to sweat bullets.

And listen for rescue noises. Only there weren't any.

'What are you going to do with her?' That's Walter, the concerned one.

'Shoot her and dump her in the slough.'

Which slough, I wondered. There are dozens of them. On the other hand what did it matter, it was only a theoretical point of interest.

'Which slough?' Walter asked.

'Down around Grand Island, I know a place.'

It's pretty down there, I thought. In the summer it's a wonderful place to go boating. Hot, fun. Tonight it would be cold; the water would be even colder. I shivered. Not that I would notice for long, the bullet would take care of that.

I was slated to be a delta dump. Funny, it wasn't how I fancied going out.

'Here.' Walter held out my gun awkwardly to Everett. He shook his head.

'Take it with you. We'll dump it later, after she's taken care of.'

Dump the gun, dump the girl. I shivered again. Inside. I had too much pride to let them see.

'Get outa here, we're right after you.'

Everett waved his gun at me. I looked around at my kitchen. For the last time? I felt the tears in my eyes, hot, stinging. I made them go away. Everett snapped off the light and we filed out. I didn't consider running for it. The .25 was hard against my spine and it's tough to miss at that range.

'See you at the wedding tomorrow. I'll try to get to the church on time,' Everett said and laughed. Walter didn't.

Neither did I.

Thirty-Seven

Everett held a gun on me while Walter ran a couple of rounds of duct tape around me and the bucket seat of his Toyota truck. Simple but effective. I wasn't going anywhere.

'Sorry, Katy.' He looked at me and chewed his lip. 'I wish it didn't have to come to this. I really didn't want to –'

I stared at him in astonishment. Not compassion surely. Guilt, I guess.

'Is the money worth it, Walter? The killings, Johnny dead, the nightmares you'll have.' I hoped he'd have.

'Little late for that, isn't it?'

Everett's voice was harsh. He shoved Walter out of the way, slammed the truck door and started round to the driver's side. Walter's face, white now in the light from the street lamp, mooned at me. He was a sorry, pathetic figure and we all knew it. It wasn't much comfort. Walter headed for his car and Everett squealed the tires, making a U-turn and heading out.

'My neighbors hate that. They're probably standing at their windows right now jotting down a description and your license plate number.'

He laughed. 'You wish.'

I didn't say anything. It was too close to the truth and it sapped my enthusiasm for snappy repartee. Everett drove in silence and I brooded. I figured I had about an hour to come up with something.

'I've never met a banker like you. You don't exactly run true to type, do you?' He laughed again. 'A suit, pleasant attitude, manners, passable grammar, intelligence, you know the type.'

'Oh, I've got the intelligence, all right. The rest I'm a little short on. Don't matter a damn, though, any more 'n grammer does. My family had property and standing and folks out our way like good old boys for a banker.

'Why, shucks, ma'am,' he tipped his baseball cap at me. 'I'm just plain folks and if you can't trust plain folks, who can you trust?' Good question. I didn't have an answer.

'I'm taking you to a favorite spot of mine. Hope this don't spoil it for me in the future.' He considered it as he took the approach onto I–80 a little fast. 'Naw, I reckon not. Amazing what money can make you forget. Hey, I'm gonna get me a power boat, a twenty-four-foot Sea Ray day cruiser, top of the line. Maybe I'll call it Katerwaul, with a K, after you.' He laughed. 'Naw, maybe not.'

'You married, Dave?'

'Yeah, why?' He looked at me with curiosity.

'Nice lady?'

'Yeah, a peach.'

'Children?'

'Three.'

'And they let you kiss them?' I was genuinely curious.

'Aw, shut the fuck up.' The silence lasted from that stretch of I–80 into I–5 South.

'Hungry, Dave? What do you say we stop for a bite to eat?' I could just see the Rusty Duck from the freeway. 'How about the Duck? They have a good selection of seafood.' My stomach growled. I really had to eat more regularly. Alma was right: three squares.

'Kiddo, *you're* going to be fish food, not vice-versa.'

How tacky. In spite of myself I shivered. We went past the J Street exit and Old Sacramento. I thought longingly of the wooden sidewalks, the cobblestone streets, the old buildings, the laughter and the life down there. I gave it one more shot.

'Cocktails on the Delta King, maybe?' He laughed. Okay, maybe not.

'You'll get a boat ride tonight.'

There was satisfaction in his voice, satisfaction and something else. Excitement? He made me sick. And that's saying something.

'They don't kiss you, they couldn't.' I'd made up my mind. He laughed again. I thought about Hank. It made me want to cry. I thought about Xerxes with his throat cut. It made me mad.

And that was better.

The city fell behind us and I–5 stretched out into the long, flat valley, floodplain broken with trees here and there. A green and white sign came into view.

STOCKTON 37
LOS ANGELES 375

I pretended I was going to LA for the weekend, or to San Diego, that was better. I twisted slightly in the duct tape and Everett glared at me, then away. I wasn't going anywhere.

Okay, forget San Diego, forget LA. Stockton. Stockon sounded fine. Or Modesto. Fresno. We took the Hood-Franklin exit. Damn. I guess even Lodi was out. For once the delta didn't sound appealing.

Everett followed the road into Hood and turned left onto 160, a winding levee road with the river on the right side, fifteen feet below, and pear orchards on the left.

It was too dark to see anything, I was playing off memory: the river, the houses often with a sprinkling of palm trees. A number of the houses dated back to the 1800s. Some were painted and patched and smartened up, others had fallen first into general disrepair and then into boarded-up and decrepit decay.

I wondered why I hadn't noticed more before. Every detail seemed precious now. I searched in the dark for what I couldn't see until it became too much for me.

'Why, Everett?'

'Why what?' He sounded preoccupied.

'It's a lot of killing.' I rephrased things. 'Is it worth it?'

He laughed. 'Money's always worth it. I started with zip, with just a name, an old name and influence, and that counts around here but . . . but no money. Money counts more. I remember what it's like, having nothing. All too well, I remember. I've had my ups and downs, quite a few downs come to think of it, but no outs. And now I don't have to worry.' He scratched his chin.

'God don't buy you an insurance policy, you know. You got to git it for yourself.' It was an interesting way to look at things.

'I don't care about you, you know.' He shrugged. The heater was blasting but I felt cold inside. Like Lisa, I didn't matter. 'Except you poked around into things too much. You know too much.'

We went through Cortland, population almost nothing, and turned right, taking a drawbridge across the river, then left again. The river was on our left side now, the land to the right. A sign told us there was a $1000 FINE FOR LITTERING.

Did bodies count, I wondered. Bodies seemed more offensive than beer cans, cheeseburger wrappers, and old styrofoam fishbait containers. Much more so. Especially mine. On that thought I tuned out for a while. I didn't mean to but I did. The truck was slowing down when I dialed back in. We were on a two-lane slough road but I didn't know where. What slough: Snodgrass, Steamboat, Georgiana, Potato? Deadman's Slough? No, wrong train of thought.

'You won't get away with it.'

I grimaced, annoyed with myself. Even a crisis is no excuse for an overworked line like that. Everett didn't notice. I kept on bluffing; what did I have to lose?

'Too many people know. The cops don't know everything yet but they will. They'll put it together.'

I spoke with more confidence than I felt. He laughed. The truck slowed down even more. We passed a small general store with a phone booth and a gas station. Dead, closed for the season.

'It's my best shot.' He chuckled at his witticism. 'Shot, get it? Get it?'

'You're something, Dave.' He looked at me suspiciously, not sure it was a compliment. Smart boy.

'I don't do anything, you got me. I kill you, I get away with it. That's how I make it. Make sense to you, Kat?'

He parked and grinned. And yeah, of course it did – sick, warped sense, but sense nevertheless.

'Now you get your boat ride. Lucky girl.'

I hid my enthusiasm well. He pushed his baseball cap back, scratched his head, grinned again, and got out. I sat there, I still wasn't going anywhere. He had a pocket knife out when he opened the door. I flinched, I couldn't help it. And I remembered Johnny.

'Naw,' he patted my arm kindly and cut the duct tape, 'don't worry. You got you a boat ride first. No sense in messing up the truck anyway.'

While I struggled out of the duct tape he stuck the knife in his pocket and pulled out the .25. I got out of the car and took a deep breath. The jukebox had stopped playing and I was out of quarters. Damn. And I was in the mood for a couple more songs. Definitely. I looked around. It was cold, damp, still. And deserted.

'No one around in hollering distance,' Everett said cheerfully. He got a pair of oars out of the truck, waved the gun at me, and we started walking. The moon was about three-quarters full, and once my eyes adjusted I could see quite a bit. We made our way from the parking lot down to a small beach.

There were a number of boat tie-ups, all but one or two empty. Everything had a shut-down, off-season look. It should, it was. I had the same look. I shouldn't, I wasn't. Not yet.

Everett waved me over to a dinghy pulled high up on the beach. 'Get it in the water.' I flipped it over and dragged it down the beach. He followed with the oars.

'Get in.'

I did, being careful not to get my feet wet. That struck me as funny, almost. Not enough to make me laugh though. Everett didn't notice. He got in, pushed the boat off with one of the oars, then settled down to row, pausing and turning around every now and then to see where we were and how far we'd gotten.

I sneezed and fidgeted and he told me to shut up and be quiet. Once he stopped and flexed his hands. Banker's hands don't have the right calluses for rowing. Finally he hit a rhythm and settled down to a long smooth stretch. I tensed, then flexed my muscles and waited. He pulled the oars in a little, rested lightly on them, then turned around to check our location.

You don't get the best kicking power from a sitting position. On the other hand I was motivated. The adrenaline rush didn't hurt either.

I let fly with all I had.

It was enough.

With my right foot I slammed into the handle of the right oar. It shouldn't have gotten away from him but it did. He was complacent, counting his chickens, his money, his bodies.

The oar flew back, landed in the water, was still for a brief moment in frozen time and then drifted lazily away with the current. Everett, in an automatic reaction, partially stood and lunged for it.

'Son of a—'

I caught him around his left ankle and heaved. He was much less graceful than the oar; he made a much bigger splash, too. Something else made a smaller splash – the gun, I thought.

Son of a what? He never finished that sentence and I never found out. I guessed, but I didn't know for sure. Of course I didn't really care. I had the other oar in my handcuffed hands and I was ready to clobber the crap out of Everett. I didn't have to.

'Help! Help me! I can't swim!'

I waited to see if he were putting me on, if it were a ruse. He went down. I laughed. And then I was sorry, sorry because he hadn't heard me.

I started paddling. It was clumsy and tough going, the handcuffs didn't help, but I was making headway. I started for the nearest bank where the current wouldn't be as strong and I could pole along if I had to. He came up again.

'Help! *Please* help me!'

Help? I wasn't even tempted. Tempted? Shoot, I wasn't even interested. Even the please didn't touch me. He was yelling and splashing, wasting energy at a phenomenal rate. The distance between us increased.

'The Y,' I hollered over his voice.

'Help! Kat, help me!'

'Try the Y. I understand they have good classes. Very reasonable too.'

I think he missed the last part. Too bad. He came up again. Too bad again.

'You're close to a piling, Dave. Go for it, it's your chance.'

He bobbed up and down, looking around wildly. It was about fifteen feet downstream. The current was with him but it would take him past it if he didn't haul ass.

'Oh, God,' he said despairingly and went down again.

'Sink or swim,' I hollered cheerfully, when he struggled to the surface again, gasping, choking, and flailing his way toward the old piling. It was pretty far gone, pretty rotten. He hoped it was strong enough to hold. I didn't care.

It seemed callous, but that wasn't a true reflection of how I felt. Callous didn't cover it. Cold, heartless, long past caring: that was a start. Hey, drag out those pom-pons. I could get into rooting for him to die. I had backup cheerers too; Johnny, Michaela, Glory.

Gimme a D – gimme an I – gimme an E!!!

How about slowly, painfully? I could get into that, too. It made me feel sick and ashamed that I could feel that way about a human being. I thought about Everett. I got over it.

Gimme a—

'Kat, help me, don't leave me here!'

He was frantic, scared, and wrapped around the piling. Dave was not the kind of guy to go down with his ship. I paddled the boat along and watched the moonlight play on the water.

'God didn't give you an insurance policy,' I flung his words at him, 'but you've got arms and legs. Hang on.'

He groaned. 'It's slippery, slimy, tough to hold on. Please, Kat, I'll—'

'It's all relative, Dave. Just think, you could be a floater by now, and you're not, you've still got a chance.' I paddled on. I didn't seem any closer to the bank but I must have been, he was farther away.

'Kat!'

'I'll send help, Dave. After a hot bath, dinner, a couple of drinks by the fire.' I shivered. 'What the hell, maybe I'll give the cops a call. Maybe they'll get here in time.'

'Oh, God . . .' His voice was weaker. I paddled along and considered, considered hard; it beat thinking about how my wrists felt in the handcuffs.

What stupidity, what arrogance to come out in a boat

when you can't swim. Hubris, the Greek would have called it, overweening pride that gets us into trouble with the gods, or with an underestimated female PI. I rather thought Everett was the kind of man who underestimated women with regularity. Live and learn.

'Kat . . .' His voice was weaker.

I didn't answer. I was tired, hungry, and cold. My wrists hurt where the cuffs rubbed. My arm muscles ached at the unexpected exertion. I couldn't let myself think about, or feel, the pain and the fatigue. I started counting paddle strokes. One . . . two . . . three . . . four . . . five . . .

When I got to a hundred I started all over. It was too difficult, even in my mind, to say one hundred and one, one hundred and two. I got to a hundred a lot of times, I didn't count them either, before I saw the beach. I was on automatic pilot then.

Once I slipped and almost lost the oar, lost precious feet as the current pulled me back. I cried over it until it took too much effort to cry, then I just counted. Finally that took too much effort, too, and I just paddled.

There wasn't a lot of anything left in me by the time the boat scraped on the beach. I started to clamber out. The boat wasn't beached high enough and the current tugged it away. I reached for the oar and slipped, fell down and smacked my chin against the edge of the boat. I tasted blood. The handcuffs bit into raw flesh. There were no tears left in me or I would have cried again.

I poled the dinghy back up to the beach and stepped out into cold calf-length water. I was back on land, not dry land, but land. I almost fell climbing out of the

water. I almost fell again trying to pull the boat out.
I didn't get it up very far but it was the best I could
do.

I wanted to sit down, to rest, but I wasn't sure I could
get up if I did. And I was afraid of the cold. I made
myself walk up the beach. One step and then another;
I didn't let myself think how far it was to the phone
and help.

In the phone booth it took me a long time to get my
wallet out of my jeans, even longer to find my phone
credit card and Henley's card. He'd given me his home
number. It was tough standing up, it was tough pushing
buttons, it was tough all around.

The phone rang for a long time. It must have been
one, maybe two in the morning. My feet got colder and
my fingers got stiffer. The wife finally answered. She
sounded asleep. Henley sounded awake when he
picked up.

'Bill, it's Kat.'

'Shit, this better be good.'

'Yeah.' I took a deep breath trying to get the strength
to go on. 'It is.' There was a long silence.

'All right, let me get on the phone in the kitchen.'
Another silence. I struggled to stay standing. My feet
didn't hurt anymore. I seemed to remember that that
was a bad sign.

'What is it?'

He sounded grumpy and I didn't blame him. I didn't
really tell the story well, I babbled, but I got all the
important details. Almost all.

'Where are you?'

'I don't know.'

'For chrissakes, Kat.' I started snuffling. 'What's the

number on the phone there?' His voice had softened. I gave it to him.

'I could hang up and dial nine-one-one. You can get the location from the despatcher.'

'Forget it, I got you covered, Kat. A patrol car will probably get there first. I'm on my way.'

'Henley!' I shouted, afraid he was going to hang up, get away from me too soon.

'Yeah.' He sounded close and comforting. 'What?'

'Bring a handcuff key.'

'What the hell for?' I was silent. 'You wearing cuffs?' He started to laugh.

Unsympathetic bastard. I slammed the phone down and snuffled some more.

Thirty-Eight

A patrol car got there first, then two more. Then a helicopter. I was in Everett's truck curled up and shivering in a filthy blanket I'd found behind the seat.

The cops wanted me to sit up, tell my story, and show them were Everett was. They didn't want to take the cuffs off. The hell with them. I pointed out, a two-handed point, where Everett was. Then I clammed up, waiting for Henley. After that they squawked back and forth in radio communication with a boat. I tuned out. Most of them took off for the beach, leaving a cop behind to watch me. He was young and nice and he took pity on me.

'C'mon, miss, climb into my car. It's warm there.' I sat dumbly staring at him. My reaction time was slow snail. 'C'mon, I'll help you.'

He hauled me out of the truck and half led, half supported me over to his patrol car. I sat in the back, behind the wire and doors I couldn't open from the inside. He turned on the engine and set the heat on high, then opened the back door and offered me a package of Lifesavers.

'Want one?'

He held them out, then winced as he saw my wrists.

312

My fingers were too stiff, and cold to manage so he unwrapped the paper and peeled off a pineapple one. I opened my mouth and he stuck it on my tongue. Things were looking up; pineapple is one of my favorite flavors. He pulled off three more and lined them up on my knee, then tossed the rest of the roll into my lap. The car was starting to get warm.

'What's your name?'

'Kat.' My voice sounded funny, weak, and feeble.

He nodded. 'I'm Jerry. Call me if you need anything.' He nodded again and closed the door.

I put two more Lifesavers in my mouth and went to sleep in the heavy car heat. Later, in the background, I was aware of a lot of lights, of loud voices and noises. I opened my eyes but it was too hard to keep them that way so I closed them again on the drone of a bored, male voice.

'You have the right to remain silent. Anything you say can and will be used against . . .'

I opened my eyes to make sure they weren't talking to me. It was Everett and he looked colder and more miserable than I by far. I closed my eyes in satisfaction and dozed off again.

'Hey, Kat!'

Henley's voice startled me out of a sleep fog. I hadn't even heard the door open. The Lifesavers were stuck to my tongue, I'd fallen asleep before they were gone, before they were even worn down.

'Give me your hands.'

I held my hands out, wincing as the cuffs rubbed. He unlocked them, turned my hands over to check, and grunted in sympathy at the worn, tattered flesh. Gently he pulled my sleeves down.

'C'mon, let's get you out of here.'

He reached for my elbows and half lifted me out, then helped me over to his car. It was difficult to walk. My feet thought they belonged to someone else. I thought so too.

'You okay?' he asked.

'More or less.'

'Yeah.' There was a note of something there. 'You're a tough kid.'

Real tough. I hoped there weren't tear streaks down my cheeks. Henley put me in the passenger seat of his unmarked car. I pulled off the last Lifesaver, the one stuck to my knee, and put it into my mouth. And shivered.

'Bill?'

'Yo.'

'Could I have the heat on?'

'Yeah, hey.' He reached over and turned the ignition on, fiddled with the heat, then picked up a paper sack off the floor.

'Here, eat this. There's a thermos of coffee, too. Are your feet wet?' I nodded. 'There's socks and slippers there. Put them on.'

'Okay. Bill?'

'Yeah.'

'Could you help me get my shoes off?'

He sighed. 'Lucky for you I'm a nice guy, Kat.'

'I know,' I said, and I meant it.

He tugged at the laces for a while, then got out a pocket knife and cut them. Good idea. I was unwrapping the sandwich, pound slabs of ham, cheese, and tomato on a french roll dripping with mayonnaise. It brought tears to my eyes. I started eating right away. Henley got my shoes and socks off and felt my toes.

'Jesus!'

'Bad?' I asked cheerfully. It's amazing how food will change your outlook. 'I can't feel much.' I tore off another bite of the sandwich.

'Put the socks and slippers on and don't stick your feet right under the heater. Rub them, warm them up gradually.'

'Okay.' I ate some more sandwich. 'Bill, you've got my vote.'

'Boat? What about it?'

'Vote.' He looked puzzled. I smiled.

'Don't talk with your mouth full, Kat,' he said disapprovingly. I grinned and chomped into the sandwich as he closed the car door.

He wasn't gone long, long enough for me to finish the sandwich and two large chocolate chip cookies. I was drinking coffee and debating the apple when he climbed in. I decided to go for it.

'Well?' I asked with my mouth full of apple and he looked disapproving again. 'Have a cookie, I saved it for you.' I held it out and he ate it absentmindedly. 'Coffee?' We shared the thermos cup.

He put the car into reverse and started backing up. I sighed with relief and said good-bye to the parking lot, store, gas station, and phone booth. It was okay by me if I never saw them again, in this lifetime or any other.

'Start talking, Kat. Make it good.'

So I did. I told him everything starting with breaking into Walter's office, though I would have preferred to let that one slide.

'Shit, and you still have a license?' I was silent. I did, but maybe not for long. 'Hey, any more coffee?' His voice had lightened up.

I poured and handed him the cup and felt a little

better. He looked at me and shook his head. 'There's gotta be a better way.'

I agreed. Fervently, as it happened. 'Did Everett make a statement?'

'Yeah, he did. He said a lot more than he should have.'

'Did he finger Walter?' I took a bite of apple.

'You got it.'

'How did Johnny die exactly?'

Henley looked at me long enough to make me nervous. He was a good driver but this was a winding levee road. I'd had enough fun in midnight winter water to last me a while. A long while. A lifetime.

'He didn't tell you?'

'Not how. He wasn't very talkative and I was preoccupied with saving my neck.'

Henley grunted. 'Walter set his son up.'

I felt the tears in the back of my eyes. It almost had to be that way but it was still tough to hear. Johnny's dad, for godssakes. I swallowed suddenly and started choking and coughing.

'You okay?' Henley asked. I shook my head and he reached over to pound me on the back. It didn't help much.

'Thanks,' I managed finally. 'I swallowed that last bite of apple wrong.' And that chunk of grief. That and the bile. 'How?'

'Apparently John told his father he was meeting with Michaela that evening. Benson turned it over to Everett who took it from there.'

'He knew John?'

'From some time ago. And he had business cards as

an introduction to John, his and Benson's. It was enough.' Yes, I thought, it would be.

'John was too trusting.' I could hear the despair in my voice.

Henley shook his head. 'That's asking a lot of a person, Kat. In similar circumstances I imagine you would have been. Me, too, for that matter. John wasn't careless, he just took the obvious at face value, and nine times out of ten that works fine.'

'I guess,' I sighed. 'And Everett doesn't look like a killer. A banker for godssake.'

It was a stupid thing to say; I knew it and immediately regretted it. As if looks had anything to do with it. I wish I could learn to just think stupid things, not actually say them. Henley let it slide.

'Everett had the training for it.'

'What?'

'Killing.'

'Military?'

'Mmmm. Special forces.'

'If he's such a tough guy, why'd he break and talk?'

'The two aren't necessarily linked.' True. Another dumb comment. I seemed to be on a roll; it was not a cheery thought. 'Who knows?' He shrugged. 'The night and the water wore him down, for sure. And he wanted to see Benson tied in nice and tight.'

'Is he?'

'Tight?'

'Yes.'

'Looking pretty good.'

'You picking him up tonight?'

He grunted. 'I could. I'd rather walk a warrant through first.'

'He's not going anywhere. He's getting married tomorrow.'

'That so? You know where?'

I did, yes. Where? He'd mentioned it, I knew, and it was tucked away somewhere in the mush that presently passed for my brain.

'I can figure it out.'

'Do that.'

There was silence for a while. We'd left I–80 and were headed across town to Orangevale and my house.

'Can I turn the heat down, Kat? It's a hundred and three in here.' I nodded and at the same time shivered. He caught it with a sideways look, 'Oh, well . . .' He cracked his window slightly.

'What time is it?'

'Four.'

That was all? It seemed like days had passed, yet it was still two hours until dawn. I yawned.

'The next time I go to the delta it's summer, I take a picnic and—' I broke off as we turned the corner onto my street.

'Yeah—' said Henley softly. 'What the hell?'

We both saw it. A dark shape sat on my doorstep, small and huddled. Two dark shapes; one was Ranger.

'I don't know.'

We parked and I got out. I was too tired to run, to fight, to cope. Fortunately I didn't have to do any of the above, I had muscle with me. Muscle with a badge. I waited by the car until Bill came around. The shape stood up looking vaguely familiar.

'Kat? God, I've been waiting for a long time and it's

so cold. Where have you been? Who's that? How come your phone doesn't work? I called and called.' She sounded tired and unhappy. 'I *have* to talk to you.' Ranger nudged my hand for a pat.

'I can't, Michaela, not now. I'm bushed, washed up, history, done, tuckered out.' I stumbled slightly as I walked up the path. 'It will have to wait until morning.'

'It is morning.'

'Late morning, then.'

'But that's it, that's what I need to talk to you about.'

'What?'

'My – Walter's getting married in the morning. I'm going and I want you to come with me. I need you.'

'Okay.'

'Kat, I need you. I—' She broke off and stared at me. 'Okay? You'll do it? You'll come?'

'Yes.'

'You promise?'

'Yes.'

'Thanks, Kat, you're a peach.'

I stumbled again, this time on the steps. Not a peach. More like a soggy tennis ball, I thought, no bounce, no zip.

'*Hey*, nice slippers.' We all looked at the big, pink, fluffy jobs on my feet. Michaela grinned at me. 'You don't have any clothes sense at all.'

I shook my head. Maybe it was true, but that wasn't it. Not this time.

'Are you okay? If you are, I'm going back to Alma's. She's worried about you. Lindy, too.' I breathed a sigh of relief; Lindy was at Alma's. 'Or do you want me to stay?'

I shook my head again. 'How did you get here?'

'I drove. The car's out back in the driveway.'

Okay. Good. Fine, I thought, and started to drift off.

'What time is the wedding?' I roused myself to ask. 'And where?'

She told me. 'I'll come here. We can go together, okay?'

'Yes.'

'In the morning, then.' She gave me a quick hug. 'I *wish* we could talk now.' She said it wistfully, hopefully.

I shook my head. 'In the morning.'

'Okay, see you.'

Henley walked me to the house and checked everything out. Then he headed for the door.

'Henley?'

'Yeah. In the morning. See you,' he echoed Michaela. I kicked the slippers off and stumbled to bed.

Dead tired, but not dead.

Thirty-Nine

The wedding was at two and Michaela was on my doorstep at twelve. I was in my underwear looking for something remotely suitable to wear to a festive occasion. I'd been doing that for about twenty minutes; after last night I was not at my best. Michaela took over.

'How about these?' She held out a pair of gray wool slacks and a silk shirt – long-sleeved to hide the gauze I'd wrapped on my wrists. I nodded, hardly looking, and started to put them on.

'Hey,' she twitched them away from me. 'I'll iron them first.' By twelve-thirty she was on my nerves. Big time.

'Kat, are you ready? We should leave now. Really we should.'

'Find me a pair of earrings that match, will you?' I ignored her comment.

'All right. Want a necklace, too?'

'Whatever you can find. Load me up in wedding finery.'

'Then are you ready?'

'Then I'm going to have a quick snack.'

'Noooo,' she wailed. I ignored it and headed for the kitchen where I dug out crackers and cheese and sliced up carrots, celery, and apples.

'Sit down and eat.' The kitchen was still a mess of pasta, rice, and broken glass. I'd swept most of it into a corner. Michaela didn't even notice. 'We have half an hour before we leave.'

'I couldn't possibly eat; well, maybe just a bite.' She sat down and loaded up her plate.

'What did you want to tell me last night?'

That broke her munching stride for a moment. Then she resumed.

'I changed my mind.'

'Don't talk with your mouth full.'

She glared at me. 'I'm an adult, Katy.'

'Sorry.' I'd forgotten. Good grief, I chided myself, how was that possible? 'Why?'

'Why what?'

'Why was it so important to you last night, and today you've changed your mind?'

She took a deep breath and sat up straighter. '*It's* just as important and I haven't changed my mind about *it*, just about consulting *you*.'

Oh. Okay, that wrapped it up. For sure, I ate my crackers in silence and wished they weren't stale.

'Is it time now?' she asked. I looked at the clock.

'Almost.' The phone rang.

'Don't answer it.'

I shrugged and let the phone machine in the other room pick it up.

'You drive, okay?'

I nodded. She jumped and hopped around like a little kid who had to go to the bathroom. It was making me nervous and cranky. On the drive she fidgeted in her seat for most of the way and then got strangely quiet and broody. I looked over at her a couple of times and decided to let it go. By the time we got to Marysville she was chewing her fingernails and making nasty little nipping sounds. I didn't say anything again, but it was hard. I get points for it, I hope. Somewhere. Sometime.

The church was a medium-size white wooden structure on the outskirts of town surrounded by an ample parking lot and huge shade trees, stark and barren now in the wisps of winter sun. The parking lot was about two-thirds full and the steps of the church spilled over with smiling, happy-faced friends and well-wishers of the bride and groom. I didn't think we were going to fall into either of the above categories.

I parked and looked at Michaela who took a deep breath and climbed out. Wordlessly we marched up to the church steps. It was just under two. I pasted a smile on and pinched Michaela's elbow.

'This is a wedding, not a funeral.'

She looked at me and frowned, then lightened up a little, not much. The seating was informal with no one to steer us to the bride or groom's side. I figured most of the guests were their mutual church friends. Michaela pushed me into the last pew on the right-hand side and bumped me all the way over towards the wall aisle even though there were a number of empty seats in front of us.

Okay. No problem It was her party. Me, I was along for the ride.

'You didn't bring a present,' I said to Michaela.

'Yes,' she answered, 'I did.'

'Where?'

'You'll see.'

There was no getting around it, she was not in a convivial talkative mood.

'It's an old one. I've been waiting to give it for years.'

I looked at her. She had no purse and her hands were stuffed in her pockets.

'It must be a small one.'

'No.' She said it thoughtfully. 'It's very big, but ...' there was a long pause, 'it doesn't take up any space.'

Aha, riddles. Only I've never been much good at them. The organ started to play and the last of the people crowded around the front door entered and seated themselves. The church was almost full. Just before the massive double doors closed a largish man in black polyester entered alone and seated himself at the end of our pew.

He didn't look like a wedding guest, he looked like a plainclothes cop with dandruff. I was betting that it wasn't Henley's brother. I was betting, too, that he had a present, one that wouldn't take up much space and would be a big surprise. Maybe I was getting the hang of riddles after all.

The music changed. At the front of the church the minister and the bridegroom entered and positioned themselves. I scrunched down in my seat. I didn't think Walter would notice me, but no sense in taking chances. As far as he knew I was dead. From the rear the bride advanced. She was attended by a plump matron of honor and her two daughters, still looking like an earthquake could swallow them up any time and it would be okay by them.

I felt a sudden wave of pity wash over me, leaving me sick and weak. It's so hard to grow up, impossible to grow up unscathed. Michaela reached out and took my hand. Her hands were cold and dry and her grip was fierce. More of the same riddle I guess. I held her cold hand in my warm one.

'Dear friends,' the minister intoned. Michaela's grip increased in intensity. Both of us would soon be white-knuckled. I snuck a peek at Henley. He looked calm, relaxed, and interested. The minister droned on. I started to ease up a little, lulled by the traditional words and the beauty of the marriage ceremony. Mistake, big mistake.

'If there be any here who knows of reason why this man and this woman shall not be lawfully joined in holy matrimony, let him stand forward.' He didn't even pause. It was a token. Had anyone ever stepped forward except in *Jane Eyre* and the movies? I wondered. 'Then by the—' Michaela dropped my hand and stood.

'I do.'

Her voice was strong and clear. Somebody tittered at the parody of the marriage vow. The rest of us were silent – stunned, bludgeoned into silence. The minister looked dumbfounded.

'My name is Michaela Benson. Four years ago I left home. I was pregnant and my father was ashamed of me. The child I bore was his grandson.' She paused. 'And his son.'

Holy shit. I thought it, I didn't say it. An audible gasp went up and bounced around the room. Michaela continued relentlessly.

'I have the proofs, the medical tests. I cannot stand here and see my – my – ' she faltered for the first time, 'my f-father marry a woman with teenage girls and not speak out. I could not bear it if – if – if it happened again.' Her voice broke. Abruptly she sat down.

The silence was loud, stunned, overwhelming. Henley broke it. He spoke as he strode up the aisle. I watched him and thought what a lousy bride he'd make; he didn't have the walk down at all. Good thing he was already married.

'Walter Benson, I arrest you for the murder of John Benson and the attempted murder of Gloria Hernandez.'

Uniformed cops materialized in the back. Michaela's breath came out in a whoosh and she sagged back against the pew, her face white and strained. Hers was a hard act to follow but Henley had done it.

'No, no, no,' she moaned in a damn fine imitation of a mortally wounded cow. 'No, oh no, no.'

'You have the right to remain silent. Anything you say can and ...'

It was the second time in two days I'd heard someone Mirandized. Clearly I was hanging out with the wrong crowd. I would have to do something about that.

Someone started screaming – the bride, I think. Her daughters ran. You can only wait so long for an earth-quake to swallow you up, then, of necessity, you take matters into your own hands. And run like hell.

There were others screaming, crying, carrying on. The uniforms had their hands on their guns and were look-ing alert. Walter had handcuffs on. His bride, in laven-dar tulle, was beating his chest and flinging her flowers around.

Nobody tried to catch the bouquet.

It was not your typical wedding.

It was, as they say in LA, a wrap.

After a bit a uniform leaned over the back of our pew and tapped me on the shoulder.

'It might be a good idea if you and the young lady left now, miss.'

I nodded, in big time agreement. Why give the lynch

mob time to get rolling, to find a rope? We both looked
at Michaela who sat with her head in her hands, moaning, still doing wounded cow sounds. She was not at her
best. I figured I was going to need assistance.

'Can you help me get her out of here?'

He nodded. 'Let's go. Upsy daisy there, young lady.'
He had a nice, firm, fatherly tone that was a little old
for him; he was probably early thirties, but what the
hell, it worked. Michaela allowed herself to be hoisted
up and bundled out. The officer moved at a brisk pace,
Michaela firmly in tow. I beat them to the car and
opened the passenger door.

He shoveled Michaela in, the smiling helpful back-
hoe approach, snapped her into her shoulder harness
and pushed the button down on her door. Then he
gently patted Michaela on the knee.

'Congratulations, you did a good job and I know it
was hard.' She looked at him blankly. He smiled and
patted her knee again. 'You'll be okay now, I know
you will.'

He smiled again, then closed the door and watched
to be sure that we drove off into the sun without a
posse of vigilantes behind us. He raised a hand as we
turned the corner. A nice guy.

'Will I?' Michaela asked.

'Will you what?'

'Will I be all right?'

I thought about it. There wasn't an easy answer; it
wasn't an easy question. I guess I thought too long.

'Will I, Katy?' She was crying. 'Will I? Will I?'

'Yes, in time, with work. The running, the hiding, the
fear, it's got to stop. That's being a victim. But you
know that,' I reached out and touched her arm lightly,

'and you've already stopped. The officer was right, you did a good job. I'm proud of you.'

Her eyes misted up, her nose ran. She smiled very weakly, like a forty-watt bulb on a dimmer switch.

'Thanks.'

'Just don't try to do it all yourself. You have friends and family.' I looked at her and raised my eyebrows.

'Yes, I know, and you're right. I'm so glad,' she added.

'And I think you should see a counselor. Sexual abuse is a tough thing to get over on your own.'

Her face went white. 'You believe me, don't you?'

'Oh, honey, of course!' My voice cracked.

'Okay.'

There was silence for a little bit, quiet, easy silence.

'We know someone who needs your help,' I said at last.

'Who?' She sounded surprised.

'Lindy. She is also a victim of sexual abuse. She needs counseling, too, and she won't listen to me. I think she'd listen to you.'

'Okay.' She sighed, then straightened her shoulders. 'I'll try.'

I smiled at her. 'Good girl.'

Sometimes it's easier to help yourself helping another. Kill two birds with one bush as Alma would say, goofing up a perfectly good proverb. Not me, I know it: A bird in the hand is – no, not that one; kill two birds with one—

'Katy!'

I snapped to attention. Michaela was pointing to the windshield, desperate and wild-eyed. Overreacting, of course. I hit the adrenaline, and the brakes, and slowed down. It was a good old boy with a pickup full of hay bales doing thirty-five on the freeway.

'Shit!'

Michaela started laughing. I did, too. We were still laughing when we got to Alma's.

'Dear child,' Alma said as we walked in. Her arms were open and welcoming. I left them there, mending fences and building futures. When I got home Hank was there. Great! Arms for me to walk into, too.

'I called you about twelve, Kat, to tell you I was on my way. I got your damn machine.'

I looked at him guiltily – oh, that call. I could hear Michaela telling me not to answer the phone and me agreeing. *That* call.

'I'm sorry.' He grinned. 'How did you get out here?' I asked.

'I caught Charity. She picked me up.'

I'm lucky in friends, I know it. And in Hank.

'I have a lot to tell you.' I didn't know where to start.

'Can it wait?'

'Yes.'

He kissed me and picked me up. It waited for quite a while. We didn't.

Forty

Michaela called me at ten o'clock the next morning. Hank and I were up, in a manner of speaking. I wouldn't have answered, didn't, in fact, until about the thirty-fifth ring. I practically snarled into the phone, a this-better-be-good attitude.

It wasn't, not good enough.

'See,' she said it triumphantly, 'I knew you were there.' I stayed quiet, it was that or blow up.

'Katy, I need your help. Can you meet me at your office for a bit?'

'Tomorrow.'

'No, today. It's a drag, I know, and I'm sorry but I really do need you. You *told* me to remember I had friends and family I could *count* on.'

I sighed, caught in my own trap. 'Okay.'

'This afternoon? About three?'

'Three-thirty and Hank's coming, too.'

'Okay, I mean swell! Thanks, Katy, thanks a bunch. Oh, and wear something pretty.'

'Why?'

'I want to take your picture.' It seemed odd. I wondered about it as I hung up.

'Hank, do I have anything pretty to wear?'

'I like what you've got on.'

He's wonderful. I turned the answering machine on and climbed back, unclothed, into bed.

'We're meeting Michaela at three-thirty, okay?'

'Mmmm.' He wasn't concentrating on what I was saying, I could tell. First things first.

At eleven-thirty we headed for midtown and breakfast at the Rubicon. We took our time; the food was good and we had plenty to talk about. The beer is great. They make it there; we could see the stainless steel vats from where we sat. We made it to my office a little past three-thirty.

There were more cars than usual. I've got my fingers crossed that the neighborhood doesn't get too upscale and price me out. The front door was unlocked. Not good. I looked at Hank, who shrugged, but tensed up a bit.

'Maybe Mr. A. is here.' And he was. He looked up from an antique adding machine he was fiddling with and waved as we walked past.

'Hiya, doll face. What's cooking?'

'Not me, I'm back burner for now.'

I opened my office door and it exploded: balloons, champagne corks, music, wild people. A roll of toilet paper went flying across the room, then zoomed back. I don't know a lot of people who will do that. Lindy was on one end, Rafe on the other. They waved and yelled; okay, that figured out right.

Alma was there, and Michaela, Bella, and Charity. Even Mrs. Rusher, proudly clutching an aluminum pan with what looked like Rice Krispies marshmallow chocolate-chip bars. I stood there, frozen like Lot's wife – only with my mouth open, Hank and Mr. A. at my back.

'What?' I finally bleated.

'It's a party, dummy,' Lindy said, 'to celebrate the good stuff. Good stuff.' Someone stuck a glass of champagne in my hand.

'And to thank you,' Michaela added.

Rafe started playing the kazoo. It was either the 'Maple Leaf Rag' or 'The Battle Hymn of the Republic.'

'Michaela's going to music school,' Lindy said. 'Isn't it great?' I looked at Michaela and she nodded slightly and smiled.

'As soon as I get everything squared away and can apply. For now I'm going to quit working with the band and,' her voice faltered, 'work on other stuff.'

'Me too,' Lindy said.

Someone filled my glass up with champagne again. Someone else gave me a celery stick with peanut butter in it. Yeech. I turned around and looked for Hank who will eat that kind of stuff. He was leaning against the door drinking a beer and grinning. I shoved the celery at him before Lindy dragged me off.

'Kat, can I talk to you?' She looked anxious. 'Look, I know you said that it would be just for a week or so that I could stay with Charity. And my time's up, but I don't want to go home or back to the streets and –' Charity drifted by, 'and couldn't I stay. *Please*, please, please!' It was an impassioned cry. Charity blinked. I shook my head.

'You can't, Lindy, it won't work.'

'Why? *Why?* I won't be *any* trouble, I promise. I *promise!*' She held up her hand like a Girl Scout. It was as obvious that she meant it as it was that it was untrue.

'Charity's not a long hauler,' I said.

'Huh?' Charity and Lindy both looked at me.

'She's good for a short pull, not a long haul. You need someone for the long haul, Lindy.'

'That's true,' said Charity. 'I never thought about it like that, but it's true.' She nodded. 'You can come and visit, though.'

'And go to shows with you?' There was a long pause. Lindy grinned. 'I promise I won't hook. I can't promise about the corn dogs and 7Up. And I can shovel shit.'

Could she ever. I didn't meet Charity's eyes, we would have lost it.

'You can come,' she said gravely.

'I am,' Alma announced. We all stared at her. She'd snuck up behind us.

'You are what?' I asked, against my better judgment. Alma had a bottle of Jack Daniel's in one hand and a cupcake in the other. She put them down on my desk and looked at Lindy.

'I'm good for the long haul. Come live with me.'

'Could I?' Lindy asked and Alma nodded.

'Could I, Kat?'

I thought about it. 'I don't see why not.'

'Oh, wow!' Lindy jumped up and down and then shyly hugged Alma. She smiled. They both did.

'We'll do it, kid. Sink or fry.' Lindy looked puzzled. Oh well, she'd get used to it. They wandered off to make plans.

'It's a good idea, Kat,' Charity said. I nodded. 'They each need someone to love.'

'Yes.'

'Alma will keep Lindy off the streets.'

'And Lindy will keep Alma out of the pool halls and bars.'

'Oh, Kat.' Charity looked annoyed. 'Be serious.'

'I am.' I was. She wrinkled her nose and drifted off.

'Yo, party girl.'

No polyester – just jeans and a flannel shirt. The dandruff was there, though, so I recognized him.

'Bill!'

He grinned. 'Update?' I nodded. 'We nailed 'em both, found blood-stained clothes and a buck knife at Everett's house.' I swallowed hard. 'You all right?'

'Yes.'

'And a gun registered to you at Benson's house. It all ties in with your story.' He looked relieved. 'We found the originals of the records you obtained at Benson's office so there's no, errr, need to bring up that angle.'

I smiled. What a guy.

'Works for me. Thanks, Bill.'

He frowned. 'Don't do it again, Kat. Burglary, Jesus. It's your license and then some.'

I nodded. 'I know.' And I did.

'And my ass. I'm not –' I nodded. I knew that, too. 'I'd just as soon collect my pension and not be a goddamned shoe salesman.'

'Yeah. You'd be lousy at selling shoes anyway. Wrong personality for it.' He stared at me for a long time, then finally laughed.

I didn't, not yet. I was thinking about Johnny. It was funny – I knew more about him now, dead, than I did when he was alive. It made me feel close to him, closer than I'd ever been because now I understood better. And it made me feel further away, because he was dead. Because that's it: no instant reply, no recall, no one more try. I was glad the case was closed. And I missed Johnny, missed him a lot.

'I got something for you,' Henley said. I looked at

him. He fished in his pocket and pulled out a Mickey Mouse watch. Across the room Lindy's eyes got big and she started towards us.

'It's Lindy's, Bill.' She stood beside me, a little behind me. He handed it to her.

'Lindy, this is Detective Henley.'

She took a deep breath and bit her tongue. I saw her do it.

'About my friend – about Lisa – have you – do you—?' She broke off.

He shook his head. 'We don't know yet, but we've got some leads, some possibilities. And we'll keep looking until we find him.'

'I'd like to know. Could you –' She stopped again.

He nodded. 'I'll give you my card and you can call me when you want. I'll tell you what we find out.'

She hesitated. 'Okay. Thanks.' Belated, but there.

'You're welcome. We found her family, they're nice people. I think they'd like to talk to you.' She looked scared. 'When you're ready, you can call me.'

'Okay,' she whispered. 'Yeah, I will.' She looked at me. 'The money? The two hundred dollars?'

'Yes.'

'I wrote a poem for Lisa, maybe it could go on her grave? Would that be okay?'

'I think so but you'd have to ask her family.'

She thought about it and nodded, then looked at the watch. 'Hold out your hand, Kat.' I did. She strapped it on and then held my wrist and the watch to her ear. 'It's still ticking.'

I listened. It was.

'Lisa and I want you to have this. We—' Her eyes filled with tears and she shrugged.

'I got it, Lindy. Thanks.' She nodded and walked off.

I blew my nose. Henley cleared his throat and swallowed the rest of his beer. 'Nice kid.'

'Yes. She's not as tough as she makes out.'

'No.'

I thought about it and didn't say what I was thinking, that Henley wasn't as tough as he made out either. Of course neither am I.

'What about Glory?' I asked.

'Who?'

'The singer in Placerville.'

'She's doing okay, looks like she'll make it.'

'Did they cop to that?'

'Everett finally got smart and dummied up. I'm guessing that ballistics will get a match on a gun we found at his house.'

'Good.'

'Yeah, we're getting the loose ends tied up. Beer, Kat?' I shook my head and he went off in search of one.

'Hey, almost forgot.' He was back, popping the top on a Bud.

'What?'

'The money Benson made with what he siphoned off the trust fund?' I nodded. 'He wants you and the kid to have it. He's got his lawyer on it now.'

I stared at him in surprise. Hot damn, I was going to get paid after all.

'I figured I'd have to fight hard and dirty to get it back for Michaela.'

'Naw, he's beaten, crawling, and remorseful. Keeps talking about squaring things with God. Me, I think it takes more than a check to make it right with God, but what do I know?'

'It's a start.'

'Damn right.'

'More champagne, doll face?' Henley winked and walked off. I held out my glass and Mr. A. filled it up. Bella walked over looking casual in a studied and beautiful kind of way.

'Hi.' I hi-ed back. 'Look, I'm sorry about the last time. I was—'

'It doesn't matter.'

'Okay. Thanks. I'd like to do a head of John from sketches I have. Do you think his family would like –'

She let me finish it. 'To have it?'

'Yes.'

'I think it would mean a lot to them.'

'Okay. Good.' She looked off into the distance for a while. 'I'm not going with Stan anymore.' She said it shyly.

'Muscle porch?' She smiled. 'Wise decision.' She nodded.

'Maybe you'd like to come to my next show?'

'Sure.'

'I'll let you know. I've got to go now.' She waved at me. 'Thanks – you know.' I nodded. I knew.

'We have a present for you, Kat.'

Charity, Lindy, and Michaela stood around smiling and giggling. Lindy's hands were cupped around something.

'Here.'

It was a little ball of gray and white fluff and it mewed.

'We know nothing can replace Xerxes but—'

'But you can start over.'

'We got him at the pound.'

They all spoke at once.

I shook my head. 'I can't. Not yet.'

Lindy stuck him on my sweater. He crawled up to my shoulder and tucked his head under my chin.

'Too late,' Michaela said.

She was right.

By five everyone was gone. The mess stayed right where it was. Naturally. Unfortunately. It took Hank and me half an hour to clean up. The kitten ate some leftover chocolate cake and ice cream and threw up on the rug, then burped and gave us a pitiful look. It was time to go home.

'Excuse me, Miss.'

I swigged the last of the champagne from the bottle, tossed it in the trash, and turned around. A five-foot-one man in a gray suit, pink cheeks, bald head, and bifocals stared at me.

'Yes?'

'Is this the office of – are you – ummm – I'm looking for – ummm – the investigator.'

'That's me,' I said, rashly risking the undying wrath of Miss Mable, my seventh grade English teacher. He looked doubtful which, considering the circumstances, was entirely understandable. On the other hand it was Sunday afternoon, not exactly office hours. 'What can I do for you, Mr.—?'

'Ummm, Smith.'

'Mr. Smith.'

I said it as though I believed it, which I didn't. The kitten was batting a pink balloon around. Uh oh. I started for it too late. The pop was loud. 'Smith' jumped a foot and came unglued on the way down, babbling, shivering. Hank snagged the kitten and the trash and

338

walked out, quietly closing the door behind him.

'Won't you sit down, Mr. Smith?'

He trembled his way into a chair, sitting on the edge, poised for possible departure. Then he searched for words. It was a long search; I decided to help out.

'What can I do for you, Mr. Smith?'

'Hmmm? Oh, ah—' He'd obviously forgotten his name was Smith. That, on top of everything else, made him look lost.

'I, uh, need to find out something.'

I nodded politely. It was, after all, why most people came to an investigator.

'This is very hard, Miss,' his voice trailed off again.

I nodded, still politely, but strained. I'd heard that one, too. I thought about Hank and the kitten and wanted to go home.

'Here, read this.'

He shoved a meticulously cut and folded scrap of newsprint into my hand. It was part of a personals column called The Meeting Place. One ad was carefully ticked off with a little blue check mark.

Modest attractive 55yr old White Christian Lady would like to meet White Christian Gentleman under 6' tall.

I looked at him.

'What do you think?'

'About what?' I was at a loss.

'About the ad, of course.' He sounded a little impatient with me. 'Do you think I could – ' He broke off. 'Do you think she—' Today was his day for starting, not finishing, questions.

339

'You are interested in answering this ad?' I asked.

'Yes.'

'And you want my opinion?'

'Yes.'

'Are you a Christian gentleman?' At five-one and white, he had the other requirements nailed down.

'Oh, yes. You see, my wife died last year and I – it's – ' He sat and looked at me. 'Lonely,' he said finally. 'Very.'

'She states four qualifications and you meet all of them. Why not?'

This was Charity's department, not mine. I thought about Hank and the kitten. I thought about love and loneliness and loss.

'I want you to check it out, isn't that what you investigators say? To find out for me. After all,' he lowered his voice, looked around and whispered, 'AIDS.'

I maintained my composure even with the ghastly specter of a fifty-five-year-old white Christian lady with AIDS looming over us. He was having more difficulty.

'There's a box number here. Why don't you correspond with her, get to know her, perhaps take her out to lunch? I'm sure you will be able to "check it out" yourself.' I smiled at him, then wiped the smile off my face and was serious again.

'Statistically the chances of a white Christian lady of fifty-five having AIDS are slim.' He looked doubtful.

'Do you really think—?'

'Yes,' I said firmly. 'I do.'

'Write to her?'

'Yes.'

'Lunch?'

'Yes.'

'But—'

'There aren't any guarantees in life, Mr. Smith.' I said it gently.

'No,' he said sadly. 'There aren't.' He took a deep breath, straightened his shoulders and stood up. 'How much do I owe you, Miss?'

'Nothing.'

'I insist,' he said firmly, on safe ground with money and services rendered.

'I don't charge for an initial consultation.'

'Oh.' Uncertain again. 'Thank you.'

'You're welcome.' The kitten mewed in the hall.

'There aren't any guarantees?'

'No.'

He shook his head sadly and started out. 'I'll let you know, shall I?'

'Do.'

He smiled and I smiled back. Then he left.

Hank and the kitten were waiting. Hank drove; the kitten slept; I thought. About a bunch of stuff: beginnings, endings, life, death, what's important. I thought about breaking into Walter's office and almost getting caught, about doing time in the slammer.

'Hank, how long would you wait for me?'

'Twenty minutes, an hour, all night, whatever it takes to keep you happy, sweetheart.' He leaned over and kissed me.

'That is *not* what I meant.' I said it with dignity.

He grinned. 'No? Okay, forty-five minutes at a shopping mall, two hours at the dentist—'

'Hank!' He laughed. 'Be serious.'

He got serious. 'What are you really asking me, Kat?'

'Five years?'

'That's a long time, honey. Better just take me with you.'

I never did get an answer. Maybe it's one of those things that you can't answer, that you can't know. Not until it happens.

Life's like that.

No guarantees.

MARTHA GRIMES

THE HORSE YOU CAME IN ON

Richard Jury is supposed to be on holiday when the telephone call comes. And in any case, what has sudden death on American soil to do with an English police superintendent? But when the victim turns out to be British by birth, and to have a distant connection with Jury's old acquaintance, Lady Cray, he reluctantly acknowledges that his marker is being called in. Enlisting the aid of reluctant peer Melrose Plant, and accompanied by the irrepressibly lugubrious Sergeant Wiggins, Jury crosses the Atlantic to see what he can find out.

Baltimore turns out to have many attractions – not least that it is the home of avant garde novelist Ellen Taylor, last encountered at The Old Silent inn. Ellen is painfully engaged upon finishing her new book, but takes time out to introduce the trio to the delights of the city – football, Edgar Allen Poe, Bromo-Seltzer and a bar called The Horse You Came In On.

A case of plagiarism, a blind and deaf street-dweller, an engaging child who bears a strong resemblance to Scarlett O'Hara – these are just some of the elements in a complex puzzle whose solution looks set to defy the combined talents of the visiting team and put an end to a very promising writing career...

A selection of bestsellers from Headline